Sages of Darkness

Howl Sage

Brock Eastman

Illustrations by Dana Loch

DESTINY IMAGE® PUBLISHERS, INC.

P.O. Box 310, Shippensburg, PA 17257-0310

"Promoting Inspired Lives."

This book and all other Destiny Image, Revival Press, MercyPlace, Fresh Bread, Destiny Image Fiction, and Treasure House books are available at Christian bookstores and distributors worldwide.

For a U.S. bookstore nearest you, call 1-800-722-6774.

For more information on foreign distributors, call 717-532-3040.

Reach us on the Internet: www.destinyimage.com.

ISBN 13 TP: 978-0-7684-4005-8

IISBN 13 Ebook: 978-0-7684-8927-9

For Worldwide Distribution, Printed in the U.S.A.

1 2 3 4 5 6 7 8 9 10 11 / 13 12 11

Dedication

Matthew,

Someday you may very well rule the world, but for now enjoy this book. I had you in mind when I wrote it.

Acknowledgments

To my wife, Ashley—I never could have finished without you. You are my rock and you keep me going. I tend to take on more than I should, but you always get me through.

To Christian Miles—your input and thought was such a blessing to have in the final days of writing. You helped me through the home stretch. I expect I'll be reading great things from you in the future. The publisher that signs with you will be very blessed.

Mike Harrigan—artist and friend. Your input into this manuscript kept me on track and got it were it needed to be.

To my friends and co-workers at Focus on the Family. What an amazing bunch of people to work with. For your support, encouragement, and for all the creative opportunities you've given me.

Endorsements

A clever blend of Percy Jackson and Fablehaven, *HowlSage* kept me up all night reading. Full of suspense, action, and gadgets—readers will cheer for young Taylor as he hunts down demons and discovers the life he's supposed to lead. Two thumbs up.

Christian Miles, age 17

Thrilling chases, advanced technology, solid friendships, and spiritual warfare; *Howlsage* is absolutely brimming with adventure! It's also told in a way that younger kids can understand and relate to. I have 5 younger siblings and the youngest is only 6. I know how hard it is to find books that grab their interests and hold their attentions, but that also have good Christian values and Biblical principals that they can understand. Not only did I enjoy reading *Howlsage* as an adult, but I know that my younger brothers and sisters will love this book as well. I can hardly wait to read it to them!

Nichole W., age: 22,
Secor Illinois

Thrilling events and vivid descriptions of characters made me feel as if I was right there fighting evil with Taylor and his friends! You won't want to put the book down until you've read the last page.

Larisa K., age:22,
Davis, CA

Contents

Preface

The Rocky Mountain range stood to my left as I drove to work one morning. The bright sun was shining and the sky was blue. But for the story that would develop next, you'd expect the dead of night.

A single word came to me, HowlSage. I wasn't exactly sure what it meant, but soon a story swirled in my mind. Howl was the wolf's call and Sage was another word for magician, so the definition for HowlSage became magician of the moon. I believe that neither magic nor a werewolf can be good, so the HowlSage would be my villain, and further, like C.S. Lewis, I recognize that demons are everywhere. To counter the HowlSage, I needed a demon hunter, and soon I had our hero, Taylor.

In the following pages of this book and continuing through the series, you will read a story that is meant to be fiction, but one that I've pulled elements into from a reality we often don't recognize for its very real and true danger.

I'm not trying to pose any theology in the following pages, and you may read things you agree with or don't. I took fictional liberties in the story and am not expressing a belief I hold or that you should. Like stories with dragons, magic, elves, or dwarves, this story is fiction. The *Sages of Darkness* series should also cause you to think, to make you reflect, to challenge how you live your life.

I also feel that too often we make light of things that, if real, would truly be nothing short of demonic—say werewolves, vampires, and zombies. These are not heroes, and because of the elements that make up these fictional species, they can never be.

For the time is drawing near and the battle for souls is being waged every day. Let us not take for granted that each of us is precious to our Lord; we are all worth fighting for.

Ashley

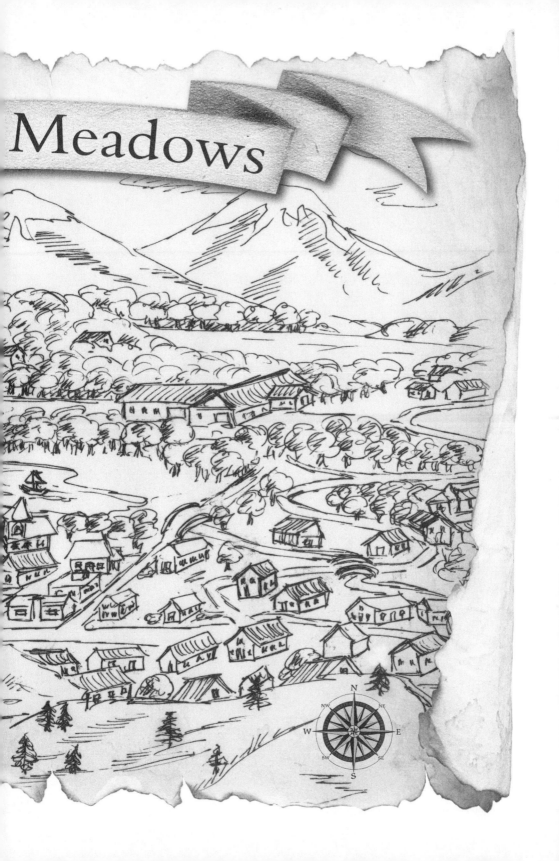

Chapter One

October 2nd
The Day After
(The Full Moon)—Monday

The scene was like that of an ill-made end-of-the-world movie. The intersection of Roth and Horton was a tangle of cars, trucks, traffic signals and signs, cargo, people, and green fire. Yes, green fire.

Green flames spewed from the front of an old blue Ford, whose hood had been smashed and its chassis pummeled two feet into the pavement. The driver escaped, but sat dazed, leaning against the roof of an overturned green SUV. The man muttered incessantly to himself.

"Hair, big, fangs, hair, blood, hair, big, fangs—"

I looked down from my perch atop the seven-story

bank building. I'd already scoured the cross streets, but there was no sign of the beast. The smile it had given only a second before it jumped told me all I needed to know. This was nothing more than a game. And I was losing.

How had they honestly thought I was ready to take the mantle from my father? We'd only just buried him, but the very next day the old man in his gray cloak arrived and said, "He has the gift. He must be trained now. The moon is to fall on Samuin."

I could still see the old monk look up at the cloudless night sky, the hood of his gray cloak falling back, revealing his bright white hair. "We have one month," he said to the man charged with my care, someone not quite as old as the monk, but still old. "The beast must be stopped." The next morning the monk was gone.

The siren of the first ambulance blared loudly as it arrived on the scene.

I had seconds to get down there and get pictures of the damage before the place was swarming with emergency personnel. Maybe then Ike and his dad could use their scientific masterfulness to tell me more about the creature.

With the prongs of my retractable grapple hooked securely on the ledge, I launched myself over the side of the building. I *had* practiced this before.

My feet planted firmly on the exterior stone wall of the building and I continued my descent, wind whistling in my ears. Five stories to go…

Four stories…

Three stories…

Two stories…

One…

The sidewalk.

The view atop had been better. I should've paid attention and looked for a clear path through the gauntlet of overturned vehicles and signs.

I'd have to make do.

A quick Bo Duke-style slide across the trunk of an orange Chevy. Around the smashed grill of a city bus. Through a puddle of nasty-smelling green liquid, and there was the old blue Ford the beast had used to cushion its landing.

I snapped a picture with my web-phone. Then another, and another. The moon's bright light exposed my hunting attire and gear to the public. Soon more police, a perimeter, a bigger crowd, news crews, and questions would choke off my escape.

A few more pictures of the impact to the hood of the Ford and of the scene around. I sprayed a neutralizing agent on the flames and they turned from green to your usual orange and red. I reached in the glove compartment of the smashed burning Ford and pulled out the car registration, and tapped the driver's name and address into my web-phone.

"Hey you!"

The voice startled me. I looked at the man who'd called out to me.

"Yeah, you. What you doin' in this guy's car?" the man said, leaving the muttering driver to confront me.

Time to go! I stepped backward and pulled the safety pin on a smoke grenade, then threw it under the car. As the white tufts of smoke billowed from under the trunk, I slid around the back of the car and disappeared into the shadows.

One of the clearest rules I was given: "Don't get caught."

I ran a short way down Roth Street and pulled out my grappling gun. A soft pull on the trigger and the hook and wire launched into the dark, midnight sky.

I made quick work of the climb to the roof. I paused to listen. A small earpiece invented by Ike's father allowed me to hear things clearly within 150 feet. The police had arrived and were already beginning to ask questions.

Then a soft, female voice caught my attention. At the ledge of the building, I looked over. A girl, only a bit older than me, was standing in the shadows. She was talking to someone, but I couldn't see whom; the person was hidden behind an emergency vehicle. I zoomed in on her with my night vision goggles. Although green and grainy through the lens, I could see she was beautiful.

Clank clunk clakkity clack!

Without a thought, my sword was before me in one hand, and my other gripped a cross on a chain as I swung 'round to meet the disturbance.

To my relief, two filth-covered rats were fighting over an old tin minced garlic can.

Back to the ledge, I looked for the girl, but she was gone. The police had extended their perimeter quite a way down each street.

I exhaled deeply, a breath that seemed to have been held in since the beginning of tonight's hunt. I had failed, and chances of me finding it again this night were very slim with only a few more hours of moonlight. It'd taken all night to track it down in the first place.

I replaced my sword back into its sheath and hung the cross around my neck, then extended the silky-feeling wings from my pack and held the small controls in my hand. My finger was on the red ignition button when I remembered how my trip here went.

Ike had "tweaked" the jet pack his dad had made *to fly me faster*. Ike was a good inventor; his dad was a great inventor.

What a disaster.

Slamming through two trees, I'd only just missed a power line, and I don't know what I would've done had both windows of my targeted building been closed.

"Be discreet; don't get caught," my trainer had said.

How was I to do that with faulty gear?

I sighed. Ike was trying, like me. He was my best friend, maybe my only, save for some adults. And our lives had gone from worrying about typical boy things like sports, pizza, and video games to—well, far from normal. We were now immersed in the very war between good and evil, Heaven and hell.

We—Ike and I—were of course on the good side. And what we fought was, without question, from hell.

Bzzzz bzzzz bzzzz.

My phone. It was McGarrett, the guy who—well, the guy who tried to keep all of this together and secret. My trainer.

I put the phone to my ear.

"Taylor, are you all right? Did you get it?"

He couldn't see it, but the frown and disappointment that came over my face would have told him the answer. "Nope, it got away."

Silence on the other side.

I knew what he was thinking. Tonight was our best chance to kill the HowlSage, while it was still a newborn and at its weakest point. Its strength and size would double every night this first week, and for every day the HowlSage remained, more demons would invade the town through the Etherpit in the mines.

An Etherpit is a gateway from the underworld, and the HowlSage acts like the beachhead commander for the invasion, clearing the way and shielding the smaller, weaker demons from hunters or Angels.

McGarrett wasn't much of a motivational speaker. Sometimes his wife would jab him, and he'd find a few inspirational words to encourage us. But most of the time, he just stumbled over his words, especially when he was disappointed.

"Ummm, well we'll get it next time," McGarrett said. "Come on back, and we'll get you prepped for tomorrow."

"McGarrett, can you send someone?"

"Can't you use your Jet Pak?"

"Naw, I think, I mean Ike *tweaked* it before I left—"

"Enough said. Me and the missus will be right over to get you. Your GPS on?"

"Yeah," I said.

"See yah in a bit Taylor, and—" Silence. "And we'll get it, don't you worry."

"Yes sir." I tapped *end call* on the screen.

I should mention that Mrs. Riley is McGarrett's wife. McGarrett you would think is a last name, but Riley is a first name, so his parents decided a kid needed one of each. Without going into too many details, let's just say his parents were different.

I waited on top of the building, my feet dangling over the side. The night was cool and cloudless, but not cold. The moon was just starting to wane, so I could see for miles over the town. It'd been full yesterday, harkening the HowlSage forth.

As I looked out over the town I shivered to think the hairy wolf-like beast was dashing through the streets heading back to the safety of its dark burrow.

Ashley Meadows is a quiet town for the most part, about 5,000 people. Set in the middle of rolling hills—what some would call mountains, but if you've ever been to Colorado you'd call these hills. Just three roads lead into town—one through a tunnel, one over a bridge, and one by ferry. It's the sort of place you'd expect existed in the 1950s; friendly, helpful people, two-lane roads, and almost no major chain stores. The town has a Starbucks and a Walgreens, but that's it. I sulked for an entire week when my dad and I first came—I wanted to be back in Paris, London, or Houston, cities that never slept, not here where the town's curfew for fifteen-year-olds is 9 p.m.

But the small-town life does have its upsides too. For example, the school lets you pray at lunch, and we still say the Pledge of Allegiance as it was written, God included. There is also a huge park at the center of town and in the middle is a large lake. The park and lake are the pride of the town, and any given Saturday or Sunday after church you'll find nearly half the residents there. Picnics, volleyball games, swimming, bocce ball, or croquet, all happen every weekend from spring to fall in the park.

The mailman knows his patrons, neighbors chat on the sidewalk and sit on their porches, and there's an old guy who drives his lawnmower down the street because his license was revoked for running too many stop signs and not wearing his seat belt. People are far more in tune to what's happening around them than in some big city like New York or Chicago. That, of course, also makes my job harder.

Several headlight beams flashed onto the street below as McGarrett's car came around a corner. I know it's him because his *customized* car has six headlights, two of which were designed especially for our line of work—slaying the evil ones of the world. There's an old saying, "You don't choose your work, it chooses you." Well, in my case that couldn't be more true.

My phone started to vibrate, signaling it was time to go.

With the grappling hook latched into place, I bounded off the roof a bit too freely, trying to speed up my descent.

Stupid move.

In order to miss a window, I shifted all of my weight to my other foot and it twisted oddly.

A moment later, on the sidewalk next to the Rolls Royce, I could feel the blood surging to my ankle as it swelled. It felt like it had its own heartbeat. As I hobbled toward the car, McGarrett stepped out to open the door for me.

"What'd you do? I thought you said it didn't—"

"It didn't," I said, cutting him off. My pride bruised as I crawled into the car.

"Taylor, how are you feeling? You look pale. You look cold. Here, drink from this thermos; I brought you some warm Tang," Mrs. Riley insisted before I'd even gotten fully into my seat. She always spoke like this, quickly making an assessment, and one that would lead you to what she wanted. In this case, for me to drink the Tang she'd made.

I slipped my seat belt on and took the mug, knowing that if I didn't I'd hear nothing more than her insistence the rest of the way home.

Home was just a few miles away toward the eastern edge of town and deep in Theodore Woods. Known as the Pink Hippo, our home was in an inn that shut down when the mines dried up. Well, they didn't actually dry up, but that's another story. The Pink Hippo had exactly 77 rooms on 7 floors, a grand lobby, a massive dining hall, a kitchen, two libraries, a clock tower, and an indoor/outdoor pool. Several out buildings also dotted the property—a horse stable, three sheds of varying sizes, and a large workshop. The workshop, built in 1983, was a new addition in comparison to the inn, which had been built in 1865. The workshop was where Ike and his dad experimented, built, and fixed their inventions, and where Mr. Riley did his research and tracking. It was also the last place I'd seen my dad alive.

McGarrett tapped a door opener as we approached the long, gravel driveway that would snake through the woods and lead to the inn. The gate swung open, and the four illuminated headlights showed us the path home.

I was looking forward to my warm bed and some tunes to fall asleep. I felt a twinge in my ankle, but it could wait until morning.

Chapter Two

October 3rd—Tuesday

I woke to my best friend shaking me. Ike wasn't exactly your stereotypical inventor. He had some of the traits though—crazy hair with rubbish in it, bright blue eyes filled with energy (like he'd just downed a venti quad-shot Espresso blended with a Monster energy drink), soot and dirt marks on his face, and a wide, bright smile.

"Taylor! So how'd it go? How'd my adjustments to the J-Pak work?" His voice was piercing to my just-wakened ear drums.

I hoped my groan might tell him I wasn't quite awake yet, and he'd get the hint to chill. But it didn't. Still, it was hard to get angry with someone so chipper.

I rolled over to look at him. I glanced at the clock.

"Six a.m.!" I shouted.

Forget what I said; I could be angry. "Ike, get out of here! I just went to bed a few hours ago!"

His smile didn't fade, but instead he shook me again. He looked even happier.

"Great, you're awake. So how did it go?" Ike asked again. He reminded me of a small terrier puppy hopping up and down for attention.

"Not great. It was a bit—well—"

Ike started to frown.

I couldn't be too harsh, even if I was mad at him for waking me. "—it needs some work."

Ike let out a sigh; his smile gone.

Could I get back to sleep? I wondered. Probably not.

I swung my legs over the side of my bed and stretched my arms and yawned.

"What's for breakfast?" I asked.

Ike answered in a rapid-fire stream of words. "Not sure, I haven't slept yet, or ate. But I'm ready to eat if you are."

I started to stand, but my right ankle gave out and I fell back into bed with a grimace on my face.

Ike looked horrified, "Oh, it was bad. My adjustments got you hurt."

"No, it wasn't the J-Pak." I sat back up. "Grab my t-shirt and jeans," I half ordered. "I did it when I was repelling down a building."

Ike shook his head and walked over to my closet and opened the door. "Which one?" he asked, but I smiled to myself, knowing what was before him.

I didn't have a lot of variety when it came to clothes. I pretty much had two styles of shirts. White tees for during the day, and black under armor shirts for hunting at night. In fact, these black shirts were a new addition to my wardrobe since I was assigned my role of hunter.

"A white one," I answered with a smirk.

Next stop was my dresser, and other than underwear and socks, there were just three pairs of jeans; all the same style and color, and a couple pairs of black athletic pants.

"How about your jeans?" Ike asked.

"Any pair is fine." I realize that some would call Ike a genius, or soon to be. But he's very short in the common sense department, which is such a cliché, I know.

He brought me the shirt and jeans and bent down to help get my right foot into my pant leg. I politely excused him and assured him I could handle it on my own. He shrugged and picked up my current good read from my nightstand, a comic book titled, *The Howling of Hamburg*.

"Research?" he asked as I shifted the pant leg delicately over my right ankle.

"Uh, yeah I guess."

Right leg in, now the left leg.

"So what was it like?" he asked.

I knew exactly what he meant. He wanted to know what it was like to face the HowlSage.

I thought for a moment. Ike was younger than me by three years. What I saw last night would frighten a grown man, no less an 11-year-old. "It was hairy; really hairy."

Left leg successfully in. I stood and used the bed for support while I zipped and buttoned my pants.

"Any fangs?"

I smiled. "Yeah, it had fangs," I said as I pulled my t-shirt over my head.

"Wow..." Ike looked up from the comic book. He had a curious expression on his face. "Were you—I mean, I know you probably weren't, but..." He hesitated.

"Was I scared?" I finished for him. "Sure, I guess I was a little bit."

That wasn't the truth though; I know you'd expect a 14-year-old to be scared of a giant hairy creature with saliva dripping from its fangs, but I wasn't. Honestly, not a twinge of fear. Maybe it was my adrenaline; I really don't know. Or maybe the anger I felt when I saw it covered any fear. But I didn't really know why.

So why didn't I tell Ike, "I wasn't scared." Because I knew he would have been, and should the worst happen and he had to face the creature, I wanted him to believe he wasn't alone in his feelings.

I slipped on some flip-flops, and Ike offered his shoulder. We hobbled to the old elevator and went down the five stories to the kitchen. As soon as the lift's doors opened, the smell of fresh bacon, eggs, and cinnamon pancakes wafted to my nostrils, which flared as they took in the mouthwatering aroma.

My stomach started to grumble, which for some reason gave me an unpleasant thought about the creature last night, staring at me with its fangs bared and saliva dripping from them, each drop sizzling as it hit the roof of the building.

"Good morning!" came Mrs. Riley's voice. She waddled over to us and hugged us both.

She was such a sweet lady, treating Ike and me like grandsons. But I knew she'd been a hunter like me in her own time. McGarrett had told me that Mrs. Riley had been injured by a *BloodSage* when she was younger. Their families had been the first team assigned to Ashley Meadows. They'd grown up together and eventually fallen in love. But not before she'd been attacked by a *BloodSage*. McGarrett, although not a hunter, had saved her. How, though, he hadn't told me.

Mrs. Riley pulled several pieces of debris from Ike's hair and sighed. "If your mom was here, she'd have you in the shower by now."

Ike smiled. His mom was not missing or dead. She was simply visiting his grandparents in Germany. That's the other thing about Ike; he's of German descent and in the same family tree as some great German scientists.

We took our seats and Mrs. Riley disappeared through the swinging kitchen doors.

I'd had two bites of my eggs and one sip of fresh orange juice when McGarrett walked in with Ike's dad—whom I should introduce as Olson Swigart—in tow. They were arguing or discussing—it was hard to tell with the two of them.

They stopped when they saw me and made their way to the table to eat.

Mrs. Riley eventually joined us and we all feasted on the wonderful breakfast. There was a firm rule when we supped—no discussion of work at the breakfast, lunch, or dinner table or any other occasion that involved food. Food was to be enjoyed without the stress of work.

When we were all done, Ike and I followed McGarrett and Ike's dad to the workshop. McGarrett updated us on some intelligence he had received from the society's headquarters.

Apparently, another Etherpit had opened up in a Chilean mine—the fifth new gateway in as many months.

Our society, known as the Legion der Dämonjäger, was founded to stand guard and destroy any demons sent through the gateway. The society's forces were quickly becoming spread thin, though. In the past, new Etherpits opened only a few times a decade. I only knew all this from my last couple weeks of crash course training, so it was still fresh in my mind. But now the pits were opening at an alarming rate and the society couldn't recruit or train new hunters and support teams quickly enough. It was the driving reason for my training starting over a year before I would turn sixteen. And it was the only reason Ike, age eleven, was told what his dad really did and allowed to start training as well. Of course we were training for very different jobs.

I still ask myself how I didn't know about the supernatural side to his work. I'd just thought my dad was some sort of secret agent for the United States government. All his gadgets, weird hours, and constant travel. I figured I was only being dragged along because of my mom's death and he had no choice. But now it turns out that he worked for a different sort of organization. One that, even though its business was highly dangerous, put family first.

So with the new Etherpits opening so quickly, it was possible McGarrett or Ike's father would have to go to Chile to get things under control and establish a guard. However, with the current creature loose in Ashley Meadows and neither Ike nor I anywhere near fully trained or of age, they might get off. The decision would be up to the society's high council, whose headship was the very monk I'd met a month prior. McGarrett looked over my ankle while Ike and his dad looked over the J-Pak; I assumed McGarrett told Mr. Swigart what I'd mentioned about the trees the night before.

You'd think Ike would be in trouble, but that wasn't how his dad was. Mr. Swigart knew, like any good inventor, that there are many failures for every success. What I didn't like about this theory was it was my life on the line, my body using these gadgets and gizmos. But so far, I'd not had any serious injuries from them. Of course I'd only been on the job for a day, and began training with gadgets two weeks prior.

The Etherpit we were responsible to guard had opened back in 1890; people were more willing to believe in the reality of demons then. The miners accidently struck into a black, bottomless pit, and when townspeople started seeing ghosts or weird things started happening, they got suspicious. The society was contacted and a team was sent. Of course, the mines were abandoned.

McGarrett said, "Be careful on it today," and wrapped my ankle tightly. He gave me an old crutch he'd pulled from storage and said to take it easy at school.

Speaking of school, I remembered that I needed to finish two more paragraphs on my history paper. I took out my tablet and started tapping the on screen keyboard.

I'd just finished when McGarrett said he'd drive us to school today instead of Ike and I riding the bus. We went out to find he'd pulled up an old World War II motorcycle with a side car. This was Mr. Riley's favorite, and Mrs. Riley's least favorite vehicle in the motor pool. Needless to say, it wasn't favored by Ike and I either. He had to sit on my lap in the side car—not exactly how we liked to arrive at school.

But there was no point in arguing with McGarrett; he already had his goggles and leather helmet on.

Being the bigger of us, I climbed in first, then Ike squeezed in front of me, not quite on my lap, which was good.

We had barely secured our helmets when gravel ripped into the air as McGarrett hammered the throttle. The sidecar motorcycle tore down the gravel road, and Mr. Riley made it fish tail here and there for an extra thrill. One thing was for sure, I had no fear when riding with McGarrett, regardless of how he drove.

Fortunately for Ike and me, Mr. Riley dropped us at the back of the school, out of sight of any of our peers. I unstrapped my crutch from the side of the motorcycle, and Ike and I headed for class just as the first warning bell rang.

The day passed slowly, and I had lots of time to think about last night's events. Was this really happening to me? I mean, was I really fighting in a secret war that had raged all my life, but although being a "Christian," I'd never truly grasped its reality? It's one thing to think you believe in Heaven and hell because you're religious and you've learned about it in all your Sunday school years, but it's another thing to stand face to face with a demon, its saliva splattering on you with every wretched-smelling breath it takes.

All this time I'd just thought my dad was some sort of government spy, but it turned out his job was far more perilous. As a boy I'd thought he was invincible, tougher than nails.

But the day had come, and alas, my dad fell. He literally fell, chasing a SwampSage into the abandoned mines. McGarrett told me the painful story of what had happened after a couple weeks of training. He and Mr. Swigart were watching my dad chase a SwampSage. The entire scene was being streamed to the workshop via the night-vision camera embedded in my dad's chest armor.

Apparently my dad had the SwampSage cornered when something else shoved him from the back. He stumbled to the left, and then the SwampSage took its opportunity and pulled my dad into the black void with it.

The next morning was when I got the news, and a few days later I started my crash course in becoming a demon hunter. I'd learned about a few types of demons so far; all had weaknesses, but I couldn't keep all of that straight.

The demon I was hunting at the moment was a HowlSage. Society's term for it is werewolf, and in recent years the public's concept of the wolfish beast has been so far skewed that some would idolize it as a hero. This simply isn't accurate; these beasts are hungry for the flesh of men, and they have one purpose and that is to serve the Evil One himself. There is no glory or goodness in these creatures.

The BloodSage is equally misrepresented today, personified as a being who can show human emotions of love, courage, and honor. Most know them as vampires, but we call these demons BloodSages. They are strategists of the underworld; seeking to create vast armies of minor demons, they fight amongst themselves to create huge territories from which they can feed and siphon strength from human sin. McGarrett seems to believe they are the most dangerous demon we face on this side of the Etherpit. I asked him what he meant by *this side*, and he shook his head and changed the subject.

The beast that murdered my dad was a SwampSage. These demons are dangerous too, but not alone—their strength comes in numbers. If you've ever heard of the Creature from the Black Lagoon, you can get a pretty good visual.

There are many more demons in existence, and Ike has sketched a few for you to see. But for now I must concentrate on learning all I can about the HowlSage.

When the bell rang for school to be out, I met Ike outside the school to wait for McGarrett. He pulled up in a short few minutes in the Rolls Royce.

Ike tugged on my shoulder. "Looks like somebody is off to Chile," he said.

There were several suitcases strapped to the roof of the gray car. Mr. Riley was driving, and Ike's dad was in the back.

McGarrett motioned me into the passenger seat, and Ike got in the back with his dad—a sign that it would be Mr. Swigart headed to South America.

A few short minutes later, we pulled into the parking lot of Ashley Meadows Regional Airport, a small airport where only a few private jets and one airline flew. Southwest airlines had purchased one of three available gates and flew one flight in and out per week. Southwest airline's current president was a member of the society.

Ike hugged his dad goodbye, then stood next to me while Mr. Riley and Ike's dad spoke. As usual their conversation looked very serious as neither man frowned once.

Mr. Swigart gave a wave goodbye and then headed through security, which we knew from the overhead announcements was at "Threat Level Orange."

"It's never going to be green again," I said to Ike.

"Probably not," Ike started.

I scoffed.

"Imagine if instead of a terror alert level, we had a spiritual warfare alert level," Ike said.

"People would just ignore it like they do the terror alert level announcements in airports," I said, and as if on cue, the announcement aired overhead again.

Ike and I started to follow McGarrett back to the car. "True, they already have the Book, they just never choose to listen to its warnings," Ike said.

We rode back to the Pink Hippo listening to the police scanner. But this night, like most others, there was no activity.

Once we got back in the workshop, Mr. Riley launched the targeting application and a large map of Ashley Meadows and the surrounding countryside appeared on the oversized plasma display in the workshop. There were several glowing spots in varying hues. Small sensory devices scattered throughout the area picked up traces of scent, sound, infrared, and visual identification, attempting to match the likeness of our current prey.

Of course, my first prey would have to be the most difficult type of demon to track, having qualities so similar to animals, especially dogs. It seemed the entire map glowed red with direct matches.

McGarrett shook his head, "Looks like we'll be busy tonight just eliminating dogs, cats, and other beasts."

Ike quickly went into action. "No we won't. Last night after Taylor returned I cross-referenced the county's pet registry with our search area." He tapped the screen on his tablet computer and more than eighty percent of the red disappeared.

"Wow!" I said amazed. "That was cool."

"Yeah, after it taking us half of last night to eliminate locations, I decided we needed a better way. This just made sense."

"Indeed, Ike, you certainly take after your father," McGarrett said. "Too bad about losing him, too."

Ike looked at McGarrett frightfully, and Mr. Riley quickly realized his misstep. "I mean, losing him to Chile for a few weeks."

"Oh right," Ike said, regaining his composure.

"It looks like we still have a resident genius though," McGarrett said as he patted Ike on the back.

"So it looks like there is still a hot spot near the mines, one near the old canning factory, and one south of the airport."

I watched as the red hue glowed, pulsing as if it was alive. It wasn't, but I knew the thing we were tracking, the thing that made the screen crimson, was.

"How's the ankle?" Mr. Riley asked as he sat in a desk chair.

"Aw, feels fine," I said, but in truth it was actually quite tender. I'd relied heavily on the crutch all day.

"Good, but are you sure?" he asked.

"Yeah." I forced a smile. "Good as before last night."

With that, the three of us headed to eat dinner before tonight's hunt. A full meal of pot roast, carrots, potatoes, and Mrs. Riley's fresh made bread with butter and jam.

Afterward, I was so full all I wanted to do was find my bed or a couch and curl up to sleep. But alas, McGarrett reminded me—of course waiting until we were excused from the dinner table—that it was time to gear up. The sun was setting and the moon would soon be in domination of the night sky.

Ike didn't come with us right away, but instead disappeared into the kitchen while Mrs. Riley was still gathering the dishes.

I went to my room and grabbed one of the black under armor shirts from my closet. I laced up my pair of black New Balance shoes and off I went.

McGarrett was accessing video from the traffic and security cams around town, trying to get a glimpse of our target. The chief of police, Chief Rutledge, was a believer and he had helped secure the feed for us. "Mr. Riley, find anything?" I asked stretching my shoulders. The mention of his name made him jump. We were all on edge these days.

"Nope, but with Ike's quick work, we've eliminated most of the locations," he smiled and looked at his watch. "We have about twenty minutes before it will awaken. I think the first place we try is the old canning factory."

"Why?"

"It has the highest reading, and the mines seem too easy. Plus, the mines always glow red. It's a rarity that they normalize, no matter the sensor settings."

I started to gather my essential gadgets into my pack, including a restock on my smoke grenades. The J-Pak hung waiting on a hook. I swallowed hard and sighed. It was the quickest form of transportation, having a top speed of 178 miles per hour. Of course I'd never tried it that fast. I wanted to, but so far my uses had been either under the watchful eyes of Mr. Riley and Mr. Swigart, or as I barreled through a tree. Not good times to push its speed limits.

The door swung open and Ike came tearing in; he was out of breath, and there was blood. Blood on his shirt, blood on his hands. Was he hurt?

I started for him when he held something out before him. Three red globes, or bags. He wasn't hurt; he'd—well, invented something I guessed.

Ike made a beeline for me. He held out his hand, a proud smile across his face. "This is chicken blood," he announced.

I looked at him disgustedly. "And?"

"I drained it from tomorrow's dinner. Mrs. Riley had already killed the chickens," Ike explained.

While fresh meat is the best, and there was no comparison to Mrs. Riley's fried chicken, the grim aspect of killing the chickens remained. I never had to do it, but I was out back once when a chicken escaped from Mrs. Riley and was running around headless. Now the saying, *Running around like a chicken with its head cut off*, has a whole new meaning to me.

I stared at Ike. "So what are they?"

"Blood Bombs. I've drained the blood into these heavy latex balloons. If for some reason you find yourself out of options, toss one of these near the beast. It should at least briefly overwhelm its sense of smell, igniting its hunger. While its busy sniffing the blood, you'll get the second you need to escape." Ike handed me the bombs.

"Thanks." The balloons fit nicely inside a small pouch that I tied to my belt.

McGarrett had turned in his chair and stared at Ike, an eyebrow raised in curiosity. "I see you're breathing and that's what matters, so I won't ask. Can you help me get the J-Pack outside? Your dad undi—*modified* it while you were at school."

By modified, McGarrett meant tweaked, but tweaked back to its original state.

I hobbled after them; my ankle felt worse. I assured myself it wasn't fear.

I pictured the beast hunched over, its fangs bared, its bright green eyes staring me down. I knew it'd been about to pounce when I pulled my sword from its sheath.

McGarrett and Ike were near the car. Ike was looking over the J-Pak.

"Taylor, come over here; we're losing time," McGarrett warned.

I stood straight and they lifted the J-Pak into position, releasing its weight onto me.

Suddenly, my ankle buckled and I fell backward onto the J-Pak. A searing pain shot up my leg and I jerked in agony, but the jet pack straps over my shoulder held me down. I couldn't move, stuck like a turtle on its back.

McGarrett and Ike released me, but Mr. Riley frowned and shook his head.

"This is going to be a bit of a setback. You can't go out on that leg."

Ike helped me to my feet and I winced, then felt liquid running down my leg. I looked down and saw blood.

"Looks like the contraption cut you as well," McGarrett said and shook his head. Clearly he was frustrated, but had to act like he was concerned about my injuries. "Have Mrs. Riley look at that."

Ike began to laugh.

"It's not funny; Taylor's seriously hurt. We have just 27 days left to stop the HowlSage, before it reaches its full strength. Have you forgotten what the creature's purpose is? It has the power to summon minor demons. It could gather an army by the full moon and then we'd be hard pressed to stop even half of the demons from escaping into the countryside," McGarrett scolded.

"I'm sorry." Ike pulled the pouch away from my belt. He opened it and showed it to Mr. Riley and me.

One of the blood balloons had burst. I was covered in chicken blood, but it was better than my own.

"One of the bombs I made for Taylor," Ike whispered sadly.

McGarrett frowned, "Well either way, get inside and have Mrs. Riley look at your ankle. I'm going to listen to the police scanner for a while. Let's hope since it is still only two days old that it's not feeling too frisky."

Ike helped me across the driveway and up the grand front staircase of The Pink Hippo. We stepped into the quiet lobby and I stopped to take off my blood-soaked shoes, socks, and pants. No need to drip chicken blood all over the carpet.

"I'll meet you in the library," I said to Ike.

"OK," he said sullenly.

"Ike, don't worry. I'll get it. It's not your fault I got hurt," I explained.

"But he's right, we can't let the HowlSage live to the full moon," Ike started. "His venom will become potent and he could spread hate throughout the town."

I knew what Ike said was true, but it was worse than even that. A HowlSage was a Magnum level demon. There are several levels, the Masterum, Supremus, Magnum, Quantus, Regulus, Minor, and Microus. The HowlSage's tactical purpose was to act as a landing party and general to a battalion of demons. The creature would come through and act as a strongman, guarding the Etherpit and allowing demons of lower levels to come through safely.

"I know, but I'll get it. We have time," I reassured Ike.

He forced a smile.

"I'll see you in a little bit."

Ike headed for the library and I headed to my room.

After changing into fresh clothes, I found Mrs. Riley in the lobby sitting near the fireplace. I showed her my ankle; which was now purple and swollen. She made an almost clucking noise as she evaluated the damage.

"Well dear, it's off to the infirmary with you. We need to put a splint on and wrap it."

We went up to the second floor where the walls between several of the guest rooms had been removed, making a large medical ward. There were seven beds and scores of medical equipment—some a bit outdated, but then updated by Ike's dad, making it better than what the local hospital had available.

I laid down on one of the beds, and Mrs. Riley gathered her necessary supplies. I rolled my pant leg up far enough for her to access my ankle, in hopes of avoiding a gown.

She applied some salve, rubbing it in a little less gently than I would have liked. My leg involuntary lurched a couple of times, for which Mrs. Riley apologized, but assured me it was necessary to work the salve deep into my skin, thereby allowing it to seep into the tissue.

She placed the splint on each side of my ankle and then began wrapping. And wrapping. And wrapping. Soon the affected area looked like I'd grown a melon-sized growth just above my foot.

Of course, walking now became an art, but there was no more twinge of pain when I stepped down. I could put all my weight on both legs, but it was a challenge not to bump the right ball of bandage against my left foot, causing me to stumble.

I hobbled my way to the biggest of the two libraries, probably one of Ike's favorite and one of my least favorite rooms in the old inn. Two stories of paper, as in books, surrounded the circular room—most really old, from the 19th and 20th centuries. In other words, very few that I would actually read.

I did find a few books intriguing, like *Frankenstein*. Now that was an interesting story—man trying to play God, but realizing God cannot be played.

Sure enough, Ike was seated comfortably in an overstuffed chair, one with a few bite marks from the Riley's former dog, Gruff. There were at least a dozen books open on the ground surrounding Ike's chair.

I knew these books weren't left over from a time before; they'd been skimmed just tonight. When Ike was looking for something he was like a machine.

"Ike!"

He jumped at least a foot when I said his name.

I laughed. "A little edgy are we?" I asked.

He shook his head, "You shouldn't do that to a guy. And—and you would have startled too, if you'd just read what I did."

"Oh yeah, let me take a look." I walked over to Ike and he offered me the current book.

"It's from 1834," he said.

"Oh really." I turned it over in my hand, half laughing inside at the fact that a book written in the early 1800s could at all be frightening. I read the cover: *The HowlSage Haunting.* So?"

"Read the subtitle."

"*How the hunter became the hunted.*"

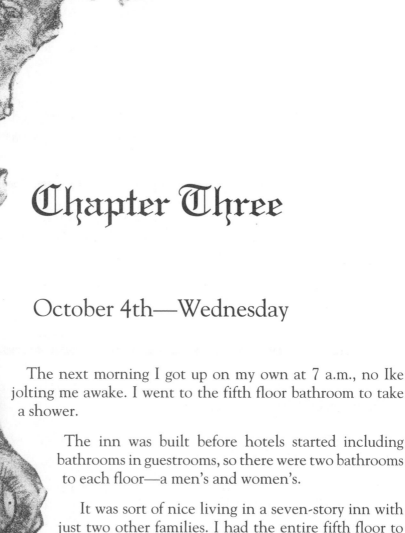

Chapter Three

October 4th—Wednesday

The next morning I got up on my own at 7 a.m., no Ike jolting me awake. I went to the fifth floor bathroom to take a shower.

The inn was built before hotels started including bathrooms in guestrooms, so there were two bathrooms to each floor—a men's and women's.

It was sort of nice living in a seven-story inn with just two other families. I had the entire fifth floor to myself. You'd think it'd be lonely, but not really. Ike and his family were on the third floor and the Rileys on the first. Sometimes we'd have guests from other chapters of the society and they'd stay on the fourth or sixth floor. Really, I didn't spend much time on my floor; mainly just to sleep and wash-up. But sometimes if I wanted to get away, it was nice.

I wrapped my ankle with plastic to keep it dry. I was known for lengthy showers. There was something about the water running on your face, the steam swirling round. It gave me clarity, helped me feel cleansed and refreshed.

I dried off and undid the plastic from my ankle. A thick layer of steam filled the room. I wrapped my towel around me and stepped into heavy air. The mirror was completely fogged over and I could barely see my reflection.

With an extra hand towel, I wiped a path dry. *That was bett—*

My body involuntary jerked backward, my brain sending a defensive message to my muscles before I even consciously knew what was happening.

I ducked, rolled, and popped to my feet, five feet away from the threat.

There, staring at me, was the furry beast, the creature I was hunting. The HowlSage.

I was armed with nothing more than a towel. It brandished razor claws and fangs; each set two inches in length.

I made quick work of the towel, twisting it into a whip. It might work. A damp towel had a powerful snap to it.

What was I thinking; the towel wouldn't even penetrate the thick brown matted coat of the beast.

In three seconds I would launch myself backward and through the door.

One…

Two…

Roar!

Its furry head was in my face and on me before I had a moment to react. I grabbed at its ears and twisted, in the only offensive maneuver I knew. I'd seen it done in James Bond films a dozen times.

The head came loose; I'd ripped it clean from its torso.

Wait.

Laughing?

Out from the steam stepped someone I'd not expected. It'd been a month since I'd seen him at my dad's funeral. With curly brown hair, chocolate skin, and at six-foot-seven, my cousin Jesse could easily pull off a HowlSage when shrouded by steam.

He looked at the twisted towel on the floor and started laughing even harder, grabbing hold of the nearby counter to brace himself as he howled uncontrollably. Maybe howl wasn't the right word to use in this circumstance, but either way he was thrilled with the results of his prank.

I scowled, reached for my towel, and wrapped it tightly around myself. Picking up the fake werewolf head, I turned it over in my hands, observing it. Clearly he'd recently been to a Halloween costume store. They'd popped up everywhere in the last month. I exhaled an angry sigh and tossed the mask at Jesse. It bounced off his side, throwing him into another fit of laughter.

My cheeks flushed as I walked out of the bathroom. Angry no, embarrassed yes. But yet happy—Jesse was here.

Back in my room I got dressed in my usual school attire and waited. It'd only be a moment yet.

Sure enough, the door creaked open, and the now wet, soggy werewolf head poked around the open door, speaking in a mocking voice. "Tay Tay, I'm gonna get you. You'd better get your towel."

I threw my pillow at the door; it bounced off and rolled aside as Jesse entered the room.

"So you're here," I said.

"Yeah, I'm here. Surprised?"

"A little."

"Scared?"

"You wish."

"So I hear you've got a HowlSage on your hands."

"Yeah, sure do. And with dad gone, it's me left to guard the Etherpit."

"Naw, it's up to us," Jesse said with a half smile.

"You've been sent? You're not just stopping on your way to another assignment?"

Jesse shook his head. "Nope, since I turned eighteen I make my own rules. I go where I want to."

"Ha, your parents would never…"

"My parents nothing; I'm an adult now."

A knock on the door interrupted the banter.

"Can we come in?" came the sweetest voice I knew besides my mom, sweeter than Mrs. Riley.

In walked my aunt Mary and uncle Matt. Quite the pair, you see. My aunt Mary had dark skin and was taller than my uncle, whose skin was as pale as the moon three nights ago.

I looked at Jesse and shook my head, then mouthed his line about making his own rules.

My uncle snorted. "Don't worry Taylor. We overheard Jesse's little comment about going where he wants to. We'll see if he can pay for that car on his own."

Jesse blushed.

"Did you drive here?" I asked.

"Yeah, Dad and Mom drove separate," Jesse explained.

"We're off to New York. I've got some research to do at the Museum up there," Uncle Matt explained. "But Jesse here is going to stick around and hopefully be of some assistance to you."

I stood from the bed immediately. "Really!" I exclaimed, sounding like a little boy who'd just found out he was going to Disney World. Which was a bit more excitement than I wanted to reveal. I knew full well that Jesse would let that go to his head. "I mean—cool."

"We do wish we could stay longer," my aunt said sweetly. "But Matt is needed immediately to look at a sarcophagus. Traces of a Sage were detected."

My uncle Matt sighed. "We were in Egypt just a few days ago when the decision was made to move it to New York. I said we should just leave it there. But I was overruled."

I did wish they could stay, but knew that my uncle was one of the top archeologists in for the Legion der Dämonjäger. He once hunted, but lost half his right leg to a bite from a BloodSage. To stop the spread of the venom, he'd had to remove it on the spot. I'll save you the gory details of how he did it. But that's why he could no longer hunt. But by applying the field experience he had, he could sense things others couldn't.

"We only stopped by to make sure Jesse arrived as intended," my uncle Matt looked over at my cousin with a frown. "Your aunt and I will be off for New York in just a few minutes actually. However, Jesse is here for the remainder of the hunt."

A wry smile crossed Jesse's lips. "That's right, lil' cuz. Me and you hunting together."

I nodded, relieved I wouldn't be alone.

Together we headed downstairs for breakfast and feasted with Ike and the Rileys. It seemed Mrs. Riley had tripled her breakfast effort. There were seven types of pancakes and four syrups, eggs, bacon, sausage, biscuits, hash browns, and yogurt parfaits.

After the early feast, I knew Ike and I would still be off to school.

I tried convincing McGarrett to let me stay home, due to the ankle, but he wouldn't have it. Said something about education coming first, and hunting second.

Ike and I wanted Jesse to drive us, but his parents said they'd be leaving shortly and wanted to clarify some things with him first. That meant lay down some ground rules and consequences.

School crept by, literally second by second. I couldn't concentrate knowing Jesse was at the inn and I was stuck at school. Boring. But then I headed to history, and there she was. The girl from my first night of hunting, the one I'd seen from the rooftop.

I slipped behind her and followed, not in the stalking sort of way, but just made sure I took the same route she did. I never quite got in front of her to get a clear look, but I was sure it was her. Of course I couldn't be one hundred percent sure; it was the middle of the night from a roof high above and through grainy green goggles that I first saw her.

I lost her as the warning bell rang. I did a one-eighty and quickly hobbled down two more halls to get to class.

Maybe following her hadn't been on my way.

A few more classes and school was out. I loitered near where I'd seen her, but she never came.

Ike and I went outside to find Jesse awaiting us. He'd left the top down, even though the temperature was hardly over 50 degrees, but I didn't care. Ike complained a couple of times, but eventually ducked into his shirt much like a turtle does into its shell.

Mrs. Riley was in the workshop and she'd brought in a tray piled with sandwiches. She quickly looked over my ankle and told Jesse and I to eat. McGarrett had some substantial intelligence on the HowlSage; we'd be off before it got dark. She'd brought down my hunting clothes and set them in the changing room.

Usually I'd be suspicious of an adult sifting through my stuff, but not Mrs. Riley.

Besides, I had nothing to hide.

I stepped out of the changing room in my black attire. Ike helped me strap on the J-Pak, and we restocked my utility belt with needed supplies, including new blood balloons.

Ike gave me two thumbs up, signaling I was ready.

McGarrett still hadn't shown up. Apparently, he'd driven out to the location to verify the intelligence. He called to let us know what he'd found and that we'd be headed to the mines tonight.

The workshop door opened, but it wasn't McGarrett.

"You look like a Halfling version of Batman," Jesse teased as he entered. I took one look at him and smiled.

"And you look like a giant Hershey's kiss in that tin foil getup of yours."

Jesse laughed. He pressed something on his wrist, and dissipated from the bottom up.

I felt a tug on my arm, and then a shove from the opposite direction.

"Thanks to the latest military advancements, I can now appear invisible," Jesse's voice said from behind me.

Wham! I felt a solid punch to my chest armor.

"Quite the abs you have, Tay," Jesse mocked, knowing I was wearing body armor.

Suddenly his silver form appeared again, this time sitting in a chair several feet away.

"Nice," I said.

"The quick moves are mine; the suit is my mom's invention. It's even made of real silver, so if that beastie decides to bite into me, it'll be its last."

"Yours too," I reminded him.

"Maybe," he argued.

"Probably," Ike added.

I'd forgotten he was in the room; it was easy to do with Jesse here. Jesse and I had history; we were cousins. His personality dominated when he was around.

Jesse laughed. "So McGarrett's still not here?"

"Here I am," came the older man's voice as he entered. "Are you both ready? We need to head out now. It's quite the drive, and we need to be in place before it gets dark."

Ike started to follow, but McGarrett waved him off. "We need you to stay here and monitor. See if there are any anomalies in the tracking system."

Ike frowned, started to speak, then stopped. Staring at his shoes, he turned and stalked toward the large display of glowing screens.

Jesse stood and punched my arm. "Come on. Tay, we've got a HowlSage to dispatch."

A few minutes later, we slid into the back seat of McGarrett's Rolls and were off.

The twinge I'd felt in my stomach for Ike was gone the moment Jesse flipped on his iPod and streamed it through the car's stereo. It may have been an older car, but it too had many modifications.

It was getting dark. Our destination was still in the distance; freshly fallen snow created layer of powder on the road. It seemed the higher altitudes of the mountains always saw the icy gifts from winter first. The narrow road had been chipped from the side of a cliff. Barely more than two lanes wide most of the time, each curve made it impossible to see oncoming traffic and passing was unadvisable.

We were still jamming out to our tunes when something crashed into the left side of the Rolls, pushing us across lanes and toward the guardrail. McGarrett swung the wheel to the right, pulling us away from the steep cliff.

A large boulder rolled in front of the car, a mist of snow trailing behind it. Another crashed into the side of the Rolls with a resounding crunch. McGarrett swerved to keep the car from spinning off the cliff and then hooked the wheel hard to miss the debris ahead.

"I guess the HowlSage woke up from his nap!" Jesse shouted. He opened the skylight and stood up, his head poking out.

"Up there!" he shouted, but his voice was muffled by the wind. "Stop the car!"

The Rolls still screeching to a halt, Jesse was out through the roof and scrambling up the side of the cliff like a spider. I'd never seen anyone so skilled at free climbing.

"Taylor, what are you doing!" McGarrett spun in his seat to look at me. "Get going, Jesse didn't come all this way to do your job for you."

He was right, but part of me knew that Jesse wouldn't mind being one on one with the beast. His ego seemed to underestimate challenges at times.

I climbed from the car and pulled my gear tight.

Here goes nothing.

I released the wings and activated the J-Pak.

A microsecond later I was zooming up the side of the cliff past Jesse. I smiled sarcastically and gave him a thumbs up.

The beast had disappeared, but he couldn't be far from us. Landing atop the cliff, the wings snapped into a lowered position. Split branches revealed where something had darted into the foliage and large, clawed footprints led the way through loose dirt and pine needles.

Jesse, still visible, was thirty feet below and still climbing.

He wouldn't wait for me, I thought, so I bolted into the woods which were surprisingly dark for how much moon still remained in the sky.

My light assisted in my search, and it wasn't hard to spot all the destruction the beast had carelessly done by thrashing through the woods.

These beasts certainly weren't covert.

A pile of large boulders came into view and I slowed down.

Snap!

I turned—the sound had come from behind me. The twilight glow of the woods made it hard to see. I put on my night goggles and scanned the area. I looked back toward the rocks and heard the softest of growls coming from the pile. I crept forward.

I heard it again. Slightly louder.

A few more steps. I slid my blade from its sheath. I was ready, a quick slash and stab maneuver played out in my mind.

Something rustled the branches behind me again. I quickly looked, but there was still nothing.

The growl had turned to a consistent hum ahead of me. Like the buzz of a thousand angry bees.

Crack!

Beside me; I turned to face it. Still nothing was before me. I scanned the branches of the trees, there was nothing above.

Almost there.

"Watch out!" someone screamed from beside me.

The words had barely registered in my brain when my body was catapulted through the air. I thudded to the ground, but kept hold of my sword. The branches above me shifted as something leapt toward where I'd been.

And there in my place, standing upright on two thick, muscular legs, was the HowlSage. It'd grown bigger in the two days since I'd seen it. And from what McGarrett had taught me, it would continue to grow every day, its venom potent if we didn't kill it before the full moon.

This was the first time I'd truly looked at the beast. It was more than eight feet in height, bulging lumps of muscle on its arms and legs. A thick coat of brown, matted fur covered all of it, but thinned on its chest, replaced with leathery skin and a solid six pack set of abs. Its muzzle came to a point, housing two sets of razor sharp fangs. Its ears came to sharp points, looking more like cat ears than dog. Eyes glowed of their own accord, like two yellow bulbs. The HowlSage's brown, moist nostrils flared as it caught my scent and smelled for fear, something I hoped it wouldn't find. Two-inch claws on its feet and hands were its primary weapons; its fangs were reserved for conversion through the injection of venom. A small tail, not worthy of the name, wiggled on its rump.

I knew only by driving my silver sword directly through its heart could it be dispatched. HowlSages were different from the horror film werewolves—they couldn't be killed by a so-called silver bullet. Werewolves were fake, their creation based on peasant sightings dating back to medieval times. But the society had done a great job of ensuring their reality remained as a myth wrapped behind the mask of the werewolf. If just anyone knew that these demonic sages existed, they might try and control them, use them for their own sinful plans. The greatest example of this happening was during World War II with Hitler's S.S. They were deep into this demonic stuff, and they had thousands of Sages in their service.

I looked at the beast and pushed myself to my feet. I squeezed the hilt of my sword and held it before me. Staring at its silver blade, it looked like something King Arthur might have used. I'd need to be quick and accurate.

Grrrrr. The HowlSage growled and lowered its head.

For this to be over, I was going to have to get a lot closer than any sane person would like. I took a deep breath. My muscles tensed as I prepared to charge forward.

Its oversized hairy shoulder jerked backward and a bloody gash appeared along its forearm. The beast swiped its long hairy arm through the air, then growled.

"Uhhh," someone grunted. I watched an area of snow compact as if a body landed there.

Jesse, I knew immediately.

The beast let out a vicious howl and took off into a mad retreat, but stopped as something plunged into its matted fur. A long wire stretched from the HowlSage to where I assumed Jesse landed.

The HowlSage screamed in anger and yanked the cord toward it. What I assume was Jesse crashed upward into the branches of a tall pine, likely holding onto the other end of the wire, his body's weight of no consequence to the HowlSage.

A twinge of fear struck through my mind like lightning, and in that moment the HowlSage growled fiercely and darted into the woods. The sound of tree limbs being ripped apart would be easy enough to follow. But my feet wouldn't move and my mind wouldn't make them.

I heard someone groan overhead.

The cracking, snapping noise slowly trailed off—I was losing the demon.

"Hey, get me down," I heard Jesse say. "I can't get my arms free."

My cousin was now visible, hanging upside down from a tree branch. The cable pinned his arms to his body and then wrapped around his right leg and up around a tree branch.

"I'll come back for you," I started.

"No, get me down, dude," he called. "This hurts."

I wanted to laugh at Jesse's precarious position, but I couldn't. I'd felt something I'd not expected and I was ashamed of that. What was worse, I knew the HowlSage could outrun me, and even if I flew overhead using my night goggles I'd not likely be able to see it through the dark trees.

We'd failed again tonight, and the best thing I could do was get Jesse down and check on McGarrett.

Chapter Four

October 5th—Thursday

I awoke to sore muscles and a shiver. It was earlier than I'd like, but nonetheless I ached too much to sleep. I stalked down the hall toward where Jesse was staying. The door was cracked and I could hear him snoring.

If not for the disappointment of last night and my aching muscles, I might have burst into the room to startle him awake.

The morning sun sent a warm glow in through a window at the end of the hall. It provided a pretty good view of Ashley Meadows. The small town was still in slumber. Only a few trucks and cars drove the streets, milk delivery, newspaper, etc.

The setting was surreal; you'd never know that demons lurked in the shadows and that a powerful one was growing, biding its time to lead an army against the town's residents. It was such a different dimension to the picturesque town.

A hand on my shoulder startled me and I spun around.

Ike.

"Don't do that!"

He stepped back, his expression hurt. "Sorry."

I sighed, "Sorry, Ike, I'm just on edge. What are you doing up so early?"

"I was just upstairs praying. I've been worried about Dad. Today will be his first day on site. If the Etherpit opened the day after the full moon, it's likely a HowlSage that they're facing."

I understood, but didn't offer any condolences.

"Plus Mom won't be back for at least another week or so. I tried calling her last night, but the whole time zone thing makes it hard to get a hold of each other…"

"Have you sent her an email?" I asked.

"Yeah, and she responded, but I'd like to hear her voice," he said.

I felt that ache in my stomach, the one that would come in weak moments. I hadn't heard my mom's voice for several years now, and I would never hear my dad's again. Ike didn't realize how blessed he was to have both his parents. I had neither.

I stopped myself from saying what was on my tongue. Sometimes it's better to listen.

We stared out the window at the town. The sun's rays were growing stronger, highlighting the town in a pink hue.

Something latched onto Ike and jerked him away. My breath hitched.

Jesse held Ike in a bear hug. "A bit on edge, are we?" he asked in a teasing tone. "That's two days in a row that I've given a good scare to someone."

I barked a laugh, regretting that I'd decided not to attack him this morning.

Jesse released Ike, who scowled and stalked off down the hallway.

"Someone can't take a joke," Jesse said purposely loud enough for Ike to hear.

I shook my head and left my cousin in the hall as I headed back to my room to dress and head for breakfast.

After eating, Ike and I headed off to school. Jesse decided not to take us, and McGarrett had headed out to the scene of last night's attack. He needed to take some pictures and see if he could find any fur samples. So Ike and I were stuck with the bus.

My ankle felt a lot better and hoofing it down the driveway to the bus stop wasn't all that bad. Ike explained to me that he'd tried calling us last night. The hillside along the road we were on started to glow red, but when he tried to call and warn us he couldn't. He even tried using the backup HAM radio. But nothing seemed to work. He couldn't explain what had happened, but he checked and the communication systems all seemed normal this morning.

The bus arrived a few minutes later and we took seats across from each other.

Several more stops and we arrived at school.

The day was uneventful; I barely passed a math test, but aced my history paper.

And what was worse, there was no sign of the girl. I realized how few friends I had when I asked all three of them if they'd seen a new girl and all said, "No." I knew I needed to be a bit more social, but to some I was still the new kid. I'd only been in Ashley Meadows for two years. I tried to remember the saying my dad had often quoted, something about friends and outside.

Ike and I loaded onto the bus and waited for our departure home. Kids of all ages piled on. There was just one school in Ashley Meadows and it handled K through 12.

My heart skipped a beat—there she was. Just as the old yellow bus grunted and jerked forward, she stepped out of the school. I stood as if I might leap from the bus, but obviously that wouldn't work. For one, the bus driver would order me back to my seat, and second, what did I expect to say? I'd never been introduced to the girl.

"Hey, my name is Taylor and I was watching you from a rooftop at midnight a few evenings ago."

Right. That probably wouldn't come across very well.

As the bus pulled away, I saw her walk over to a small electric pink scooter and put on a helmet. The bus turned down another street and she was out of view.

I apparently had acted funny, because Ike was staring at me, an eyebrow cocked. I filled him in, knowing he wouldn't judge me and he'd keep my secret. After all, at only eleven, he hadn't really become interested in girls yet.

He sat and listened, but didn't have much of a reaction. Just shrugged and said he hoped that she'd be my *friend* someday.

Back at The Pink Hippo, Ike and I checked the workshop but neither Jesse nor McGarrett were around. The Rolls was gone and so was Jesse's car. We crossed the short distance from the workshop to the inn.

The driveway to the inn looped around a large rotunda, where cars could circle and drop off passengers and luggage before parking. Ike started for the center of the rotunda where a large fountain sat spraying water. I followed.

The fountain was the namesake of the inn—three oversized pink hippos wallowed in the water in varying positions. The pink paint that once adorned the copper animal busts had mostly peeled off, but a few flecks still remained. The fountain was a scratchy green and white color; that's what happens to copper after it oxidizes. I only know about oxidization because Ike explained it to me. Apparently the Statue of

Liberty is also made of copper.

Ike reached in the fountain and moved his hand around as if searching for something. A moment later he pulled out his web-phone and tapped the screen. I looked over his shoulder and watched as a video played on the screen.

"What are we—?"

Ike held up his hand. "Watch. Listen."

The video zipped by in fast-forward mode. Ike quickly tapped the play button as McGarrett stepped out of the workshop. He walked to the Rolls, and Jesse came out of the workshop dressed in his silver suit. Neither of them said anything, but both got in separate vehicles and a moment later drove down the lane. The camera rotated, following the cars until they disappeared out of sight. It even zoomed in as far as it could.

Ike tapped the device off and slid it back in his pocket, then reached in the water to touch something in the fountain.

"What was that all about? How'd you do that?" I asked.

Ike smiled, happy that he'd impressed me. "I've placed several cameras all around the inn, my own security surveillance. McGarrett doesn't know about them," he explained.

"And neither did I."

"Nope, nor does my dad or mom," he said. "They're secret."

For some reason it didn't concern me that Ike had covertly planted cameras all over the inn; instead, I felt honored that he'd shared it with me. Although, why not before now?

"You can't tell anyone, not even that cousin of yours," he explained.

"I won't," I promised. "So, what's in the pool?"

"Oh, there's a switch that turns the streaming signal on and off. If I left the stream open, McGarrett or my father might have detected it. So while the camera remains active and senses motion, I don't allow its wi-fi to transmit."

"Way beyond me." I smiled at him, a real genius, and three years younger than me. "Where do you think they went?"

"Not sure, but it looks like they were doing some recon; Jesse was dressed in his hunting clothes. Maybe they're hoping to find the HowlSage sleeping in its den."

"How long ago did they leave?"

Ike pulled out the phone again and checked the time stamp on the video. "Looks like noon."

"Hmmm, and they're still not back yet."

"Nope, there were no more records, besides you and I walking up the drive."

"Well, I guess we should just wait. How about we see if we can snag a snack?"

Secretly, I was miffed that they'd gone somewhere without me. I mean, I remember what McGarrett said about school first, but still. We had a little more than 27 days to find the foul beast, or risk it spreading hate and bringing forth a small demon army. That seemed a bit more serious than my studies.

The sun dropped and still no sign of McGarrett or Jesse. We tried calling, we even tried tracking them. But the signal was still messed up. Ike explained that it seemed to happen at sun down, and the problem hadn't existed the previous day before sundown either.

We asked Mrs. Riley where they'd gone, but she didn't know. I could tell she seemed a bit nervous. The three of us ate together and Ike and I decided to go to the library afterward.

I was getting angrier by the moment—an entire night of hunting wasted. I was stuck home. I'd considered gearing up and flying out on my own, but Ike reminded me we didn't know where the creature was due to the dead signal. I could search all night and never see a sign of the beast. It'd just end up being a waste, and if they returned while I was gone, there would be no way to contact me.

More so, I was angry at Jesse for going without me. We were supposed to be partners, cousins, blood. Instead, he was out having fun, taking the glory probably, and he'd eat it up if he got the HowlSage on his own. His head would explode with pride.

It wasn't until nearly midnight when the Rolls sped up the drive. Ike and I saw the headlights from the library window and raced downstairs.

The Rolls skidded in the gravel driveway as it grinded to a stop. The door swung open and McGarrett nearly toppled from the car. He was bleeding, and Jesse was nowhere in sight.

Mrs. Riley ran down the stairs to her husband. "What's happened?"

He looked up at her. "I'm fine. Really, it's just a scratch and a bump."

I noticed that there was a large hole in the windshield of the car. This was a great shock, as the windshield wasn't your standard car safety glass—it was reinforced bullet-proof.

This was bad. I watched Ike climb on to the hood of the car. He had his web phone out and was taking pictures, surely running calculations of some sort.

The moment had gotten away from me.

"Where's Jesse?" I asked.

McGarrett looked at me. "I don't know. We got separated."

I took a step forward. "Why did you leave him?"

"Had to—" He took a deep breath. "Look in the trunk."

I ran around the car and popped it open. I'd never seen anything like it. It shimmered in the moonlight, mesmerizing. All thoughts of Jesse vanished from my mind.

Ike joined me and we both stared at the magnificent thing.

Before us was a wide jeweled belt. Chains of white diamonds surrounded a fist-sized ruby.

I looked back at McGarrett. "Where did you find it?"

Chapter Five

October 6th—Friday

I repeated my question, "Where did you find it?" It was but a few seconds into Friday, but the day had already started grimly.

"We'd noticed something odd in a section," McGarrett took a deep breath, "—of the old canning factory. The levels were higher than they'd ever been, but it was still daytime. So we decided to investigate immediately."

I felt an odd sense of guilt for being so angry that they'd left me behind. "Then what happened?"

Ike had disappeared to the workshop, and Mrs. Riley had gone to retrieve some bandages. McGarrett sat on the ground, his back against the car.

"The canning factory was dark—not like shadows or nighttime darkness, but dark as in the absence of hope or anything good. It was cold. An eerie mist swirled within the building and voices whispered in the mist," McGarrett's voice trailed off. "The voices whispered hateful things.

My heart sunk, and thoughts I would have never had before began to slip into my mind. I saw things, things of pure evil." He stopped and took a deep breath, his eyes closed. "I'd entered with Jesse, but he had gone invisible far before we reached the door. I stood there and felt entirely alone." McGarrett's voice was weak as he continued. "Then it came. I don't know what it was, but it blocked my exit. Shrouded in a gray mist, the thing moved forward. I backed away from it, and tripped over a large beam. Suddenly Jesse attacked, still invisible, but I knew it was him. His sword glowed green, appearing only momentarily as it sliced into the gray mist. There appeared to be nothing inside. The mist separated, but reformed quickly." McGarrett stopped for a breath. "He yelled for me to run; I turned and crawled out of reach. But it didn't matter. I watched as the sword wielded by an invisible hand appeared each time it sliced and slashed through the mist. There was one thing to do—I knelt, bowed my head, and began to pray. My eyes closed tightly." McGarrett swallowed. "What seemed like hours but was a matter of minutes passed as I prayed. I felt the darkness lift, I felt a sense of relief, of someone holding me. When I looked around, the gray mist was gone. I was alone and I knew that Angels had to have been the ones holding me. I called for Jesse, but he didn't answer."

Mrs. Riley had returned with bandages and a warm, wet cloth. She began wiping and dressing her husband's wounds.

He spoke again, "I went back to the car and retrieved a sword mightier than the one Jesse had used."

I knew exactly what he was speaking of—he meant the Book.

"I walked into the factory, praying aloud, searching for Jesse. I'd never realized how large the building was, and I had to search every inch of it. If Jesse was still invisible, but—" he stopped.

I knew what his next word would have been if he'd continued.

"Hours passed and I knew the sun would disappear soon, when I remembered something your father and I had discovered. There had been an old sewage drain that we'd sealed together. But before we did, your father had walked its entire length. A side tunnel had been dug, connecting it to the mines, but no man had dug this connection. We planted some sensors and then sealed the factory side of the drain."

It was hard to hear him speak of my father. They'd had more adventures together than I had, but more than that, it made me miss him.

"When I reached the old drain, I found the seal had been destroyed. Something had broken through." McGarrett looked at me. "Taylor, I would have climbed in and gone after, but my body won't allow me to do what I could long ago."

I nodded to let him know I understood.

McGarrett stared at the ground. "Instead. I went back to the Rolls and made for the mines—"

Mrs. Riley interrupted, "You know you aren't—"

Mr. Riley broke in, "—I had to, the boy had been taken, I assume. I might have been his only hope."

"Wait, might have?" I asked.

"Yes, but not yet. I sped to the mines like a banshee, which for all I knew was exactly what we had faced. I blasted through the old chain link fence to entrance seventeen, one of the last that has not collapsed. Darkness had fallen, so I knew I had to be even more cautious. The HowlSage would now be awake and stalking the hillsides."

Ike suddenly ran up to the car wearing thick sparkling gloves. He reached into the trunk and lifted the belt out. I admired the glittering jewels once again.

Ike walked to the front of the car and set the belt onto the hood. Mrs. Riley looked at it, as did McGarrett.

"Yes, we must get that inside and safe," McGarrett said, and climbed to his feet as if no injury had ever riddled him. "Quickly, everyone to the workshop."

The four of us went inside and McGarrett ordered all of the windows and doors to be sealed.

"What about Jesse?" I asked, ashamed I had forgotten him at the sight of the belt. There was something possessive about the thing, as if nothing else in the world existed once you caught sight of it.

"Yes, as I was saying," McGarrett started again. "I walked into the mine and followed it deep into its depths. For how long, I don't remember. I searched many off shoots of the tunnel; whenever I would come to a dead end or a collapse, I'd turn and go back to the main branch of the mine. Deeper and deeper I went, then I heard something. Soon, out of the darkness, Jesse appeared. No longer invisible, he turned and fired something into the darkness. An ear splitting roar howled from the black. He looked at me and shouted, 'run!' I didn't, he ran to me and pulled something from an old burlap sack."

"The belt," I said without thinking.

"Yes," McGarrett nodded. "Jesse gave me the sack and ordered me forward. He fired blindly into the darkness again. A new howl erupted. Jesse was hitting his target—and a moment later I saw it. The HowlSage erupted into view, enveloped in the eerie gray mist I'd just seen. Together we ran for the entrance of the mine. I was slower, so Jesse continually stopped and fired at the beast to delay it. Once or twice he attempted to use his sword, but it glowed green each time it entered the mist and the HowlSage didn't try to avoid the sword, but took the blows. I knew we were facing something more powerful than we had before—the silver in Jesse's sword should have turned the HowlSage into dust, but it had no effect on the creature."

"The silver didn't affect the HowlSage," Ike repeated. "That's not possible."

"It's the truth. We eventually made it to the car. I climbed inside, as did Jesse, when something fell from the sky, or dived. A beak of sorts pierced through the windshield, sending fragments of glass everywhere. That's where the scrape comes from. The beast tore its beak from the hole and reeled back for another strike; I'd never seen anything like it. Jesse climbed out of the car and swung his sword at the creature. The darkness shrouded its identity, and it flew from the hood before it could be killed.

"The HowlSage had emerged from the mine and was starting for us, but the gray mist seemed to hang back near the entrance. Jesse looked at me and I knew what he was thinking. I tried to stop him, but he argued that he had to try to kill it and that I needed to get the belt away from here. Before I had any chance to stop him—not that I would have been successful—he tore forward to meet the HowlSage. I heard a screech and felt the car rock as the beak of the creature pierced the roof of the Rolls," McGarrett stopped for a breath. "I slammed the car in reverse and tore from the mine property, my destination The Pink Hippo. I looked out the rearview mirror, but there was no sign of Jesse, the HowlSage, or the gray mist."

I sighed and listened for the sound of tires on gravel or the slamming of a door, as if expecting for Jesse to arrive any moment.

"What of the flying thing?" Ike asked McGarrett.

"I'm not sure; it didn't attack again," he said.

"What is the belt?" I asked. "I mean, is it special or something?"

"Not sure yet, I need to run some tests." McGarrett stared at me. "Jesse never said where or how he found it; we were too busy scrambling for our lives."

The hours passed slowly. McGarrett wouldn't let us leave the workshop. The building provided more protections than the many-windowed inn. We were literally sealed within. Of course I knew, as did Ike, that the defenses only worked against physical threats, which meant ninety percent of our enemies could still get to us.

McGarrett had been busy analyzing the belt as Ike looked on. Mrs. Riley hovered over me, trying to comfort me. "Jesse is more than capable of handling himself against a five-day-old HowlSage," she assured me.

Knock, knock, knock.

I awoke with a start, lifting my head from where it rested on a computer panel. Using an old hard drive for a pillow hadn't been a good idea.

A few feet away, McGarrett flipped to the screen that monitored the workshop entrance.

He was looking ragged, but clearly it was Jesse. He'd returned.

McGarrett clicked a button and the door opened. The bright sunlight from the outside blinded me as I looked to see my cousin. Jesse hobbled forward; a tear in his pant leg revealed a deep gash. He sat nearby and looked at me as I lay in a sleeping bag on the floor.

"Glad you had a good night's sleep," he teased.

Typical that Jesse would still have a sense of humor.

"Yeah, well what else could I do? I was stuck in here, because you ran away."

He smiled then looked to McGarrett. "Is it safe?"

"The belt? Yes, we have it here. I've run some tests, it certainly has the signs," McGarrett said.

Jesse frowned.

Signs? Signs of what? I wondered. I was about to ask, when Jesse groaned painfully.

"What is it?" Mrs. Riley asked. She'd already started to clean the wound. "Is it a bite?"

We all knew the implications of the question, and if it was a bite, we knew the consequences that waited.

"No," Jesse answered. "A branch got me."

Everyone sighed in relief.

"So it got away?" I asked.

"It did, but I chased it all the way to the river where it slipped into the murky water and disappeared. The sun was nearly up."

"What of the mist?" McGarrett asked.

"Never left the cave, and I blocked the HowlSage from reentering."

"And the flying thing?" Ike asked.

Jesse shook his head.

"All right, now that Jesse is back and the light has returned, it's time for…" McGarrett started.

I waited for him to say, "It's time for school." But that wasn't to be.

"—one of the missus' wonderful breakfasts. Then off to bed for everyone," McGarrett finished.

"You mean no school?" Ike asked.

"Not today. Everyone needs rest; this weekend is going to be challenging to all of us."

We all went to the dining hall and in ten minutes food started streaming from the kitchen as Mrs. Riley brought one dish after the other. Jesse looked as though he might doze off at any moment, and although I'd gotten a little bit of sleep, I could hear my pillow calling me.

There was to be no hunting that night—sleep all day, relax to a book or movie, and then sleep some more. We'd get back to it Saturday night.

Ike woke me about 2 p.m. I agreed to go with him to Coal Chase Lake, which stretched across the back side of the property. It was a great place to spend an afternoon.

We outfitted ourselves in fleece jackets, hats, and gloves and made our way through the woods behind The Pink Hippo. It was a good three-mile hike on dirt paths winding through pine forests, the smell of which made me feel alive.

As we hiked, we talked about the hunt, and Ike shared a couple theories he had about the gray mist. He believed it was some form of demon spirit that had been defeated or banished. As for the flying thing, he wasn't sure yet.

I just hoped I didn't have to fight either one.

As we arrived on the shore we looked out over the lake. The greenish blue water stood out against the cold gray sky. The lake hadn't frozen over yet, but we were certainly not going swimming.

An old wooden row boat would be our transport out onto the water.

The lake was dotted with several small islands; Ike and I had named each one. There was *Pine Needle Island* where a small glen of pine trees had created a three-foot covering of needles. *Croaking Flat*, where we'd discovered an entire colony of frog burrows. On *Cedar Point Island* a single cedar tree stood in the center, from which we'd hung a rope, creating a swing to jump into the lake from.

Ash Isle was a wide, flat pile of rocks. Ike had determined that it'd been used by a Native American tribe in some sort of burial ritual at one time. The isle was cleared of trees, and he'd discovered fragments of old pottery and even some bone fragments a few feet below the top layer of rocks. I never had asked what caused him to dig in the rocks.

But our favorite island was *Doughnut Rock Pool*. No, it wasn't where we made mud pies or rock doughnuts when we were younger. It was a fairly large round island with a warm pool in its center—well, warm in the summer. The pool sat in the middle and the colder lake water couldn't get to it. The sun would heat it all day, leaving it lukewarm—perfect for swimming. The pool itself couldn't be seen from the lake, as it was surrounded by large lilac bushes, which added a sweet fragrance to the air. It was always sort of our private hideout, a place where Ike and I could just hang out.

We decided to land on the island of *Doughnut Rock Pool*. The lilac bushes were totally leafless, and we fought our way through the branches that still provided cover for the pool. The water of the pool was slushy with ice, which made sense since it wasn't nearly as deep as the lake and the October temperatures had been dropping every day. I teased Ike that we should polar bear swim, but he went into a detailed explanation of the risk of hypothermia and how neither of us would be able to row back from losing the feeling in our limbs. I conceded and we decided to go to *Cedar Point Island* where we could at least climb up into the tree and look out over the lake.

We made our way past *Ash Isle* which was on our way to *Cedar Point Island*. As I rowed by, Ike called for me to change direction and land. He'd seen something shiny on the island.

He leapt from the boat before the bow even touched the rocks. When I reached him he was using his foot to uncover something buried deep in the rocks. It was shiny and had three curves and a base.

"Do you know what this is?" Ike asked.

I shook my head.

"It's a candelabra."

"A what?"

"A candle holder," he clarified. His brows were narrowed and I could tell he was thinking. "It looks oddly like one of the silver candelabras that sits on the mantle in the small library," he explained.

I shrugged. "You've lost me."

"Well, what is it doing out here?" he asked.

"I don't know, are you sure it's from The Pink Hippo?"

"Ninety-nine percent sure, but either way what is a candelabra doing out here?"

"Maybe a miner stole it a long time ago and buried it here so he could come back for it later. Then he got arrested or shot and never made it back," I said suspiciously. It was fun to say outlandish stories like this to Ike, it usually got him all excited, but this time it didn't work.

Ike frowned at me. "Good story, but no," he said and paused. "No this was placed here recently. I've been over this island with a metal detector before, and nothing has showed up. This would have definitely shown up."

I kicked a loose rock at my foot. "OK, so someone brought this out here and dumped it."

Ike sighed. "Well let's take it back and see if the one in the library is missing."

I agreed, and as Ike can be a bit impatient, we headed back for The Pink Hippo immediately.

Ike was right, it matched the candelabras on the fireplace mantle, but the three originals were still there, evenly placed across the mantle. I could tell he wasn't satisfied, but I decided he could investigate on his own and headed for dinner.

Chapter Six

October 7th—Saturday

A howling wind rattled my window and woke me from my sleep. I slid out from beneath my warm covers; a fire was lit in the hearth at the far side of my room. I rubbed my eyes, but the fire remained. It wasn't my imagination. Maybe McGarrett had lit it.

Rhythmic breathing was coming from a chair sitting near the fireplace. Who had visited me at this late hour? What time was it?

As if on cue, the clock tower's bell began to chime.

One. Two.

No more.

Who could possibly be up that late, or early, after the previous morning's events?

I went to speak, but the

words hung on my lips, stuck like peanut butter.

I crept closer to the chair. The breathing increased, a wheeze to every breath.

In an instant the shaggy head of the HowlSage turned to peer around the side of the chair and stared me down. I didn't even jump at the snarling lips and hairy face, I knew it was Jesse and his fake head again.

But then its lips curled, baring bright white fangs.

It was real!

I backpedaled quickly toward the door.

But it spoke to me, "Taylor, welcome. Come and sit next to me. The seat is empty," he motioned for the chair opposite him.

I shook my head, but still could not speak. I couldn't run, or move at all, for that matter.

The beast beckoned me forward with one large, deadly paw.

I stepped closer to it as my mind screamed "No!" But my legs would not obey.

Every step took me nearer, until I could smell the beast's rancid breath. The HowlSage remained sitting, it didn't advance on me, nor did it feel like a threat.

I sat in the chair across from it.

"Taylor, you should know something. You are a skilled adversary," it said, its voice a low growl, yet I clearly understood every word. "Your cousin can not match your abilities; he is far weaker than you."

Again words moved to my lips, but couldn't get free.

"You and I could be a strong team; we could rule this city." The HowlSage laughed. "Heck, we could rule this world, if we wanted. Imagine having anything you wanted the moment you wanted it. That's what power can get you, and we would be unstoppable."

I felt something cold on the back of my neck. Suddenly an icy gray mist slid over my shoulders and pooled near my heart.

"Let us in," the HowlSage whispered. "We can change you."

A bright light flashed across the room. Lightning. A storm was moving in.

My voice found itself. "You would change me to evil," I said.

The HowlSage's laugh rumbled with the thunder. "What is evil?"

The gray mist swirled around me, enveloping my head.

I tried to think. What *was* evil? Who decided what evil was?

Lighting flashed again. The thunder shook the windows.

The HowlSage's eyes flashed, its fangs gleamed with saliva. "Join us, Taylor. Bring us the belt."

"The belt?"

The demon nodded.

My legs found strength and I was again in control of them. "I'll get it for you."

Another flash of light, and for the shortest moment my father's face appeared before me, a sword in his hand. His lips moved but I couldn't hear what he said.

"What is it, Dad?" I asked, my voice a fraction of its usual volume.

The HowlSage snarled and then appeared to smile. "Yes, your father. We can bring you to him. We have him. He is…"

I never heard the next words the HowlSage spoke—the room swirled about me in a shining white light.

My head ached as my eyes truly opened. I was sitting on the floor. My bedroom door was closed before me.

What had happened? Was that for real?

I looked around the room; the fireplace was black. The early morning sun glowed behind heavy curtains. There was no storm and there was no HowlSage.

I ran my fingers through my hair and pushed myself up. A dream, a nightmare perhaps?

I'd heard about this side of the battle, but I had yet to experience it.

I remembered something the demon had said: "*Yes, your father. We can bring you to him.*" Was there any truth to that?

I gathered a change of clothes and went to wash up. The bathroom was already filled with steam when I entered, and I heard Jesse singing. He stopped when I let the door slam shut.

"Good morning, cuz," he said from one of the shower stalls. His voice sounded guilty—he'd been caught singing.

"Morning," I said, and stepped into the other shower.

What would it hurt to ask Jesse about the dream, or at least see if he'd ever experienced anything like that?

Before I could ask, his water turned off.

"Don't take too long, we've got a lot of work to do," he said. "I went for a jog this morning and McGarrett was already at work on the car. Ike was busy working on something as well. You're the last awake."

I frowned. Weren't any of them as tired as I?

When I reached the breakfast table everyone was long gone, but there was still a covered plate waiting for me. Lukewarm but still tasting good. Mrs. Riley was nowhere in sight, and I ate alone for the first time in I can't remember how long.

Outside The Pink Hippo everyone was busy. McGarrett was pounding a piece of sheet metal across the roof of the Rolls. Ike had the J-Pak out. Actually, he had two J-Paks out. Mrs. Riley had Jesse's *tin foil* suit laid out across her lap, and she was stitching the torn sections back together with some weird looking tool. Jesse was sharpening his sword and I saw mine lying next to him on a crimson cloth.

"Aye, Taylor, glad you could join us," McGarrett called.

I nodded. "What can I help with?"

"You can help me with the windshield. That's my next project."

I did so, and the rest of the morning, noontime, and afternoon were filled with repairs and preparation. We took only one break for a short lunch, and then didn't finish until four. There was only an hour before sunset, and it was time to locate the HowlSage.

The new tactic was to wait for it to awaken and watch for its movements. Generally this would be considered dangerous, as it was always best to reach the HowlSage in its first hour of awakening. That was when its senses were not to their full strength, or so we'd been told. The truth was we actually knew very little about HowlSages that lived past a couple of days. Sure, the society had tracked many of them in the past, but few made it past their first day and the ones that had were long ago, before good records were kept. Nearly one hundred percent of HowlSages were banished back through an Etherpit on their first day of life, if you could call it that. So my failure posed a significant threat—with each day it would grow stronger and we could only assume what it may do or try.

McGarrett assured Jesse and I that he was confident we could overcome it together.

Another reason for the new tactic was to be sure the HowlSage was as far from the mines—and the gray mist—as possible.

Jesse and I were fitted with the J-Paks that Ike had been tweaking. The boy scientist had taken a myriad of spare parts, and literally in only a few hours duplicated my J-Pak.

I made sure to take the original pack. I wasn't about to be the first one to test out Ike's copy, which probably included some "improvements." Jesse was oblivious and had no reservations about strapping the newly-built contraption to his back. He didn't know Ike's history with modifications.

McGarrett gave us a few quick pointers. He told us the last location of the HowlSage and the direction it had been heading.

Right for town.

The residents of Ashley Meadows were about to sit down to dinner, spend time as a family, and then tuck themselves in. Likely front doors would remain unlocked, and even some windows would remain open to allow the cool autumn breeze into their houses.

If only they knew what lurked in the shadows of the streets.

As had happened the previous nights, our ability to communicate was disabled at sundown. Even the tracking software had failed tonight. We were totally blind, and would be out of touch once we left The Pink Hippo.

Jesse and I had no choice but to start the hunt; McGarrett and Ike would work on the communications issue. If we didn't hear from Mr. Riley, which meant he hadn't fixed it yet, we were to meet him in the park at 3 a.m., where he would be waiting.

"All right, are you ready?" Jesse asked, grasping the small controls to his jet pack. I nodded, and he pressed the ignition. I clenched my teeth waiting for the pack to explode, but it didn't. Instead Jesse lifted into the air and suddenly throttled it, shooting off like a rocket into the midnight sky.

I pulled my night vision goggles up, smiled at Ike, then pursued Jesse.

We rose over the woods and turned for Ashley Meadows. The ground zipped past below, and I noticed that Jesse was slowly pulling ahead of me.

A sign of Ike's modifications working?

Jesse signaled for me to stay high, while he went lower.

It would be hard to spot the beast in the dark shadows of the town. It was hard enough when we had sensors delivering us real-time data, but now we were flying blind.

We'd been scouting for fifteen minutes with not a hint of the HowlSage.

It was going to be like finding a needle in a haystack.

Then something caught my eye, and I turned for a better look.

A creature was running through a yard, hairy yes, large no. Just someone's dog. The fifth I'd spotted tonight. Another sign of a lax small town—animal control didn't exist.

But wait! I throttled down my J-Pak to see better, and to my horror I watched the dog lift into the air and fly twenty feet across the road and into the hedge of the neighbor's house. I twisted my night vision goggles to zoom in, and there in the yard was the HowlSage.

It scanned the yard before it, and then stepped around the corner of the house.

I sped up and dropped altitude to reach Jesse. I signaled that I had spotted the beast and we turned to head back.

Through some choppy, on-the-fly hand motions, I signaled that I would land on the roof and he should land in the front yard.

Jesse nodded and in the next moment he went invisible; even the J-Pak disappeared—a sign Ike had thought of everything.

I touched down in near silence on the shingled roof and made for the side where the HowlSage was last seen. As I neared one of the eaves, I heard something whispering, but in song. I crouched and peered over the side of the roof like a gargoyle on a cathedral.

The HowlSage was standing near a window, its head bowed.

I started at the sight of a hand reaching from the window and holding out a locket of sorts. Who would be working with a demon? The HowlSage took the red jeweled locket in its paw, bowed lower, and slowly crept backward. I heard the window shut and its lock click.

My sword slid slowly from its sheath at the pull of my hand. I was about to launch myself down on to the demon, when a set of claws grabbed me from the back and yanked me into the air. Instinctively I swept the sword over my head in an arc.

I glimpsed the HowlSage out of the corner of my eye, running away.

Where was Jesse?

I felt a claw dig into my shoulder, a hot searing pain. My sword nearly dropped from my grip; I switched hands; a claw dug into my other shoulder. What had me in its grasp?

Twisting my neck, I couldn't get a clear look at the creature. It screeched as it lifted me higher into the air. My arms were succumbing to numbness and I could barely hold the sword, much less use it for defense.

Below I could see houses moving past. We were headed east—no, north. I realized that in our flying around town tonight, I'd not kept track of our location. Without our communications and tracking devices, we were literally blind.

I slid my sword back in its sheath seconds before I lost the remaining feeling in my arms. There was nothing I could…

My entire body jerked left, as did the beast holding me. Something had plowed into the creature.

Over the rushing wind, I could hear Jesse's voice. "Are you OK?"

"Does it look like it?" I yelled.

I heard him laugh, and then my body dropped out of the beast's clutches. I was free-falling to the ground.

I looked up to see a silhouette of the largest flying creature I had ever seen. It wasn't a bird, or a plane, and it certainly wasn't Superman. This thing looked more like a dragon, but without fire blazing from its lips.

I was still falling. My arms were numb, but some feeling was returning. It took all of my will, but I forced my right hand to the J-Pak controls. The wings spread wide and the engine fired up. I slowly started to rise again.

We were over the mines now, miles from town.

My muscles tingled in my arms. I looked for Jesse and the flying thing. They had disappeared into the dark sky.

"*Eeeeeeekawe*," screamed the creature from above. I looked up, but a layer of wispy clouds blocked my view. My heart sank as I remembered the eerie gray mist. But these clouds were light and airy, not like the thick heavy mist of my dream or described by McGarrett.

I broke through the clouds and saw Jesse. He was visible and the winged thing was gone. He came lower to me.

"I didn't kill it!" he shouted as we hovered a thousand feet in the air.

"What was it?"

"I don't know. Any sign of the HowlSage?"

I had totally forgotten about the hairy demon. "No."

"Let's go, we need to find it," Jesse reminded me.

"Sure," I said, and remembered what I had seen and heard. The hand. The song. "When I saw it at that house, someone was giving it something."

His eyebrows narrowed. "What do you mean?"

"Someone was singing to it, and gave it a locket or something."

He looked shocked. "Someone gave this thing a necklace, and it didn't try to bite the hand?"

I shook my head. "Do you remember where the house was?"

We looked toward the town a few miles away. The chase had taken us away from the house, and without our tracking program there was no way to know where we'd been.

"Did you see who the person was?" I asked Jesse.

"No, I never made it around the side of the house. I was distracted when a car stopped in the middle of the road to help some poor dog that was limping across."

I shook my head and nearly cracked a smile, although clearly now was not the time for humor. "The dog was alive?"

Jesse nodded.

"I saw the HowlSage pick the thing up and toss it across the street like a baseball."

"Yikes," Jesse said.

"Yeah. I was watching this dog run across a lawn when suddenly the HowlSage appeared."

Jesse rubbed the stubble on his chin. "Let's do another circle around the town, but if we don't see anything, I think we should head back. McGarrett has to be told about someone giving something to the HowlSage."

"Why?"

"Haven't you ever read *The HowlSage Haunting?*"

"No."

"Well, you should," Jesse said. "Let's do a few loops around town, and see if any of the streets or houses look familiar."

Our tours around town proved to be of no value and we returned to The Pink Hippo where I shared what I saw with McGarrett and Ike.

McGarrett shook his head. "This hunt will be far worse if there is a human involved."

I scowled in confusion.

"Haven't you ever read—?" McGarrett started to ask.

"*The HowlSage Haunting*, I know," I finished for him.

"I was actually going to say, the section on Human Interaction in the society's hunting manual?"

I shook my head. "No we haven't gotten there yet."

McGarrett frowned, "It wouldn't hurt you to read ahead you know."

I felt a guilty pain in my gut. I hadn't really given this training thing one hundred percent commitment.

"I need to call headquarters and let them know about your sighting right away," McGarrett explained.

"Wait, there's more," Jesse said. "The flying creature attacked us."

"It was a lot larger than I'd originally thought," Jesse said.

"I thought it sort of looked like a dragon, but it never shot fire or anything," I added, but no one seemed to care.

Mr. Riley shook his head.

"Do you know what—" I started, but was cut off.

"No time now, I've got to report this." Clearly, he knew something about this beast, but wasn't ready to share with me.

I looked at Jesse, but he shook his head.

Ike gave me an odd stare and winked. "I'll be right back," he said, and left the workshop.

"I'm going to make the call now."

I started to lift off the jet pack when I remembered the beast piercing my shoulders with its claws. I tried to get a good look at the wounds. I didn't see any blood, or rips in my shirt. I felt around with my fingers, pressing where there should have been sore tears in my flesh, but there was nothing.

I was sure the flying thing had wounded me. I remembered the pain, the loss of feeling in my hands and arms. I'd been sure that the nerves in my arm had been severed.

I asked Jesse to look. He didn't see anything, either.

With McGarrett on the phone and our bodies aching, we decided to go relax until he needed us. We knew we would not be headed back out tonight. So we headed to the swimming pool and hot tub.

The pool was original to the hotel's first days; there were very few of its kind left in the world. Decorated with thousands of small tiles in ornate patterns, it was a long rectangle, creating the perfect canvas for the jungle mosaic across its bottom. Several pillars rose from the middle of the pool to support a domed roof high above.

The hot tub was large and square, easily fitting twenty people if you wanted, its middle sported a half-submerged hippopotamus, which was pink in color. The hippo sported bubble jets, one of which was comically placed near its butt. It so happened that this jet also turned on first, so for at least a few seconds it looked as though the hippo was breaking wind. I almost could picture the builder rolling across the floor of his home, laughing in hysterics at his crafty inside joke.

Jesse and I swam several laps in the cold, refreshing waters of the pool, and soon our relaxation turned into competition. We were racing across the pool, freestyle, then back stroke, then butterfly. 100 yards, 200 yards, 300 yards. We were exhausted when we finally pulled ourselves from the pool.

I laid back, my chest rising and falling with every deep breath. I could hear Jesse next to me, heaving.

"Jess?" I asked.

"What?" he responded weakly.

I turned my head toward him, "Have you ever seen a girl, and known right away you liked her?"

He didn't laugh, which I'd expected him to do. But he didn't say anything for a good minute. When he looked at me, he looked sad.

"You know, Tay, I actually have."

"What happened?"

"When I saw her something would come over me. She seemed to glide past as if walking on air, her hair glowed golden, and her eyes sparkled. Regardless of where or when I saw her, I could smell roses..." Jesse's voice trailed off as he looked toward the ceiling.

"Did you ever—you know—talk to her?"

"Sure, and I was so nervous when I did, all I could say was, 'Hollow.'"

"Hollow?"

"I meant to say 'hello,' but it came out 'hollow.'"

I laughed inside, careful not to let it out for Jesse to hear. He was actually for once being serious, and it just so happened to be for something I actually wanted his advice on. "You didn't give up, did you?"

He turned and looked at me in the weirdest way. His eyes shimmered as if he was going to cry, and he stared at me longingly.

"No, of course not," he smiled at me proudly. "You know me better than that. I'm Jesse Rivers, girl glue."

"Did you say girl glue?" I asked.

"Girl glue, that's what they called me at school."

I thought it a weird nickname, but I suppose it sort of made sense. The back of his yearbook was always filled with lots of comments from girls, and he had had many a girlfriend.

"So what'd you do next?"

"Well, I waited for her outside school one day, and when she came out, I broke into song. I knew she liked Baylor McLaw, so I sang her latest love song."

"You didn't."

"Sure did."

"And?"

"Well, let's just say, I still have a one hundred percent record of getting the first date."

I laid my head back. A lump had formed in my throat. Did I have enough nerve to sing? Could I actually carry a tune? And how was I supposed to know what kind of music the girl would like if I didn't even know her name?

I heard Jesse's wet footsteps heading toward the hot tub, so I got up and followed him.

We broke into a fit of laughter as soon as the jets came to life, because so did the hippo. Bubbles were blasting out in an angry stream. I laughed until my gut hurt.

Finally, I sat back in the hot water to contemplate my girl situation and the song. Jesse's eyes were closed, and I thought I'd asked enough for tonight. It'd been a good talk, the most serious we'd ever had.

When we were done, we changed and headed back for the workshop. I found Ike sitting on the steps of the inn. Jesse continued on, but I stopped to find out what the boy genius was doing. After all it was October and cold, and Ike wasn't wearing his coat as usual. Another example of street smarts versus book smarts.

"What's going on?" I asked.

He sighed, but didn't say anything. I could tell he wasn't in a good mood.

"Dude, it's cold out here. You should go inside, or get a coat or something." Realizing I sounded a little too much like a mom, I added, "If you get sick, we won't have anyone to keep our gear in repair. And I need my stuff to work when I fight." It was an OK recovery. Not the best, but decent enough that he'd buy it.

He nodded and stood.

"What's wrong, why are you acting so bummed?"

His lips pursed together and his eyebrows narrowed into a scowl. "You left."

"What?"

"You weren't in the workshop when I came back."

"So?"

"I said, 'I'll be right back,' and you left."

"Oh…Sorry, I didn't—"

"Of course you didn't. I'm invisible when he's here."

Now I was confused. Where was this coming from? "Who is 'he'?"

"Jesse! Your best friend!" Ike turned and stormed up the stairs of the inn, disappearing behind its doors.

I thought about going after him, but decided against it. Was he jealous?

I shrugged it off and headed for the workshop.

Chapter Seven

October 8th—Sunday

I slipped on a pair of pants, put on a white tee, and made my way downstairs. I was thankful that today there would be no hunting. It was Sunday, and today was our day of rest. Mrs. Riley still liked to cook, but it was never work to her.

The smell of bacon and eggs reached my nose before the elevator doors even opened. Like a zombie in a trance, my legs pulled me to the table. McGarrett was sipping coffee and Ike was waiting patiently to eat. Jesse came in shortly after me, wearing jogging clothes. He'd been out for another run.

Mrs. Riley joined us and McGarrett blessed the meal. As was the rule, we couldn't speak of work, so I couldn't ask about my dream, nor could Ike fill me in on whatever he had gone off to research last night. I'd realized much later in the night that Ike was probably upset about me going swimming, because he'd gone to discover something on my behalf. I'd try to make it up to him later.

After breakfast I changed into my Sunday best, a dress shirt and khakis. These clothes were not stored in my bedroom, but instead kept in a closet near the laundry, where Mrs. Riley pressed them before every use and kept them smelling fresh.

Something about the teen boy smells that my room possessed might leech into the clothes. I didn't think my room smelled, but I guess I'm just used to it.

The drive to the church was quick. Ike and I rode with Jesse and Mr. and Mrs. Riley took the Rolls. He'd tried to convince his wife to ride in the motorcycle's sidecar, but she had politely declined.

The church service always seemed the same. No offense to the pastor, but there was such a regimen to Sunday.

Greet.

Pray.

Sing several hymns.

Announcements.

Pray.

Offering.

Special song, a duet or solo usually.

Sermon.

Pray.

On occasion there might be an altar call, or communion, but for the most part every service was the same, at least to me.

Ike always took lots of notes and I listened as best I could. Most of the other kids chatted with each other, texted, or played games. I knew from my interactions at school that several of them didn't really live the life you'd expect from a so-called Christian. Ask any one of them about their extracurricular activities and you'd understand. I guess I had little room to talk; my prayer life had really dropped off after my dad fell. And I suppose I wasn't one hundred percent focused on my spiritual walk.

Frankly, I was mad at God, I was mad that He'd taken both my parents from me and then turned around and expected me to fight for Him, to risk my life. How was that fair?

I shivered. It felt as though someone was hovering over my shoulder, listening to my thoughts.

Regardless of my current emotions, I believed. I'd asked Christ into my heart, and I had the assurance of where I was going. But supposedly most of these other kids had as well. They certainly didn't act like they were Christians. Were they going, too? I mean, what does it really mean to be a Christian?

Jesse jabbed me in the side and whispered, "You look distracted."

I was, but I didn't want to tell him why. "Oh, yeah. Just thinking about last night," I lied.

He nodded and continued to listen. His Bible was open in his lap, but I never once saw him look down at it. He was just staring at the pulpit.

After church, we went to the park and ate a picnic lunch that Mrs. Riley had packed. The weather was warm and sunny for October.

After we'd finished, Jesse lay back on a blanket, earbuds in, listening to tunes as he drifted off to sleep.

The Riley's were sitting up at a pavilion talking to some other townspeople. I recognized the mayor and his wife, Chief Rutledge, and another husband and wife who had visited The Pink Hippo a few times before, the Friggs.

Ike and I decided we'd head down to the skate park. I'm pretty decent on a board, and Ike's good on his blades. However, the ankle twisting incident a few days ago stopped me from any skateboarding. Instead I decided to sit and watch, maybe give a few pointers to Ike. I knew that spending this time alone with Ike would make up for last night's frustration, and if I had a chance I'd ask him about what it was he'd looked up.

To my surprise and I suppose delight, the girl from the first night of the hunt appeared.

She was riding along on a bike and stopped on the path no more than twenty feet away.

Was this my chance? I stood and took a deep breath, trying to gain enough courage to shout to her.

I saw her look back and wave to someone.

My heart sank as the person she waved to came into view. A boy her age, maybe a little older, came riding down the path. He didn't have a helmet on; she did. And he looked, well, cool. My belly churned. Competition with a boy I don't know for a girl I don't know. Yeah, that's normal.

She took off before the other boy could reach her. I heard her laugh as she disappeared down the trail into the woods. The boy stood and then hammered on the petals, cycling as fast he could. As he passed he turned to look at me, but his face was shadowed under a hood.

"Ouch!" I called as something hit me in the shoulder. I looked down to see a pinecone.

"You missed it!" Ike yelled. He was rolling toward me, hands on hips. "Dude, I did what you told me and this time I didn't fall."

I smiled. "Sorry, man."

"What were you looking at?" he asked.

"Just a girl."

"A girl?"

"Yeah, the one I told you about. She was just here."

He looked around and then back at me curiously. "Tay, I think you're seeing things. It's just you and me."

"She rode off into the woods on her bike," I said.

"Oh, well, do you want me to skate after her?" he asked.

"Nope, she had someone with her." My voice sounded down, more so then I intended. But I had remembered the boy with her. Obviously, she was taken.

"If you're that sad about her leaving, I really will go after her."

"It's not that she left, it's who she left with," I said, looking toward the woods.

"Who?" he asked innocently.

"Some kid."

"A boy?"

"Yeah."

Ike's voice suddenly sounded chipper. "Well, maybe he'll be your friend too!"

He really didn't get it. It's what made him so refreshing at times, and annoying at others. In this instance, it was the former. I forced a smile and we went back to our picnic area.

Jesse was asleep on the blanket, but Mr. and Mrs. Riley were sitting on a bench swing nearby, talking. The others had left.

Chapter Eight

October 9th—Monday

School.

I never looked forward to school before, but now that I was on the hunt it was worse. How was I supposed to concentrate?

I sat there watching the second hand on the clock slowly tick by. Why they even included this hand on clocks I'll never know. Especially in schools. The number-one thing kids want when they're in school is to be out. So it's like these clocks were made to torture us.

I decided I needed to use the restroom, so I raised my hand and got the pass. Really, I just needed to stretch my legs in the hall. The teacher, Mrs.

Diordean, looked annoyed, but I was annoyed at learning about Greek mythology. I mean, seriously, you want to waste three weeks of my life teaching me about some fake—immoral by most accounts—myths. Why?

So I stepped into the wide green and white halls of David Louis High. The school had been named for a town founder.

I went to the bathroom, and then detoured to the library before heading back to class. I needed a bit more fresh air. Besides, the librarian is pretty cool, I knew I could loiter a bit without drawing any suspicion. I stopped by a newly-added section of graphic novels, for research of course.

I fingered the spines; none seemed to jump out at me. Maybe I'd go further into the library, see if I could find anything on monsters—one of those old classics, like *Frankenstein* or *Dracula*.

This part of the library consisted of floor-to-ceiling shelves, tightly packed together in rows and all butted up against a cold brick wall. You were lucky to squeeze between the shelves and were in trouble if someone came into the row after you. There was no way to get out.

I found the section titled *Classics*; our librarian had arranged the library shelves in his own *easy* to find categories. Some made sense. Others, like *Blues*, not so much. As far as I could tell, this was just a collection of books with blue spines.

I found Mary Shelley's *Frankenstein* and slid it off the shelf. There were actually two editions—an illustrated and non-illustrated. I, of course, took the one with pictures. Easier on the eyes.

And then I noticed an eye looking at me. Gray—no, blue-gray. I couldn't be sure, but a moment after I looked up, it disappeared.

Who was looking at me?

I slid my body down the tight aisle and peaked around the corner and down the aisle the eye had been in.

No one.

Nothing.

I looked around the library's lobby of overstuffed chairs and wooden tables.

The librarian, Mr. Skogerboe, sat at the main desk, a newspaper hid his profile from view, and a cup of coffee was in his hand. Two kids sat at a far table—both had headphones on, neither looked like they'd moved for a while. Another kid sat at a computer, but he was a bit rotund, and just by looking at his body, the eye didn't seem to fit.

It—I know it sounds farfetched as I only saw the eye for a microsecond—but it was a girl's eye. I was sure of it; ninety-nine point nine percent sure.

But there were no girls to be seen in the library. Two exits were all that led out, so I would have to make a choice.

I chose wrong. The hall was empty, but that wasn't the worst of it. I stepped out of the library and right into Mrs. Diordean.

"What are you doing, Taylor?" she asked, arms crossed.

I stumbled for words. "Uh, ummm, well. I."

There was no good excuse I could come up with and aside from that, I'd be lying. Which was wrong.

"Back to class, Mr. Rivers," she said.

I began to tromp down the hall, when around the corner came the girl. She looked me right in the eyes. And walked past.

Her eyes were the eyes. Well, the eye that I saw between the books.

I turned to follow, to stop her, but Mrs. Diordean was right there.

She put her hand up and then swiveled it to motion for me to keep going. My sentence was set and I was headed to my cell.

I had to wait after class, at which point she questioned my wandering and sentenced me to after school detention.

This wasn't good, because that meant I wouldn't be free to leave until 5:30. The after school detention program was two hours of sitting at a desk. You could work on your homework, but if you weren't doing that, you could do nothing else.

I knew this would throw some serious kinks into tonight's hunt, but the damage was done.

I only had a moment to tell Ike about my charges, before I made my way for the assigned room. He shook his head and promised to tell McGarrett and Jesse.

As I headed back into the school, the halls were already empty with the exception of some loose pieces of notebook paper, a couple broken writing utensils, and an abandoned maintenance cart.

I sighed, knowing I couldn't put off my punishment any longer, and started for the right classroom.

A light overhead flickered, giving off that annoying buzz that fluorescent lights do as they die. I looked up as the light went out. The hallway seemed darker than it should have, and the air seemed, I don't know, heavier.

And then a laugh echoed through the hall.

I froze. All but one light went out, the remaining one flickered on and off rapidly.

A silhouette appeared just outside the pulsing light. The person stood about my height, but was covered in a dark cloak. The person laughed as they lifted something into the air—it looked oddly like a farmer's pitchfork. Then its sharp tips seemed to gleam with a self-illuminated red glow.

The figure began to speak, "You are known. You are seen. You are f—"

A burst of light shot from behind me, hitting the cloaked figure square in the chest. The body flew backward and slammed into a bank of lockers, then crumpled to the floor. I turned to see the maintenance man standing there, his hands cupped together and pointing toward the figure.

Had the light come from him? Had he attacked the person or thing who'd threatened me?

I looked back to the injured body on the floor, but it was gone. The cloak was there, but it was nearly flat on the ground, its occupant gone, missing. But where?

I turned to my savior, but he too, was gone.

And then the lights came back on and I was standing in the hallway alone. There was no one in sight. I stepped to the abandoned cloak and bent down to pick it up.

When my fingers touched the fabric, it felt like I was running my hand over a hot coal. I yanked my hand back in pain. The black cloak began to sizzle, and then it burst into flames, deep red flames.

A second later it was gone. Not even a burn mark on the floor remained. There was no sign that a fight had even taken place. The only sign of the maintenance man was his cart in the middle of the hallway.

What had happened? Was it just my imagination?

"Mr. Rivers, you are late for your detention," a voice said behind me.

It was Mrs. Diordean.

"You owe me another twenty minutes, Mr. Rivers," she growled and then added with what looked like a satisfied smile, "For your tardiness."

I sighed, probably a bit too loudly and followed her to the assigned detention cell, err, room.

As the seconds clicked by, I thought about what had happened. Clearly it wasn't the HowlSage; it was too early in the day, too much sunlight. Besides, the figure had been too small to be the beast. My size, in fact. Maybe a bit taller.

I remembered the dream I had had a few nights prior. I had to tell McGarrett about it. He needed to know what I had seen, what the HowlSage had said to me—about joining, about my father.

The seconds, minutes, and eventually hours ticked by; the other students left while I finished out the additional twenty minutes.

Didn't Mrs. Diordean have anything better to do with her time—or her life, for that matter? She sat up there like a perched bird, grading papers with her red pen. Surely she had a cat or something to get home too.

I felt an odd twinge in my heart at the mean thought, but shrugged it off.

Finally I was released and I literally ran for the door, but stopped to check the hall for anything suspicious before darting out of the detention room.

No cart, no flickering lights—the coast was clear.

I figured I would have to call McGarrett or walk home. But when I walked into the cold night air he was already there, waiting beside his Rolls. The expression on his face was all I needed to know that he wasn't pleased with me. I hoped if I told him about the hall battle he'd loosen up a bit.

He didn't. In fact, his expression grew grimmer and he said nothing. He didn't even try to provide an explanation as to what it might have been. Instead, he motioned me into the car and we drove a few blocks away, down an alley, where we stopped and got out.

He took my gear from the trunk and fitted me up right there on the spot.

"Jesse was supposed to rendezvous overhead fifteen minutes ago, but you were late. I am hoping he'll make another pass," McGarrett said.

"So I take it communications are still down."

"They are," he admitted. "Here he comes."

I certainly didn't see or hear him, but I knew McGarrett had a sense about these things, or at least better ears.

Sure enough, I felt my hair ruffle a bit and then heard the soft thump of Jesse's Keds touching down beside me. Jesse made himself visible and gave me a very sarcastic grin.

"Way to go cuz," was all he said.

I nodded.

"You guys should get going," McGarrett interrupted before we could start bantering. I looked at him, but he wouldn't look me in the face.

We shot into the sky, Jesse invisible, and me nearly so with my black getup. It had to be very tough for anyone to see me from the ground. The sky was dim with only half a moon remaining.

It was hard to think that just seven days prior we'd had a full moon. And, including tonight, there were just twenty-two days left in the hunt. Twenty-two days and the HowlSage would be fully grown, its venom potent, and the moon full. That would be like the perfect storm striking Ashley Meadows, and not even a fully trained and well equipped team of hunters would be able to easily defeat it.

While the darkness helped mask my soaring through the chill air, it also provided cover for the HowlSage below, casting odd shadows and providing dismal light.

Jesse informed me that our primary goal was to find the house where I'd seen the hand. He wouldn't tell me why this took priority over finding the HowlSage, but I knew if there was a human involved then our situation was far more perilous then we'd originally thought. I wanted to think that this extra involvement might have been reason for my failure the first night, but I knew that wasn't true.

Finding the house, though, was literally like searching for a needle in a haystack. While not a big town, I had little recollection of what the house or street had looked like and neither did Jesse.

Our battle with the flying creature had taken us far away from the house, and with the tracking software inactive that night, we had no markers of our locations. Normally they were carefully recorded. Worse, I seemed to be experiencing memory loss when it came to the event. I could not picture anything from that night.

Nearly an hour passed with no sightings of a familiar house, street, or dog.

We decided on one last patrol of the town before heading back to The Pink Hippo.

As we approached the exit from the highway tunnel that lead into town, I saw it. The HowlSage was loping along the ditch toward the tunnel. I signaled Jesse, who saw it as well. He flew in close to me and shouted over the noisy rush of the air.

"You go over the ridge and cut it off; I'll follow it through," he said.

Having screwed up once that day already, I wasn't about to argue about who got to do what. So I obeyed and flew higher, gaining altitude in order to clear the rocky mountain range that separated Ashley Meadows from the rest of the world.

Ten minutes later, I was hovering over the entrance to the tunnel.

Five more minutes and still no HowlSage. Worse, no Jesse.

Three more minutes and I became worried, so I dove into the tunnel. No traffic at this hour of the night. But before I'd gotten a hundred yards in, I saw Jesse limping along on the side of the tunnel.

"What happened?" I asked as he approached. "Did it get away?"

"Never had a chance to get at it. My left engine just shut off and I flew into a spiral. I nearly became a pancake on the front of a semi-truck. The creature leapt on to the truck and rode it back out of the tunnel." Jesse stopped beside me. "I'm going to kill that Ike when I get back. He nearly killed me."

I felt a lump in my throat. I was nervous for Ike, but I also knew I hadn't warned Jesse about Ike's, well…short-fallings.

We found a pay phone and waited for McGarrett to pick us up. Unfortunately, Ike had decided to come along. Jesse chewed on him like a piranha on a goat that had made the ill-fated choice to drink from the wrong river.

I said nothing.

Chapter Nine

October 10th—Tuesday

No demons attacked me at school the next day, which was a good thing. I don't want to sound boring, but I'd prefer to be a normal kid whom normal things happened to.

I just wanted the day to be uneventful. To have some sort of normalcy—but at lunch I saw her.

It was the grainy green girl with blue-gray eyes. These were the two biggest recollections I had of her. First sight through my night vision goggles, and the second moment a single eye staring at me between two book spines.

Now she was here before me and she wasn't green. She was alone at one of the lunch tables, the perfect opportunity to meet her under normal circumstances.

This was my chance. I decided against bursting

into song, whatever Jesse had said.

It was time to get over this unjustified fear I had of introducing myself to her. She was just a normal girl my age, right?

Was I kidding?

I stared at her again. The way she bit into a sandwich made it look like an art. On second thought, maybe I did need a song.

I shook my head, I was getting away from myself.

Breathe.

What was happening to me? I'd never felt this way and as far as I knew never acted this off center.

I motioned for Ike to find a separate table, and like the good friend he was, he didn't ask any questions and found an empty table. He even gave me a little smile of encouragement.

I felt my throat constrict as I approached. And with each step another pebble of anxiety dropped into my stomach. Within three strides, it was full of boulders.

I cleared my throat in preparation.

Then out of nowhere—quite literally nowhere—a boy appeared. The same one from the park.

He didn't even look at me, just sat across from her and bowed his head.

I made a ninety degree course change as if I'd innocently been maneuvering between the rows or lunch tables. I found my way to Ike and sat next to him.

I'd been ravenous with hunger moments before we'd entered the cafeteria, but now the food on my tray wasn't remotely appealing. I'd declined Mrs. Riley's homemade meal for a shot at the cafeteria's BBQ rib sandwich. My favorite and the only lunch the school made that I liked. But now the piece of meat sat on its bun, brownish-orange goop dripping off of it in a rather disturbing way.

I pushed my tray away.

"Can I have it, if you don't want it?" Ike asked.

I shrugged.

Ike pulled an empty baggy from his sack lunch from home, and lifted the sandwich to it. He pulled each side of the bun away from the meat, letting the brown patty slip into the baggy without his hands ever touching it. The sides of the baggy were now streaked with goo.

"Perfect."

I didn't ask.

As I looked at the boy and girl sitting together at the table, alone, I wondered, *What made him so special?*

"What are you looking at?" Ike asked.

I sighed. "Nothing."

He followed my gaze. "You're looking at her." His voice cracked. Ike cleared his throat. "You know, you shouldn't be letting yourself get distracted by her. She's just a girl. And you need to be concentrating on the hunt. We're running out of time."

"I don't care," I said, in more stern a voice than I'd wanted. "I didn't choose the role of Hunter for myself. I don't even know if I want it."

Eyes still on the boy, I saw his cheek twitch with a slight smile.

Ike shook his head. "Of course you do. I'd love to be you."

"No you wouldn't. You don't have a clue what it's like being me. You don't have to put your life on the line every night."

Ike lowered his head. I heard him sniffle.

"Look, I didn't mean too…" I started.

"No, I don't know what it's like to be you. But you're wrong. I'd gladly put my life on the line for the cause. I believe in what we've been called to do." With that he stood and walked out of the cafeteria.

I didn't see Ike the rest of the day, not until he boarded the bus. He chose a seat at the front, and left me alone in my row toward the back. I can't even remember the last time he didn't sit across from me.

Ike didn't even wait for me after being dropped off at the gate in front of The Pink Hippo. Instead, he maintained a good ten yards ahead of me as we walked up the drive. I knew he really wanted to keep his distance, as my strides were longer, and at the same pace I could always catch him. He was nearly jogging by the time we reached the stairs of The Pink Hippo.

"Ike, wait up," I said. I watched my breath roll from my mouth in a hazy cloud. I hadn't realized how cold it was today.

He turned to look at me.

"Look, I'm—"

Kaboom!

Ike nearly leapt out of his shoes and I ducked low.

A plume of black smoke hurled high into the air from behind the workshop.

Ike and I ran to investigate the source of the blast. As we rounded the side of the building, we heard a groan. It was Jesse's.

We found him sprawled out on his back, covered in black soot. Several tears marred his clothing, and bloody gashes ran the length of his bare arms.

The door at the back of the workshop burst open and McGarrett came into view. He looked at me. "What happened?"

"I don't know!"

Jesse rolled to his stomach and pushed himself to his hands and knees. "Canister," he whispered.

"Canister?" I asked, then looked at Ike. His face had turned the color of his wide eyes—a deep shade of green.

Ike was shaking his head. "Not...shouldn't have...wasn't ready... didn't know."

I looked toward a spot in the yard where a hole, several feet deep, had been gouged into the ground. Black smoke rolled up from it as an eerie purple flame sputtered from its center.

McGarrett had gone back inside the workshop and returned with a fire extinguisher, but a second before he began showering the purple flames, Ike found his voice.

"No, don't use that! It won't work. It might make it worse." I'd never heard Ike speak in such a deep, commanding voice. "I'll get something for it."

He ran for the door and disappeared into the workshop.

Jesse let out another groan, so I went to him. I wasn't exactly sure what I could touch, his arms and the front of his legs looked singed. His clothes looked like they were melted to him in some spots.

"Can I help you?"

"No," he groaned, his voice rife with pain. "It burns."

Ike appeared with two sacks of white powder, one under each arm. He gave one to McGarrett and instructed him to use it on the fire, and then started sprinkling the second onto Jesse, who shook his head and started sputtering as the dust got into his mouth.

"What the…? That's disgusting! What are you doing?" Jesse cried out. "You almost killed me with whatever that was, and now you're covering me in who knows what. Get away from me! I've had it with your worthless inventions! They don't work!"

Ike stopped his powder delivery.

I wanted to say something, but at the same time I agreed with Jesse. Or at least I thought I did. Ike had lambasted me at lunch for taking interest in that girl and not showing a desire for my calling. But he wasn't following his calling either. I mean, if he was, would he mess up so much?

Ike's eyes grew cloudy with unshed tears.

McGarrett seemed not to have overheard; he was attending to the purple flames, which were dissipating as he spread the chemical powder over them.

Ike dropped the bag and broke for The Pink Hippo. Or at least that's where I assumed he was headed.

I stared at Jesse, having realized how cold he'd been.

Jesse glared at me. "It was true and you know it," he said, an edge to his voice.

I didn't nod or shake my head. I was frozen. I didn't know what to say to my cousin. Ike was my friend. He'd been there for me to help with my mistakes more times than I could remember. At the same time, Ike had nearly killed me a few times, and someone needed to rein him in. Jesse had a right to be mad—it was our lives that were on the line every day, not Ike's.

I offered Jesse a hand and pulled him to his feet. He didn't cringe as I'd expected.

"Does it hurt?" I asked.

"It did, but it doesn't now," he admitted.

But neither of us would admit that the white powder was the likely culprit for the disappearance of the pain, not to mention the purple flames.

"We'd better get you inside and have Mrs. Riley take a look at those burns and scrapes," McGarrett said.

"Sure thing," Jesse said as I put his arm over my shoulder and guided him toward the inn.

There was no sign of Ike as we walked into the inn, and Mrs. Riley hadn't heard him come in.

In the infirmary on the second floor, Mrs. Riley looked over all of Jesse's wounds. She put some salve on them, wrapped them, and sent us downstairs where she'd made dinner. We waited for Ike, but he didn't show, so Mr. Riley said a prayer and we ate without him.

After dinner, we went to the workshop. I'd be flying solo tonight.

"What happened?" I asked Jesse.

He frowned. "I can't remember."

"I mean, what were you doing? What was it that you had?"

"I don't even remember."

McGarrett cut in. "That was a new agent Ike was working on. Something to—"

The phone rang.

McGarrett picked it up and listened. "Yes," he replied. "This is he. Oh, I see. Thanks for letting me know."

Mr. Riley hung up the phone. "That was Chief Rutledge. There's been a break in."

"Where?" I asked.

"Hoobler's Jewelers."

"Huh?" Jesse said.

"Why does that matter to us?" I asked.

"Because, while the cameras are blank, several strands of hair were found caught on the broken glass. Animal hair, to be precise."

I nodded. "The HowlSage."

"Such is my suspicion," McGarrett said. "Let's go, we need to get a sample. Jesse, I want you to stay here this time. Hold down the fort."

Jesse didn't argue. "No problem."

A police line had been set up around the front and sides of the building. The breached window was in the alley. I followed McGarrett under the police tape, where we found Chief Rutledge talking to a detective.

"McGarrett," the chief said with a nod. "I thought you might be interested in this."

Mr. Riley nodded back. "Sure. What you got?"

Chief Rutledge walked us over to the window, and with gloved hands picked up a piece of glass.

The shard of opaque material was strewn with strands of brown hair or fur. The hair was too thick and dark to belong to a human.

The detective handed McGarrett a pair of gloves. Mr. Riley slid them on and the police chief handed over the shard.

"There's hair all over the glass, as well as inside," the detective said. "Too much for a human. It had to be animal. But we're not sure why. Or how."

"Was anything taken?" Mr. Riley asked.

I watched as he looked over the shard and pulled a few strands of fur away from the glass.

"Yes, in fact. Mr. Hoobler has already taken inventory and here is what's missing," the detective said, handing over a list with several orange highlighter marks across it.

I read the document from beside McGarrett. There were several descriptions as well as some sort of item number listed beside each one. But what caught my attention was the handwritten notes next to all the highlighted items. In most cases the jewels had been removed and the gold or platinum casings left behind.

"We think this must be a well-planned setup. Someone is trying to pin this on an animal perhaps," the detective said. "But how could anyone think we'd believe an animal could tear apart the jewelry and selectively remove the gems? Especially when taking into account that only certain types of jewels were stolen."

"What types?" Mr. Riley asked.

"Rubies, white diamonds, and opals," the detective said.

"It's rather peculiar. Not like anything I've seen before. That's why I called you," the police chief said.

McGarrett nodded. "Peculiar indeed."

Chapter Ten

October 11th—Wednesday

My eyes shot open. I rolled hard to my left and off the far side of my bed, crouching in my boxers, ready for action. I'd even swept the dagger off of my night stand to oppose the creature.

Ike smiled at me and cocked his head to the side. "I didn't realize that you're always ready to fight."

I exhaled an angry breath. "Ike! What are you doing?" The red glowing digits on the clock displayed five a.m.

"Yes, but," he started. "I have something very special to show you. I just finished it."

"Just? You've been up all night?"

"Not quite; I took three forty-five minute naps," he said matter-of-factly.

"Oh."

"Are you ready?" he asked, eyes bright with excitement.

"Sure, I guess," I crawled back into my bed and pulled my covers back over me. "Go on, but then I'm going back to sleep."

Ike nodded and pulled out a small silver canister. "This is what you sort of saw last night. But it wasn't ready then. It wasn't in a proper container."

"You mean the purple fire and explosion that nearly killed Jesse?"

Ike frowned. "You could look at it that way, but he shouldn't have even been messing around with it. It was clearly labeled 'do not touch.'"

"You know Jesse, warnings don't do much to deter him."

"I guess," Ike said, but then continued with his display. "All right, here we go." He held the canister out in front of him.

I used my index finger to shift the invention away from over my bed. He smiled and swiveled a small silver cover off the top of the container.

A slithering stream of purple smoke lifted up from the canister in a long wispy chain. It curled upward a few feet and then started to spread out. Ike shifted his other hand to the left. The smoke followed the movement of his hand, which I then noticed was covered in a metallic glove. He shifted his gloved hand back the other way and the smoke moved again.

"Whoa!" I said. "That's cool."

"You want to try?"

"Sure, but...but what's the point?" I asked. I knew there must be one, but I certainly couldn't figure out what the purple smoke was supposed to do.

Ike started to remove his glove. "Well, it's still in the test phase. But I think this will help with our gray mist problem. You know, that weird stuff that makes the HowlSage impervious to our usual forms of attack."

I nodded and took the glove. The purple smoke had continued to slowly sneak from the canister, creating a large cloud over my bed. It shifted left as the glove was transferred to me.

I jerked my now-gloved hand right, then left, then right again. Each time the smoke shifted directions. It didn't seem to go faster in relation to my hand movement, only directionally. I moved my hand up, it followed. I moved my hand down.

Ike reached out and grabbed my wrist, moving my hand back up. "No, not yet. Keep the smoke away from fabric for now."

I looked at him peculiarly. "So what is this stuff?"

"I've mixed together some of the main weapons used to kill demons. Clearly the gray mist is powerful, so it's not one of the lower tier demons."

"What did you use?" I asked, still watching the purple smoke follow my every move."

"It's one part garlic powder, one part silver sulfate, one part salt or sodium chloride, one part magnesium, and one part holy water. While it won't kill a demon in physical from, like the HowlSage, my theory is that the gaseous forms of these demon-killing methods, put in contact with whatever type of demon the gray mist is, will kill it or vaporize it."

"Wow, that sounds really…ingenious."

Ike was beaming. "Thanks."

"OK," I said. "So, how do we get it back into the container?"

"Simple." Ike reached under the bottom of the canister and tapped something. "There's a button under here."

I felt the glove on my hand lose something. I wasn't sure what, but something seemed to leave its metallic fabric. The smoke began to suck back into the canister. I couldn't hear anything, but something was pulling the purple cloud back into its container.

Ike smiled as the room cleared. Clearly this invention was something he was proud of, something he had worked really hard on.

I counted on my fingers. It'd only been six days since we learned about the gray mist, and yet Ike appeared to have already created something he thought would help combat it. And it seemed to work. Even Jesse would have to be impressed with that. Maybe all the tension between them, the fighting, would stop, or at least they could come to terms.

The smoke was nearly back in when the canister gave off a high pitched whine. It started to rattle, and then shake, and then it shot out of Ike's hand like a rocket.

We both watched as it flew up, curved over Ike's head and right toward my closet. It disappeared into the darkness of the clothing repository and...

Crack! Boom!

A flash of purple lit the room, followed by purple flames and black putrid smoke dispatching from my closet.

Once again, I rolled from the bed and prepared to evacuate, but apparently Ike had come prepared. Because he darted from my room, but returned a microsecond later with two bags of the white powder he'd used the day before.

He started throwing handfuls at the fire, and within a moment the flames died down and the smoke stopped billowing from my closet.

I walked over to observe the damage and stepped in front of Ike.

Total destruction lay before me. There was nothing but blackened walls and the remnants of a single hanger melted to the metal pole that stretched across the closet. All of my white and black shirts had gone up in smoke.

I turned and looked the few inches down at Ike. I felt the temperature in my face rising, my palms were sweating. My muscles began to twinge as blood and adrenaline coursed through them.

Ike had about two seconds to run from the room, before I'd unleash my fists on him. He must have known it, because he backed away and ran.

I took several breaths, trying to regain some vestige of calmness. I'd nearly gotten there when I realized I was only wearing boxers and every shirt I owned had been in that closet.

I was through the door in pursuit of Ike without a second thought.

"Where'd you go, you little—?" I caught myself. I heard the elevator door slide shut. He'd escaped.

Jesse stepped out of his room. "What's all the commotion?" he asked.

I groaned. "Ike just burned all of my shirts."

A smile slipped across Jesse's face and he started to laugh.

"Come on, it's not funny. What am I going to wear?"

"You're right, it's not funny. Not if you had to go to school with that scrawny body exposed." He laughed harder. "I'll let you borrow a shirt."

I followed Jesse in, knowing that I likely would hear about this loan every day for the foreseeable future. He tossed me a bluish shirt with some weird design on it.

"Thanks," I said.

"It's about time you started dressing with a little more style," Jesse said.

I supposed it was true; Jesse certainly did have a knack for staying with the most current trend, from clothes to music to the latest buzz words. I'd thought the word "stellar" had had its day, but he used it a few times, and sure enough I heard it on at least two television shows within a week of Jesse using it. It was sort of weird how in style someone could be, but appear to not put any effort in doing so.

At breakfast Mrs. Riley mentioned that Ike was feeling sick and would be staying home for the day. Her expression told me there was more to it, but she didn't expound. Instead, she provided me a sack lunch and sent me on my way.

I figured that with everything that had happened over the last few days, all of Ike's invention mishaps, and with mine and Jesse's ill treatment of him, he was probably hurt and embarrassed. But with all of my shirts destroyed and several near-death experiences still fresh in mind, I wasn't ready to console him.

I got the once over from several different girls in the first minute of entering the school; a few looked twice. All that had changed was the shirt I wore. I hadn't changed my shaggy hairstyle, or put any cologne on. Just a different shirt.

It was weird how style could change people's interest in you. In or out, for that matter.

The morning passed slowly otherwise, and at lunch I sat alone eating my lunch. A ham and Swiss sandwich, red grapes, pretzels, and carrots. The perfect sack lunch in my opinion.

A hand brushing through my hair caught me off guard. I turned to look and nearly fell out of my seat.

It was her.

"Hey, do you mind if I sit down?" she asked.

The lump in my throat stopped me from speaking. Instead, I jerked my head left and right, then, realizing I'd nonverbally said "no," I nodded.

She smiled at me as if I was a strange curiosity. I nodded again and forced out a single word, "Yes."

She giggled and sat. She had long brown hair, those blue-gray eyes I'd seen, and yes, both were blue-gray in color. She wore light blue skinny jeans, with a few factory-created worn spots, ballet flats, a pink and lime green striped shirt, with an unzipped purple hoodie overtop. She was even more amazing than I'd realized before.

I hadn't truly processed the infatuation I had with her until that moment. What had been driving my desire to meet her all this time? Clearly, it'd been her looks.

"So, what's your name?" she asked.

"Tay—Taylor," I bumbled out my name like a two-year-old learning how to speak.

She smiled and waited as if I should get the lump out of my throat. I didn't.

"Well, my name is Melanie, but you can call me Mel," she said.

"Hi, Mel," I forced out. Was that seriously the best I could do? I'd been waiting more than a week for this chance, and I was quickly biffing it.

"Hi, Taylor," she countered, purposely sounding as awkward as I had. "Tell me, why'd you switch it up?"

"Huh?"

"The shirt?" She looked me over. "It's blue today. I've never seen you in anything but white."

"Oh, yeah," I said. I felt myself smile; she had noticed me before.

"Well, I like the variety. You look good in blue. Any reason for the change?"

I laughed—well, my voice sort of squeaked out a giggle. Again, not my best moment.

"It's quite the story."

She started to make herself comfortable as if she was ready to listen. She pulled a sandwich and a pack of Oreos from a gray and pink argyle backpack. "Go ahead." She twisted the lid off a thermos and dipped an Oreo into it.

Milk and Oreos.

She took a bite and I involuntarily licked my lips. For the Oreos of course.

"So—well—you see, I've got this friend. Well, acquaintance." I felt a small sting in my heart as I said that, like I was betraying my best friend, which I suppose I was. "And he invents things."

"Yeah?" she said.

"Well, this morning he brought this canister thing into my room." I stopped. Wait, I couldn't tell her about this. First off, she'd never understand. Second, I wasn't supposed to share this sort of stuff with anyone from the outside, especially not someone I'd just learned the name of a few minutes prior. "You know it's really not that great a story," I said.

She smiled and took another bite from her Oreo. "OK, but why'd you swap your shirt?"

I tried to think of a good answer that wouldn't draw any more suspicion.

"Well my regular shirts weren't available at the moment. So I borrowed this from my cousin."

"Cousin? Does he go here?" she asked.

"Oh, no, he's out of school. But he's staying with us," I said.

"That's cool. So, where's that little guy who is normally around?" she asked.

"Sick. He's the inventor I mentioned."

"I see."

"And where's your guy?" I asked abruptly and a bit more forcibly then I'd intended.

She laughed. "Oh he isn't 'my' guy," she said using her fingers to make quote marks.

My heart leapt. A sliver of hope glowed before me.

"Naw, sometimes it feels like we're together, but not officially," Mel explained.

I felt my heart sink back into my feet. "Ah."

She smirked. "Oh, it's nothing like that." Her hand slipped over mine.

What was happening? Was I dreaming?

"No, he isn't my type." She looked into my eyes with those mesmerizing blue-gray orbs. I felt a warmth radiating from her hand unlike anything I'd ever felt before.

Several minutes must have passed, or been lost, because the bell rang.

Lunch was over and we had precisely five minutes to get to class. I couldn't afford another detention.

Mel clearly didn't want to be late either. Because before I could even say goodbye, she'd packed her things and left the cafeteria.

I sat still for a moment, dumbfounded. I had no idea what had happened in the last twenty minutes. I went from being strangers with this girl, to her touching my hand?

I made my way to class in a daze, which held my mind for the next few hours until school was over. I decided to wait around as long as I could for her to come; even standing near the scooter I knew was hers, but she didn't come through the doors, and my bus was about to leave.

I boarded and stared out the window like a puppy dog, until the school disappeared from view.

As I walked up the lane toward The Pink Hippo I felt something hit me in the back. I turned and saw a pinecone sitting in the middle of the gravel drive.

Something hit me again. I turned.

Another pinecone.

"Nice shirt," came the voice from overhead, and a moment later Jesse became visible. He landed next to me. "McGarrett fixed my J-Pak and I was just testing it out."

I smirked. "Any sign of Ike?"

"Naw, that little pipsqueak is still 'sick.' But you and I both know he isn't sick. He's embarrassed at his constant screw-ups."

I knew I should feel bad that Jesse was berating my friend, but I didn't. After all, his recent series of cataclysmic mistakes nearly cost me and my cousin our lives. Killing us was supposed to be the HowlSage's job, not Ike's.

"McGarrett is sending us to the canning factory tonight," Jesse explained. "So let's hurry and get you suited up. I left a spare shirt in the workshop changing room for you, and Mrs. Riley brought down some hunting pants and shoes."

"Thanks," I said. "You gonna hunt tonight?"

"Yah. The burns are already healed up."

I nodded. I wasn't sure if it was Mrs. Riley's salve or Ike's white powder.

We rode into town in the back of the Rolls. The idea was to drop us off a short ways downstream from the abandoned factory, then make our way to it.

It was dusk, which impeded my vision. Jesse was already invisible, but I could see imprints from his footfalls in the soft dirt next to me. A steam was rising from the river running next to us as the water cooled in the chill night air.

"Hey Jesse, that isn't the gray mist stuff, is it?"

"Doesn't look like it to me," came Jesse's voice from beside me.

As we approached the factory, we were surprised to see a light glowing through a few of the windows. Was someone inside? If some civilians were, they had no idea the danger that lurked nearby.

Jesse motioned for us to slow down, I crouched low as we crept forward. The light seemed to flicker and then it disappeared.

Jesse pushed open the old rusted door that he and McGarrett had entered previously. The metal base screeched across the concrete, announcing our presence to anyone within a mile, or at least that was what it sounded like.

The factory was three stories tall, most of it open from floor to ceiling. There were pieces of machinery in some areas, with ladders and balconies. The back portion of the factory was sectioned off into three floors of offices.

Jesse and I moved deeper into the abandoned factory in our search. It reeked of garlic, which was the prime product being canned here. It wasn't the yummy smell you get when someone's baking garlic bread; this scent was rancid. Near certain machines I'd get a particularly good wiff and almost hurl.

An odd sensation kept me looking back at the door every few moments. Sounds fair; I mean the thing we were hunting was also hunting us, but this was different. There was someone or something else here. I could sense it.

"Let's split up," Jesse said.

"Are you—" I stopped myself. I couldn't sound like a wimp. I wasn't scared—or was I? For the first time since we'd started this hunt, I realized that maybe I actually was scared.

I thought I couldn't be, that fear did not affect me. But the risen hair on my arms and the shivers running down my spine said differently.

"Am I what?" Jesse asked.

I puffed out my chest. "Ready," I said, covering my fear.

"Yeah," he whispered. He was invisible, so in actuality I already felt somewhat alone. "I'll head toward the offices; I'm probably better suited for close-corner combat than you are. You search out here. If either of us finds it, I'm sure the other will know. If we don't, we'll meet up at the entrance to the tunnel."

"OK."

Of course, I didn't see him leave, but I knew I was alone.

As I said, the factory was almost cavernous, the third floor lined with windows, some cracked, some only fragments left.

Where had the glow come from? It made little sense as I estimated what windows we'd seen the light shining through as we'd approached. There was no platform in this section of the factory. The lower floors of the factory had fewer windows, but none of them had been lit up.

I walked over. There were shoe prints in the dust that cloaked the floor, smaller than mine, but not Jesse's and not HowlSage prints either. The marks left by the shoe soles were in an odd pattern as if the wearer had danced, or spun, or...something. Then the prints left the circle.

So I followed. But they disappeared where the dust did. I felt a cold draft and looked up. Several of the windows were missing in this section of the factory. I determined the wind must have swept the dust away.

I continued in the general direction the trail had been leading when I heard something on the air.

A voice, chanting. I turned to see the owner, but there was no one.

The chanting continued. It was similar to the song I'd heard outside that house a few nights prior. But the voice was different. Deeper. I'd heard the HowlSage speak in my dream, but...

Shouting erupted behind me from the third floor of the offices. Jesse!

I darted for the stairs to help. As I did, out of the corner of my eye, I saw it—or someone.

It was my size, cloaked in black, in the shadows of one of the old machines. I turned to look. It held something shiny in its hands.

A dagger?

My hand was on the hilt of my sword, but the cloak swirled and a second later the person was gone. Either in the shadows, or literally vanished into thin air, but gone nonetheless.

I heard Jesse shout again. He was challenging the HowlSage. I started up the first flight of stairs.

"Finally I've got you cornered, you stinking hairy beast. Where's your misty comrade?"

A loud growl rumbled and I felt the staircase railing shiver.

"That's the best you got?" Jessed called.

I figured he was still invisible. I pictured him circling the creature that was probably over nine feet tall by now.

I reached the second landing on the staircase.

Roar!

"Whoa!" I heard Jesse yell. "That was close, but not close enough."

Something banged against the wall.

"Throwing things, are you?"

I twisted the handle of the door, but nothing happened.

I saw the wall of the room shake and heard something smash against it.

"Not nice. Take this."

I pictured Jesse slashing at the HowlSage with his sword.

Suddenly the staircase shook violently and I looked down to see the lower landing and set of stairs crumbling to the ground. The second landing and staircase leading to the third floor shook and started to fall.

Within a second, the landing I stood upon dropped sharply at an angle. I reached for the door and held on tight. The only thing stopping the landing from dropping two stories was the bolts anchoring it to the third floor, and they wouldn't hold long.

I spread the wings from my pack out and started the J-Pak. Letting go of the handle, my body slid off the landing and I let the J-Pak lift me into the air. I hovered for a moment, looking for anything that might have caused the collapse.

It was there, the cloaked figure. It had a chin, a human-looking chin. It held a dagger in its hand and I knew the weapon had been used to slice through the old metal supports. This was not your typical knife.

The knife was silver, and in its hilt was a large red ruby.

A crash resounded overhead, pulling my attention upward. Time seemed to slow down.

Glass flew through the air, and I watched as Jesse's body was launched through a third floor window. He was visible and he was falling. I dove to catch him, but I couldn't get there. My hand only caught his arm a moment before he slammed into the wood-plank floor, slowing him down only a bit.

Still standing just a few yards away was the cloaked figure. Even in the shadows of its cloak I could see its gleaming eyes.

Jesse groaned and I looked at him.

When I turned back, the staircase saboteur was gone.

I looked toward the third floor. I wanted to attack the HowlSage, but I stopped myself. If the stalker hadn't left, he might come back to finish off Jesse. And Jesse was hurt bad.

A short moment later, the HowlSage came to me. Leaping from the third floor, the demon landed ten yards away. It snarled and then let out a deafening howl.

Jesse's eyes opened wide and he pushed himself up. The HowlSage started for us. I slid my sword free of its sheath and stood before my cousin. The beast stopped five yards away and rose to its full height. Its eyes narrowed and flashed yellow.

It was ready to strike.

But then its ears perked up. It slowly turned its head. Something had changed its mind. The beast stepped backward slowly.

I knew this was my chance. I dashed forward at the beast, when I heard a grinding noise overhead. I looked back—the bolts holding the landing I'd been hanging from were coming loose, and Jesse lay directly below.

I dashed back to my cousin and pulled him away from the point of impact. We'd barely gotten clear when the landing crashed to the ground with a metallic noise that sounded like a thousand cymbals crashing together.

I looked back and the HowlSage was gone. It'd gotten away, and for some reason I felt relieved.

Chapter Eleven

October 12th—Thursday

It turned out Jesse had only sprained his ankle; my last-minute grab had been just enough to stop him breaking anything or, well, dying.

School went quickly and I didn't see Melanie—I mean Mel—anywhere. Which was disappointing. I wanted to feel her hand run through my hair again.

Weird how I'd only talked to her once for all of twenty minutes, but it was like I had to see her, feel her touch.

It didn't happen today though; she was nowhere.

Ike was still sick, and Jesse was laid up. So when I returned to The Pink

Hippo after school, I was on my own with McGarrett.

"Taylor?" McGarrett asked.

"Yah?"

"Do you feel up to hunting tonight?"

"Of course," I said.

"I mean, with Jesse hurt, the communications still down, and Ike sick, we can't provide you a lot of support." He paused for a moment. "Your job is more dangerous than it's ever been."

"OK, but really, can it get much more dangerous? I'm fighting a demon either way," I said.

Mr. Riley frowned.

"I know what you do is essential," I corrected. "I'm not saying it's not. But the task at hand is always dangerous. I'm always a moment away from—" I swallowed hard.

"Death," McGarrett finished. His expression changed from serious to kind. "Taylor, can I ask you a couple questions?"

"Sure."

"How is your Walk?"

I felt my heart drop into my knees. He wasn't talking about my ankle. I knew exactly what he meant, spiritually. "Ummm fine," I lied.

And there, with those words, I proved my walk wasn't what it was supposed to be. I'd lied, which was a good indicator my walk wasn't where it should be.

"You're sure?" he continued. "I know I'm not your parent, but I am responsible for you. And I guess I've been lax in keeping up with you."

"You've—we've been busy," I said.

"No, I don't want to make any excuses for it. I have to do better at mentoring you."

I nodded. "All right."

He smiled. "Now, are you absolutely sure you're ready to go out tonight?"

I pulled on a black pair of gloves. "Yep."

"Good. With the sensors not functioning correctly after dark, we don't really have any updates on the HowlSage's movements tonight. One place we haven't been thoroughly checking is the park." McGarrett tapped the keyboard in front of him and a large city map appeared on one of the screens. "I've mapped out the sightings we've had of the HowlSage and some possible paths it would have taken to get to those places. At least four of the routes would be through the park, so tonight I want you to spend some time checking there." McGarrett stopped and held out a folder for me to look at.

I opened it and found several grainy images of someone in a cloak. "Who is it?"

"We don't know, but the images were caught by a camera in the park. Some wildlife photographer set the camera up to track the Canadian geese, and when he saw this suspicious figure in the background of his pictures he decided to let the police know."

I handed the pictures back to Mr. Riley.

"The chief brought these to me after they stationed a patrolman there, but they never saw the cloaked figure. It might have been a one-time thing, but I think with the likelihood that the HowlSage is moving through the forest, and your sighting last night, these images are of the saboteur from the factory."

I nodded. McGarrett was right; he had to be.

We went outside and I strapped on the J-Pak.

"Since you're alone tonight, I want you to check in every couple hours."

I sighed.

"I mean it. Use a pay phone or fly back here, but I want you checking in."

"A pay phone, really?"

"There's one at Yoder's Fuel Station and one at the IGA grocery store. Our cell phones aren't connecting at night for us either. In fact, calls are getting dropped at dusk for everyone in town. Apparently, several cellular companies have sent crews up here trying to fix the issue, but they can't figure it out," McGarrett rubbed his chin and looked up into the night sky. "The Chief says that their dispatcher can't get a hold of the patrols at night either. His men have to come by the station to check in every so often. Only landlines seem to be working."

I nodded, but McGarrett looked me in the eyes. "Taylor, I mean it. I owe it to your parents to watch out for you. I can't do anything about you hunting, it's your job, it's who you are, but I have to try my best to make it easier and safer for you."

I laughed unintentionally, but he did as well. We both knew my job wasn't safe and it couldn't be.

"I will call, or come back to check in," I promised.

"Good. Now get going. The sun is nearly set."

I touched the controls to my jet pack and blasted into the air. I gave it a little more power than needed, partially because I was tired of all the sappy talk, but also because mentioning my parents had made me want to find and kill the HowlSage as soon as possible.

Ashley Meadows was mostly dark. I headed for the middle of town where the park and lake were located. I had my night vision goggles on, knowing that I was again looking for a needle in a haystack. It was hard enough to find a big hairy creature bounding through the woods, but someone my size in a cloak, now that would be impossible.

Two hours had passed with no sighting. So I made my way to the gas station and landed. I found the pay phone, an old, rusty thing, and inserted a couple of quarters to make my call. It was weird holding the handset to my ear and hearing it ring.

"Hello," I head McGarrett answer.

"Yeah, it's Taylor. I'm just checking in. Haven't seen anything yet."

"All right. Thanks for calling. You need anything?"

"Nope, but I'm heading back to the park to look."

"OK."

I hung up and started for the back side of the gas station. I'd decided to ditch the J-Pak and wings there, so as not to draw suspicion to myself at the pay phone. It was one thing to be dressed all in black, but to have a jet pack strapped to your back was too much for a civilian to handle. Especially since the underside of the gas station canopy glowed like a tanning bed.

I took off again and started flying a zigzag pattern over the woods.

Then I saw it. Not the HowlSage, but the figure. I only caught sight for a brief moment, and it was only the slightest movement that got my attention. I brought myself to a hover position and used one hand to zoom the night vision goggles in.

Nothing.

I flew lower in the direction it'd been walking. I went slow.

I saw some bushes moving near a trail. I knew I'd have to be on foot if I wanted to track the figure, so I landed.

I stepped forward into the underbrush silently and found myself on a path, the beginning to which had been shrouded by bushes. Just twenty yards ahead, a silhouette moved forward on the trail.

I crept along for several minutes following. The figure turned and walked between two pine trees. I'd lost sight of it for the moment. Not wanting to walk into a trap and find the person waiting for me, I dropped to my belly and crawled under one of the trees, staying near its trunk and shrouded under a blanket of needle-covered branches.

A small gap in the branches allowed for me to see what was ahead. Before me was a clearing lined with pine trees, like a greenish-blue ring of spires. Immediately within the pine circle were rocks—large round rocks ringing the clearing—and in the center was the figure, on its knees, bowing.

Up and down, up and down.

I heard it whispering, chanting as I had heard it the night before. I couldn't understand what it was saying.

The figure stood and looked into the sky, which I realized was visible. The clearing extended far up into the atmosphere. Above us, only a sliver of the moon showed. A few more days and it would be new moon, which meant the Earth's satellite would disappear from view.

The figure pulled a dagger from its cloak. The same as from the other night, ruby hilt and all. The knife was set on the ground in the center of the circle, and the figure knelt again, bowing up and down, up and down.

Suddenly the radio on my wrist squealed to life.

"Testing," came the voice. "Testing, one, two, three."

I slapped my hand over the radio, but it was too late. The figure looked toward me. It scooped up the dagger from the circle and dashed wildly into the pine trees at the far side of the circle.

I leapt to my feet in pursuit, but as soon as I broke through the trees there was nothing, no one in sight. The wielder of the knife had given me the slip and there was only one person to blame. I knew whose voice had spoken over the radio—it'd been Ike.

Chapter Twelve

October 13th—Friday

I scrubbed my wet mop of hair a bit harder than usual. Partially because there were pine needles trapped in it from last night, but mostly because I was still angry at Ike. He'd interrupted me before I'd had the chance to apprehend the cloaked saboteur.

Not even the five minutes of radio berating I'd given him had made me feel better, nor could Mr. Riley calm me down when I returned. I was so tired of getting that close and then failing. I was ready to kill the HowlSage, to unravel the mystery of the cloaked figure and the gray mist.

I heard the door to the bathroom open. "Morning Tay," said Jesse. "You're up early."

"Yah, I couldn't sleep." I

poured some shampoo into my hand and worked up a lather.

"Me either." I heard the shower in the stall next to me turn on.

I stroked my fingers through my hair.

"Any tests at school today? Math, science, history?"

"Nope, nothing."

I closed my eyes as the suds ran down over my face. The shampoo smelled of the ocean, some brand Mrs. Riley had picked out no doubt. But I wasn't ever particular, so long as I didn't smell like flowers or cotton candy.

"Still mad about last night?" he asked.

For a moment, the only sound was the water from the two showers.

"Yeah, I am. I was so close."

"I know how you feel. I feel like the two of us should have gotten this thing by now. You know what the average life of a HowlSage is?"

Free of shampoo or soap, I shut off my water and dried off. "Yes, I know…"

"One day," we said in unison.

I heard Jesse sigh. "We'll get it, though."

"We'd better. Or the River cousins are going to look pretty pathetic."

Jesse laughed, "Almost as pathetic as when you tried to kill the HowlSage with your towel."

And to think I was going to go back to my room and get dressed, letting Jesse finish his shower in peace. "Is that so?"

Jesse didn't say a word, just laughed.

"You'll get yours, buddy," I warned.

"As long as Ike doesn't mess it up," he retorted, and I couldn't help but laugh at that.

"I'll see you at breakfast," I said, and started for the door. I pulled it open and let it shut. But I stayed inside the bathroom. I waited for Jesse to start singing. His choice—"Sunshine Flavors."

Halfway through the second verse I turned on the ice cold water in the sink. I took the bag out of the garbage can and set it softly on the floor. The rubbish bin wasn't very big, and the antique faucet was in a nice swan neck arc. I let the cold water fill the trash pail to the brim, then tiptoed to the shower. He never saw it coming.

With one quick swing, the water flew from the bin, over the curtain, and onto Jesse.

"*Ahhh!*" he cried as the curtain to the shower buckled and wrapped around Jesse's falling body. Apparently the cold water had caught him so off guard, he'd thrown himself out of the shower, but the curtain blocked his exit.

A second later, Jesse lay on the tiled floor wrapped in the shower curtain. The look he gave me told me I'd better run, and now. I sprang for the door, dropping the trash can in my wake. I'd at least have a few seconds while he untangled himself from the curtain.

I was to the elevator and inside before he could even get out of the bathroom.

I was safe, for now.

I headed for the seventh floor, so I could sneak back around down the stairs and to my room to get dressed. The seventh floor had an atrium with a glass ceiling and lots of plants growing. Mrs. Riley grew a lot of her own produce there in the winter. It was a very peaceful place, with a fountain and other areas to reflect. But what was most interesting was a door that led nowhere—or so it seemed.

In the center of the large room, the door stood in a frame, attached to no walls—you could walk all around it with no need to go through the door. But to someone who understood its purpose, the door was significant. Much like the gaping Etherpits that appeared deep in the caverns and mines of the earth, this door led somewhere. Those Etherpits provided entry for demons into our world, this door and others like it around the world provided a way for Angels to enter. While not limited to these entry points, they were a representation to us as humans that the Angels were always ready to join in the battle with us.

To my surprise, I found McGarrett on the seventh floor kneeling in the garden. He was praying aloud and I'd caught him mid-prayer.

"Lord, please let Taylor see. Let him remember that You are in control and that You care about him. Open his eyes as I cannot. Amen."

I felt guilty. Mr. Riley had been praying for me. Me, the one who let him down in the hunt so far. I slowly stepped backward and then made for the stairs where I could make my way back to my room and avoid Jesse. But most of all I didn't want McGarrett to know I'd heard him.

When I entered the dining hall, I saw Jesse. But he made no attempt to get me. His revenge would come later, probably when I was least expecting it. Ike wasn't there and I was sort of glad, because Jesse would have made some sort of sarcastic remark to him I'm sure, further complicating the situation.

"So, are you going to be able to hunt tonight?" I asked.

"No, I—" Jesse stopped mid-sentence. Mrs. Riley had come in with a plate of waffles.

I nodded at him. There was no talk of work at the breakfast, lunch, or dinner table, ever, final answer, period.

"Anything interesting at school today?" Mrs. Riley asked, setting down the waffles.

"Nope," I said and forked one on to my plate. "Maybe the lab project in chemistry, it might be cool."

Jesse snickered. "Yeah, just don't get carried away like Ike and blow something—"

"That's enough of that," Mr. Riley warned.

"Yes indeed," Mrs. Riley interjected. "He's under enough strain with his parents being so far away. And besides that, he's younger than you."

We all looked toward the door as it slammed shut.

"Oh dear, he must have heard us," Mrs. Riley said as she got to her feet.

We all knew Ike must have stepped through the door as Jesse made his comment. He'd heard and retreated before anyone could stop him.

"Hun, let him be. He's a boy, he doesn't need to be coddled," McGarrett said.

She sighed, but continued after Ike, the door swinging shut behind her.

"I keep telling her it's just his nerves. We're all on edge these days. You know we're nearing the halfway point. The HowlSage must be nearly eight or nine feet by now."

"Nine," Jesse clarified. "I saw all nine feet of it before it threw me out the window."

"Lucky I caught you," I said.

He scoffed at me.

I shook my head. "I was thinking I'd head back to the woods tonight."

"I think that's a great—" Mr. Riley stopped midsentence as Mrs. Riley came back through the door.

"Great waffles," Jesse offered, smothering a stack of three in syrup. "And syrup!"

"Yeah, really," I added.

We'd nearly been caught, and I doubted our guilty expressions were enough to fool Mrs. Riley.

She took her seat, but didn't add any food to her plate. Instead she just sat apparently lost in thought.

After breakfast, it was off to school. Since I had not seen Mel yesterday, I had high hopes I would see her today.

Sure enough, as lunch came around I saw her. She was seated at the table where I'd first felt her touch. I decided I'd take the same approach to an introduction she had to me. I ran my fingers down the back of her long brown hair, but before I was halfway through, an icy cold hand had clenched onto mine, and with unimaginable strength twisted my arm and brought me to my knees on the floor beside her.

I looked at the hand, the arm, its owner, expecting to see the boy who I'd seen her with in the park, who she said wasn't her guy. But no, it was her, her arm, her hand.

The grip released as I looked into her blue-gray eyes.

"Oh, I'm sorry," she apologized. "I didn't know it was you."

I shook my hand and arm. "Yeah, it is. Quite the grip you have."

"I guess those Tae Kwon Do lessons paid off," she said innocently, then changed the subject. "I'm really glad you came over." She touched the seat next to her. "Sit."

I did.

The warmth and feeling had come back into my hand. I took out my sack lunch and set it on the table. She'd already laid out her lunch.

"I looked for you yesterday," I said.

"I was sick. Just under the weather, but I'm feeling better today."

"Cool."

"Where's your little friend?" she asked.

"Who?"

"The inventor kid."

"Oh, Ike. Sick."

She nodded and dunked an Oreo in her milk thermos.

"Yeah, he's got a touch of something." It wasn't a total lie. He's got a touch of hurt feelings, I assured myself.

"Too bad."

I took a bite of my sandwich. I needed something more interesting to say. I looked her over. *Wow, she's beautiful.*

"Cool bracelet you have on."

"Oh, this? It's nothing special. Just a gift from someone."

"Let me guess, the boy?"

She blushed. "Yeah, well, he got it to make me feel better. So far it's worked."

I forced a smile. "That's good." I swallowed the lump in my throat. "He must really like you?"

"I guess," she said, then pulled another Oreo from the pack. "Here, twist with me."

She held the cookie out, holding on to one side of the sandwich.

I took the other side in my fingers and she counted to three. We twisted and the two halves came apart.

She laughed. "Looks like I got all the good stuff."

It was true; all the creamy white frosting was on her wafer. "Want some?" she teased after licking it.

"Ha, I'll pass."

I looked at the bracelet on her wrist again. It was silver, with several red and clear jewels inlayed. An inscription was etched in curvy lines encircling each of the jewels. I couldn't decipher what the words said, probably some mushy love line. Of course, the bracelet had to be faux. If not, this kid was in a financial league I couldn't compete with.

I shared my chips with her, she shared a few more Oreos, even letting me dip in her milk. When the bell rang she stayed around long enough and asked me to walk her to class. Right before she stepped in she leaned close to my ear and whispered, "Meet me outside Mrs. Mullen's room after seventh hour. You can drive me home." Then she walked into her class.

I stood like a statue, frozen at the door.

Mr. Burton gave me an odd look. "I know you love science, but you'll have to wait until seventh hour." He smiled sarcastically and shut the door in my face.

This wasn't happening. I'd hardly talked to girls before, now the first one I take interest in approaches me, talks to me, and shares Oreos with me, all within a few days. And now I get to drive her home?

Wait, drive her? I can't drive.

The tardy bell rang on the speaker, which meant I'd stood like that for at least a minute. But I didn't care. I wandered to history, ignoring Mr. Samford's comment about getting to class on time. Fortunately there was no punishment handed out.

Usually class would go slow if you were waiting for something. But it flew by instead, probably because I was in a half daze still. Unsure of how all the pieces had fallen into place.

At the end of each of my afternoon classes, I had to stop myself from walking to Mrs. Mullen's room and standing outside her door until school was over.

Finally the last bell of the day rang, and I made my way to meet the girl. I couldn't call her mine yet, but she was the girl. As promised, she came out, her pink and gray argyle backpack slung over her shoulder. I quickly offered to take it and she willingly handed it over to me. We walked down the halls; part of me wondered where that boy was. Part of me wondered if she'd take my hand, or if I should take hers.

Outside the school, she walked to her scooter and undid the small lock that had secured it to the bike rack. I looked at the buses; mine was just third in line. I knew I should go get on it. But I couldn't pass up this opportunity. Should I call McGarrett? Of course not, he'd track me down and make me come home.

No. I was doing this for me. If he was mad, so be it. I could always tell him I had detention again, or that I was attacked again. Yeah, that was a good excuse. I'd tell him the cloaked figure jumped me.

"Are you ready?" came Mel's sweet voice.

"Ummm, yeah," I stuttered. "Ready."

She climbed on her scooter and motioned for me to step up behind her. "Hold on."

I looked around. "Where?"

"To me, of course. I won't bite."

I let out an awkward laugh and took a deep breath. I wrapped my arms around her, interlocking my fingers.

Mel giggled again. "You'll probably be fine just holding on to my shoulders."

"Oh," I said, embarrassed. My face burned, and I hoped she didn't turn around and see my bright red cheeks.

"Here we go." She twisted the small throttle on her handle and the scooter shot forward. She turned, and we were off down the sidewalk.

I looked back and watched my bus jerk, then lurch forward as it started its route toward The Pink Hippo without me.

And then it crossed my mind how dead I was going to be when I got home.

We zipped down the street; Mel turned this way and that.

I soon forgot about needing to be home.

…About McGarrett.

…About the HowlSage.

We talked about all sorts of things. I learned her favorite bands, that she'd moved here from Chicago last summer, and that her parents were missionaries. I thought that was pretty cool. She'd been to Tibet, India, Iran, Malaysia, Egypt, and Indonesia, some really interesting countries. I told her my favorite bands, favorite foods, about The Pink Hippo, and that I lived with the Rileys.

She asked where my parents were and I decided to just tell her they were away. I didn't want to ruin the great time we were having with a depressing story about how I was now an orphan. It was just a half-lie, if even.

Nearly half an hour passed and we were still riding around. I noticed the sun was getting lower in the sky.

"How far do you live from the school?" I half-shouted into her ear.

"Sorry. I've passed my house at least five times," she admitted.

"Oh."

"I guess I'm just having too much fun."

That was a good thing. "No worries, I am too."

"Cool. You want to go get some coffee or something?"

I shrugged. "Sure."

It couldn't hurt to be out a little longer. The sun hadn't quite set yet.

We pulled into a parking spot at the Starbucks—as I mentioned before it was one of only two chain stores in town. There was a guy in a corner, headphones on, laptop screen glowing. Two girls sat across from each other, gabbing about who knows what. Another set of people sat around a table, all with the same book in hand: *Claiming Your Inner Self*.

At the counter, Mel rattled off her order like a professional. I looked at the menu, trying to decipher what might not make me twitch at its bitterness. I'd had a sip of Mr. Riley's black coffee before.

Mel started to pull out a little pink sequin wallet, when I grabbed her hand.

"No, let me get it," I said. Maybe this wasn't a planned date, and maybe she drove me around, but I was certainly going to show that I was capable of treating her right. I pulled out my wallet, and opened it. A few ones, some notes, and that was it.

She smiled. "It's all right. We'll go Dutch today."

"Dutch?"

"Pay for yourself."

"OK, sure." But was the small amount I had going to be enough for even me?

I ordered something small and cheap and got back change of three cents, which I quickly dropped in the tip jar with a smile. The barista nodded a half-hearted "thanks" and I went on my way.

We found an empty set of chairs and sat down.

I watched her take her first sip. I did too. The coffee was raw-tasting, bitter, black. I forced myself to swallow and hoped my expression hadn't given away the fact that I wasn't a big coffee drinker. Clearly she was.

"So what is it Taylor likes to do in his spare time, evenings, weekends?" she asked.

I knew this would be a tricky answer to give. I couldn't tell her what I was currently doing, and if I told her something not true, she might want to join me sometime. And besides that, I didn't do much other than hunt. If there wasn't a HowlSage, it might be a SwampSage, a Goblin, Wormink, or any other sort of demon.

"Well, I like to read."

"You do? Like what?"

"Just about anything."

"Have you read the latest series from Bethanie Freyer?"

"Who?"

"You haven't heard of Bethanie Freyer? She only wrote the best-selling series ever."

"Oh, uhhh." I looked down at my steaming cup of coffee. "I'm more into comic books and graphic novels."

I expected her to frown, to be disappointed in my lack of higher level literature; instead she smiled.

"That's cool; the publisher actually just started releasing the saga in graphic form," Mel said, then sipped her drink. "I'll bring you one on Monday."

I smiled, relieved that she didn't take me for a complete moron. "Cool."

The sun had long set by the time we left and headed for home. When we arrived at the gates of The Pink Hippo, she stopped. I hopped off to push in the code to open the gates.

"You mind if I leave you here? I really need to get home," Melanie said.

I shrugged. "No problem. I'll see you on Monday."

"See you then." She twisted the throttle and shot a few loose pebbles out behind her. And with a wave she was off down the dark road.

I watched the scooter's headlight beam disappear before starting up the drive. And then a frightening thought entered my mind. What if the HowlSage attacked her? She was all alone in the countryside.

I had to protect her, even if she didn't know it. I'd get the J-Pak and fly over her until she arrived safely home. The gravel crackled under my feet as I sprinted for the workshop. As I slammed open the door, McGarrett turned and glared at me.

"Where have you been, Taylor?" he shouted.

I stopped dead in my tracks.

"It's eight at night. The sun has been set for hours."

"I—"

"No excuses tonight," Mr. Riley ordered. "Ike is missing. He's been gone since early this afternoon. And Jesse is investigating something at the ferry even though he's still injured."

My heart sunk at the news of Ike. "Missing?"

"Mrs. Riley and I haven't seen him since lunch. And his rollerblades are gone."

"Blades? He wouldn't have used them to go to town," I said.

"He must have, because he isn't here," McGarrett said. "We'll talk about why you were late later, but for now get changed. We need to find him."

I quickly suited up and McGarrett fitted me with the J-Pak.

"Check the woods in the park. Mrs. Riley said he was pretty upset about giving you away and making you lose sight of the cloaked figure."

I nodded and blasted into the air. My destination was set. The park and the circle in the woods.

Melanie! I remembered. She'd hopefully be nearing town by now, it wouldn't hurt if I shifted my route enough to check in on her.

I followed the road, and a moment later I saw the little scooter she was driving. She hadn't made it very far, maybe half a mile, which was unusual. I'd left her nearly ten minutes ago; why hadn't she gotten very far?

She seemed to pick up speed and it only took another fifteen minutes for her to cross into Ashley Meadows proper. At that point I felt assured that she'd make it home. The HowlSage had crossed into town several times, but she was a far less likely target in town than in the winding dark forest of the countryside.

Now for the park.

My radio spurred to life. "Taylor?" It was Jesse.

"Yeah?"

"I'm still at the ferry, but I'll join you as soon as I can. Glad you could help." His last line was clearly a jab at my tardiness.

"Sure. I'm headed to the park to look for Ike."

"I just don't get that kid…"

"Lay off, will yah, Jesse?" I scolded. "He was just trying to help."

"Sorry man."

I felt bad for jumping him, but Ike was lost and, well, I felt somewhat responsible, especially if he was at the stone circle in the woods.

"It's fine. I'm just—just worried. That's all."

"I get it. I'll see you when I can."

The radio went silent and I veered toward the park. I knew right where I was headed and didn't waste any time looking for Ike as I went. If he was in the park, he'd be at the stone circle.

Dropping through the woods would be difficult, so I landed on the trail again and made my way down the paths I'd followed the cloaked figure on the night before.

As I entered the circle, there was nothing. No sign of Ike, no HowlSage, nobody wearing a cloak.

The trees stood like guards ready to arrest me, but the stones circled me like a protective boundary the pines could not breach. It was an odd arrangement.

I stepped to the center and looked around, then studied the dirt floor for any prints. Ike had been here, I could tell by the marks of the stars on his Converse shoes. The HowlSage had been here too. Whether they'd been here at the same time was impossible to tell.

I looked up as a branch snapped in half overhead. Someone dropped out of the trees, a rope wrapped around their waist.

"Ike!" I yelled, then lowered my voice. "Ike, where have you been?"

"Here." He shrugged. "I've set up some surveillance."

"Surveillance—why didn't you tell McGarrett? Why didn't you have him come with you?" I asked in rapid fire style. "It's too dangerous to—"

Ike held up his hand. "Stop it! I'm not a baby. I'm nearly completed and I did it without anyone's help." He unhooked the rope from around his waist. "I can take care of myself."

"Well…" I started.

"You and Jesse act like I am no use. You think just because you're hunters, that you are more—"

Ike stopped ranting. I watched the color drain from his face. He looked like a ghost.

"What is it?" I asked, but I needed no answer as I heard the low growl of a creature, of the HowlSage.

My instincts took over. I rolled forward in a somersault toward Ike and twisted as I sprang up, my sword ready in one hand, and my other behind me protectively in front of the boy genius. I faced the beast.

The HowlSage had gotten larger. Its fur was dark and sleek, shining in the pale ambient moonlight that shown down through the circular gap in the trees. It snarled, exposing its full set of fangs, each more than three inches long now. I watched as it curled its fingers, and heard its knuckles crackle; it was ready for business. It wouldn't be fleeing this time.

"Ike, stay behind me," I commanded.

Roar! The HowlSage's deafening scream raised the hair on my arms and sent shivers through my stomach, my heart, and then I felt a lump in my throat.

I was scared, frightened. How?

I had to be strong. I backed closer to Ike, but still in front.

"You—you can't win!" I called, but my voice had cracked; I'd given off a clear sign of fear.

Grrr! Arrrooough! The HowlSage let out its signature howl, it was about to attack and I was not ready. My arms were cold, numb. The sword felt heavier than it should.

Frozen in place, I knew my legs weren't going to do their job if called upon.

A shadow blotted out the little light there'd been in the circle. I looked up and saw something winged circling overhead. It wasn't Jesse. It was the flying thing.

I heard Ike whisper something behind me, "It's the Raptoryx."

"The what?" I started to ask as I looked back at the HowlSage, just as it hunched and launched itself into the air, soaring at me like a bullet fired from a rifle, fast and on target.

All I could do was shove Ike to the ground, hoping to get him out of the way, and move my sword in a defensive position before me.

The HowlSage dropped short of my sword, swiping its large paw upward in a direct hit on the hilt of my sword. I felt it slide from my weak sweaty palm and into the air. It twisted and clanged to the ground a few feet away.

Weaponless, I stared into the beast's cold, yellowed eyes.

"You can't turn me. Your venom isn't active yet."

It growled, but the growl sounded like a laugh. It bared its fangs again. All it need do was lurch forward and bite; there was little I could do to get out of the way.

To my surprise, it stalked backward, slinking closer to the center of the circle, and continuing.

"Ike, look, it's leaving—don't worry." I glanced for my sword and saw it nearby. Keeping my eyes on the HowlSage, I edged toward my weapon.

The HowlSage was nearly to the stone line now. I knew that I should pursue it, I should attack it. But not only was my strength gone—I'd felt fear.

Besides that, I couldn't leave Ike; he was clearly scared.

"Ike, I won't leave you," I said as the HowlSage backed into the spruce trees and disappeared as the pine branches closed around it. "It's OK now, come closer to me."

Silence.

"Ike?" I turned around and to my horror there was no Ike. I was alone in the circle, only a twisted rope hanging from a branch high above remained.

"Ike! Ike, where are you?" I yelled. I remembered my radio. "Jesse, quick, I need you here. Ike was just here. And so was the HowlSage. Now he's gone."

"Who?" came a frantic reply. "Who's gone?" It was McGarrett.

"Both of them," I said.

"Taylor, I'm almost to you. Two minutes. I'll search from overheard. Do you know which direction he went?"

"No! And watch out—the winged thing is back."

"Thanks for the tip."

"Jesse," McGarrett started. "It's a Raptoryx."

"But I thought—" Jesse started.

"I did, too. Ike identified it. It can only mean that—" McGarrett continued.

Was I the only one that didn't know what a Raptoryx was?

"He is returning," Jesse finished.

"Trying," McGarrett corrected. "The full moon will land on Halloween, and tonight is Friday the 13th. Everything is aligning as needed."

"Didn't Ike realize what today was?" Jesse asked.

"Who is returning?" I interrupted with a shout.

"Not now, Taylor, we have to get Ike," McGarrett explained. "I'll call the chief, have him send his patrols to put a perimeter around the park.

I'm headed to Hilbert's Hill."

"I'll meet you there," I said.

Hilbert's Hill was at the very end of the only green belt, or forested corridor, that stretched from the park to the mountains. It was half a mile wide and ten miles long, stretching out of Ashley Meadows. Hilbert's Hill was the high point in a road that crossed through the corridor. If the HowlSage didn't want to pass through neighborhoods, it had to use the wooded stretch.

But where was Ike? Had he gotten scared and wandered off?

As if on cue, a voice echoed through the dark woods. "We have him. He is ours. He will not live to see you again. He is gone."

My entire body felt as cold as ice; anything that wasn't numb before, was now. I felt queasy; the trees overhead began to spin. I saw the winged thing still circling overhead. My vision went blurry, then gray, then black. I felt my legs buckle and my head hit the soft dirt of the stone circle.

Chapter Thirteen

October 14th—Saturday

I slid from my bed and approached the glowing fireplace. How I got to my room, I didn't remember, but I was cold. So cold, and the fireplace looked warm. I stood on the tiles before the hearth and stared into the flames as they flickered amongst the firewood.

Fire was such an interesting thing. It seemed alive, yet it was not. No, it was the opposite—fire was death. The consumption of what once was living. But it was beautiful.

When I'd been younger, I had tried many times to control fire, to master it in some form. But I'd never been successful.

Just after my dad and I had come to Ashley Meadows and I had met Ike, he and I had been working on an experiment. The end result was one of the outbuildings and several nearby trees catching fire.

I felt my heart ache at the thought of Ike. Where was he? I'd let him down, and without my parents, he was truly the closest thing to family I'd had. Closer than even Jesse.

"I can take you to him," a gruff voice said from behind me.

I didn't jump at its words, nor did I twist into a defensive position, even though I knew the voice.

I turned and looked into the HowlSage's bulbous yellow eyes. It sat in one of the high-backed winged chairs. "Follow me," it said, but its lips did not move. Its voice was in my head. "I shall take you to your friend and then to your father."

My father?

The HowlSage had promised this before. And before it'd been a dream. I forced myself to speak, "What do you want?"

It bared its teeth in what I took to be a grin. "I want you to bring me the belt and then follow me to your friend and father."

"I can't get you the belt. It's locked away."

"You can. Don't you want to see your friend again? Wouldn't you like to find your father?"

I nodded.

"Then you must follow me."

The fire popped loudly and I looked into the flames. For the slightest second I saw Melanie's face. At least a vision of her.

"Come now, we must go," the beast said.

I looked back at it. But this time the HowlSage was gone—someone in a black cloak had replaced it.

"Follow us, we shall get the belt together." The figure stood, its face still hidden behind the cloak.

"Who are you?" I asked.

"This is not important," it said. "You will know me soon enough."

Something flashed where its face should have been.

"No, you—" the voice screeched.

The room began to swirl, flames shot from the hearth. My head started to spin and then I sat up.

It'd been another dream. I was still in bed. My body was cold, and I rubbed my arms across my bare chest and pulled the covers up to my chin. It was still dark outside. My alarm clock read 4 a.m.

Were Jesse and McGarrett back yet? I slid out of my bed for real this time and pulled a borrowed shirt over my head.

I wandered down the hall toward Jesse's room. His door was shut and when I tried turning the handle, it wouldn't move. Locked.

He was probably asleep if his door was locked.

I continued to the end of the hall, where I looked out over the grounds of The Pink Hippo. The Rolls was parked in the driveway next to the workshop.

The light was on in the building. It looked like McGarrett was in there as well; I knew Mrs. Riley wouldn't be out there at this hour of the night.

I decided now was as good as any time to tell him about the two dreams I had. This way I wouldn't forget.

As I walked to the workshop, I heard a couple people talking. It was Jesse, and the second I wasn't sure about. It didn't sound like McGarrett. Was it Ike? A glimmer of hope surged into my heart.

But as I entered the room, I saw something I hadn't expected. Jesse was holding the belt out in his hands, his bare hands at that. He jerked backward and nearly fell from his chair when the door shut behind me.

"Tay…uh, what are you doing up?" he asked as he set the belt on the table before him.

"Bad dream. What are you doing up?" I asked. "You have to be tired from all the searching."

"Of course I am, but are you feeling all right?"

"What do you mean?"

"When McGarrett and I found you we couldn't wake you. You were out cold. What happened?"

"I don't know, I just heard this voice and everything went black."

"That's weird."

I nodded. "So, what are you doing out here?"

Jesse glanced at the clock. "Ummm, I was about to take a jog. You know, get a fresh start on the day and then look for Ike."

"Let me get changed and I'll join you," I offered.

Jesse stood up. "No, no you need to rest. That's what Mrs. Riley said."

"But—" I started.

"But nothing. Don't make me wake her," he said with a half laugh.

I pictured Mrs. Riley, her hair in curlers, escorting me back to my room and lecturing me on my need to rest. I sighed and stepped aside as he walked past me, pulling a hat over his curly black hair. "I'll be back in an hour. If McGarrett is looking for me, tell him I'll be ready at 6."

I grabbed his shoulder. "Wait, are you guys going back out this morning?"

He frowned. "Of course we are. We have to find him before it's too… well, you know."

I shook my head, "Well, at least let me—"

"You'll have to take that up with Mrs. Riley." And with that he walked out of the door and let it shut behind him.

It took me ten seconds to decide to follow him. I saw an old pair of sneakers by the door and a pullover fleece hanging on a hook. I only had shorts on, but once I got running I figured I'd be warm enough.

I slowly opened the door and peeked out to see which way he'd gone. I could hear his feet on the gravel driveway. I followed, remaining just inside the tree line. This made my running a bit more treacherous—branches, stones, small animal burrows. But I did my best.

At the end of the drive, Jesse pushed open the gate and turned out onto the main road. He stopped and started to tie his shoe, then a moment later he was off and headed for town. I wanted to follow so badly, but there was no way to keep out of sight and follow him down the road. And although I didn't want to admit it, I wasn't in as good shape as he was.

I couldn't fall back to sleep and ended up sitting in a chair in the Pink Hippo's lobby. When McGarrett came through I told him Jesse had gone on a run and that he'd return at 6. I started to plead with him that I was well enough and that I could help. But I knew I'd lost my case immediately.

"It's too risky," he said. "We just don't know what effect the HowlSage is having on you. You're already younger then you should be. Ike was—is too," he corrected himself.

I slunk down in the winged chair. McGarrett came closer and sat on the arm rest.

"Taylor, my boy. I have to look out for you, and sometimes that means not giving you what you want."

I shrugged and looked down at my knees. He stood and I heard him leave through the front door. I wanted to rebel, but what he'd said had meant something to me.

While I'd not admitted it even to myself, I'd been feeling so alone in this world. With my parents gone, I didn't think there was anyone who'd ever care for me as only they could. But I was quickly realizing that this man and his wife were doing their very best, and it wasn't because they had to.

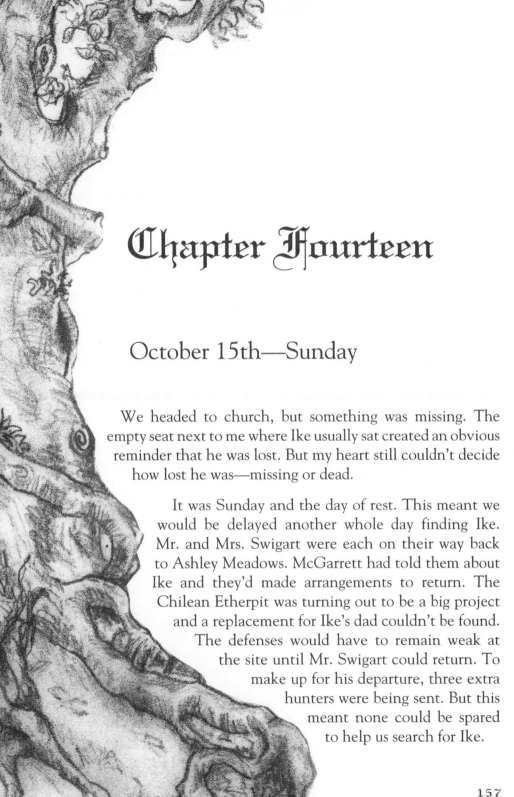

Chapter Fourteen

October 15th—Sunday

We headed to church, but something was missing. The empty seat next to me where Ike usually sat created an obvious reminder that he was lost. But my heart still couldn't decide how lost he was—missing or dead.

It was Sunday and the day of rest. This meant we would be delayed another whole day finding Ike. Mr. and Mrs. Swigart were each on their way back to Ashley Meadows. McGarrett had told them about Ike and they'd made arrangements to return. The Chilean Etherpit was turning out to be a big project and a replacement for Ike's dad couldn't be found. The defenses would have to remain weak at the site until Mr. Swigart could return. To make up for his departure, three extra hunters were being sent. But this meant none could be spared to help us search for Ike.

I had to be better tomorrow. I'd told Mr. Riley repeatedly that I felt fine, but he insisted I needed rest. Mrs. Riley had given me several cups of this nasty tea as well as a shot of something in my thigh, which hurt as I sat in the wooden church pew.

Jesse was sitting in his seat, Bible open in lap, but he just stared at the pastor, eyes glossy. I looked around. The church seemed dead to me. Its members sitting in their seats listening to the drone of the message, the next generation of members, kids, busy texting or chatting to the person next to them.

If Ike was here, he'd be taking notes. But he wasn't here, I was, and I wasn't getting anything from it.

The air was crisp with the chill of the oncoming winter. Jack Frost had started to let us know he'd be here sooner than later.

As we drove up the winding road from Ashley Meadows to the inn, my mind started to play tricks on me. As the trees zipped by, I was sure I was seeing the HowlSage run alongside us, just hidden within the tree line. But I also knew that it was day and a Sunday. Demons rarely attempted to come out of their hiding places on the Lord's day.

Jesse offered to go on a hike with me when we arrived back at the inn, but I didn't really feel up to it. Instead I decided to go sit in the hot tub and relax.

Chapter Fifteen

October 16th—Monday

McGarrett had decided to take me to school today. As we rode along, he explained a new plan to me. Tonight we would wait until midnight to begin the hunt and our search. The idea was to change it up a bit, throw a wrench into the HowlSage's and the cloaked figure's plans.

I'd only taken a few steps into school when Mel ran up to me.

"Hey there, cutie," she said and ran her hand through the back of my hair.

I gave her a smile, but didn't know what to say in response to such a greeting.

"So, do you want to hang out tonight?" she asked.

I really wanted to, but I knew I shouldn't. I needed to concentrate on finding Ike.

She reached out and took my hand. "Please!" she said with a bright smile.

I sighed, "Of course I do. But—"

"Come on Taylor," she pleaded sweetly.

I had an idea. I'd have her go up to the inn with me. Then we'd be near. "How about you come up to my place?" I asked tentatively.

She looked more pleased than I had expected. "Really?" she asked.

"Yah," I affirmed, surprised at her excitement.

"What is there to do?"

"Lots. We have a swimming pool and a library and even a game room," I explained.

"That's cool, anything else?"

I thought for a moment. "Well, there is a lake out behind the inn. We can take the boat out on it if you like."

She smiled. "Now that sounds romantic."

Romantic? Oh man.

"I'll see you after school; we can take my scooter," she offered and then started down the hall as the first bell rang.

I nodded dazedly and headed for my own class, and the day flew by. It seemed like only minutes had passed when the end of school bell rang.

As the out of school bell rang I felt myself float down the hall and to the front doors. As promised, Melanie was there waiting for me. She'd already unhooked the scooter and this time she offered to let me drive. I figured if I could handle a J-Pak I could handle an electric scooter.

We took off and headed out of town on the winding blacktop road toward the inn. The pine trees zipped by and Melanie's arms were wrapped around my waist tightly.

When we got to the gate we had to leave the scooter, because its wheels wouldn't do well in the gravel.

"So are you going to invite me up to the inn?" Melanie asked.

I looked at her peculiarly, "Well, of course I am. Why wouldn't I?"

"Well then, do it," she said.

What was she playing at? I shrugged and offered my hand. "Melanie, would you come to the inn with me?"

She nodded. "I accept your invitation to come onto the property of The Pink Hippo."

That really sounded weird, but when she took my hand it didn't matter anymore.

We hiked up the driveway and stood on the rotunda before the inn.

"Wow!" she exclaimed. "This is where you live?"

I nodded and for the first time really admired my impressive abode. It was rather big and it did have its own charm, I supposed.

"Yep, I live here with the Rileys and Swigarts."

She smiled. "So where is this boat?"

"This way," I said, and we started into the woods on the same narrow dirt path I'd followed with Ike a few days ago.

As we walked she told me more about the cool places she'd been as a missionary kid. They'd just come back from Egypt, which had been a really cool experience. She'd been able to visit and live near the pyramids, the Valley of the Kings, and the Sphinx.

I'd been to Egypt once before with my dad, but at that time I still believed he was a secret agent. I figured we were on some sort of mission for the CIA. Now I wondered why we'd been there. Had he been hunting?

A light steam rose off the lake and the sun was getting low over the mountain range in the distance. I flipped the small boat over and pushed it half into the water.

"Get in," I said, and Melanie stepped in as I shoved us off.

She dipped her hand in the cold water as I rowed. We circled some of the islands and got off onto Pine Needle Island. We sat on the thick carpet of pine needles and watched as the sun sunk lower in the sky. Then it hit me—we didn't have a flashlight and we still had to row back across the lake and make our way through the woods.

"We'd better go. The sun will set soon and it'll be dark," I explained as I got to my feet.

Melanie shook her head and tugged on my hand to get me to sit back down. "No, let's stay for a while. We'll be fine."

I obeyed, and we sat there on the island until the lake looked like a black pool of oil. Only a sliver of moon stood out in the sky. It was even getting difficult to see her sitting next to me, but I could feel her warmth. It'd been a good thing I'd chosen to wear a hooded sweatshirt to school today.

Something splashed in the water a few hundred yards away. I knew from being on the lake so often that the noise had come from somewhere near Ash Island.

Knowing what I did about what was lurking through Ashley Meadows at this very moment, I decided that it was time we got going. If something attacked, I was unarmed and I wasn't sure I could protect Melanie.

"It's probably time to go," I said again. "I'm getting rather hungry."

Melanie looked toward me. "Fine! If all you can think about is food, then take me home."

All I can think about? I hadn't even mentioned it once until now. "I didn't mean to—"

"No, you're right. I'm not worth your time. Take us back," she said.

My mouth dropped open; I could have caught a dozen flies if it'd been summer. I was glad she couldn't see. What in the world had just happened?

She didn't speak to me anymore, and I wasn't exactly sure what to say or even what I had said. I tried to apologize, but we stalked back through the woods in silence, me following her. When we reached the inn she didn't stop but continued down the gravel driveway toward her scooter.

I started to follow, but the door to the workshop opened and out came McGarrett. He walked toward me.

"Where have you been?" he asked, clearly frustrated.

"I was just—" I started.

"Who was that?" McGarrett asked

"It's a girl from—" but again I was interrupted. This time by a sharp whistle from Jesse.

"Taylor's got himself a girlfriend," he said.

Probably not anymore, I thought. I looked down the driveway, hoping Melanie hadn't heard Jesse's remark.

"Jesse, leave it alone," McGarrett warned. "Taylor, there's been a collapse," he said.

"A what?"

"The tunnel into town collapsed; several vehicles are trapped inside."

"You're kidding."

"Do I usually joke about such things?" Mr. Riley said as he started back toward the workshop.

I began to follow. "No."

"What's worse, I got a phone call from Mr. Swigart. They're inside the tunnel."

"Are they OK?" I asked as I passed Jesse, and although he'd been reprimanded he gave me a wide, jeering smile.

"Yes, actually there are at least twelve people inside the tunnel,"

McGarrett explained. "Each end collapsed, but apparently no one was seriously hurt."

"Wow. That's amazing."

"Amazing indeed, but expected," McGarrett said.

"Expected?" I asked as I followed Mr. Riley through the workshop door. I let it shut before Jesse could come in and I heard it shake as he bumped into it. I couldn't help but let out a laugh. How had he not seen it close?

McGarrett continued to speak. "I prayed for protection over the Swigarts as they traveled back to Ashley Meadows."

I nodded in understanding.

McGarrett smiled. "And apparently they have food. A vending machine supplier truck is also trapped inside."

"When will they be rescued?"

McGarrett tapped something on the keyboard and pulled up a video feed of the Ashley Meadows side of the tunnel. "The chief is saying three days. Apparently the collapse is significant on both sides, and Mr. Swigart said that as everyone gathered together more of the tunnel collapsed until they were all gathered around the vending truck. They're in a space only twenty yards wide and the tunnel is a half mile in length."

"Do they have enough oxygen?" I asked.

"Yes, the ventilation system is still working."

"That's good."

"In the meantime, we're headed to the canning factory and through the tunnel to the mines."

"We?"

"Yes, you, Jesse, and myself. And we're taking Ike's invention with us."

"You mean the purple smoke? Is it ready?" I asked.

McGarrett nodded. "I made a few tweaks and we tested it a couple of times today. We'll pray for it to work."

Chapter Sixteen

October 17th—Tuesday

Midnight had come and we were off. All three of us rode in the Rolls to the canning factory. Jesse and I were suited up in our usual gear, and McGarrett had dressed himself in one of my father's old outfits which had been slightly modified by Mrs. Riley to fit Mr. Riley's moderately larger midsection.

Seeing the old man in my dad's clothing didn't bring back painful memories; instead it seemed to comfort me in a way I hadn't expected.

McGarrett was responsible for the purple smoke canisters. I had my sword, and Jesse was invisible. We'd stay together and move straight for the tunnel, but take it slow and listen.

We moved quietly to

the ripped-up drain. Jesse was first in—being invisible had its advantages. I was next and McGarrett last. We all wore our night vision goggles, but their usefulness was limited.

The tunnel smelled of rot and mold. I almost gagged as we crossed over the carcass of an animal. What it once was we weren't sure, but clearly it'd been the HowlSage's dinner. One thing to note about the HowlSage was that it wasn't hungry for humans. No, until the full moon, it could only bite us, not infect us with its venom. Of course, its bite could kill.

We'd traveled nearly a mile through the old sewer tunnel without another sign of the HowlSage or the gray mist.

"We're nearly to the mine," McGarrett said. We approached a split in the passage, McGarrett explained that one led to the river and one into the mine.

"Taylor," I heard. But neither Jesse nor McGarrett had spoken. "Taylor," the voice came again. A whisper. "Taylor, you must turn back. Don't go any further."

I stopped and looked around. Behind us was dark, before us I could see the split and the two paths.

Jesse spoke. "Should either of us check the path to the river?" he asked.

"No, I don't think so." McGarrett tapped the screen of the device in his hand. "None of the sensors picked anything up that would signal the HowlSage has been there."

"Taylor," I heard again. Was the sound in my head? "Turn back."

I shook my head and continued forward after Jesse.

We followed the tunnel toward the mine, and the air became considerably colder. A shiver ran through my body and I rubbed my arms.

"Taylor," I heard again, but this time it was a different voice.

My body jolted backward as I ran into an invisible wall.

"Ouch," Jesse said. "You stepped on my heel."

"Well, why did you stop?"

"Did you hear that?" he asked.

"Yes," McGarrett said.

"Wait, you guys heard someone call my name?" I asked.

"No," Jesse said. "The creaking noise. It's somewhere up ahead."

I listened and sure enough, over the constant drip drop of water, there was a sound, like when someone walks across an old wood floor, or rocks in an antique rocking chair. "What is it?"

"I don't know, but let's keep going."

Our pace quickened down the tunnel. The air became frigid and I started to shiver. The water slopping over my shoes didn't help. The bottoms of my pants were wet.

Another hundred yards down the tunnel and we stopped. We'd gone too far, the sound was behind us. We started back. There'd been no split in the tunnel and nothing wooden along the way. I took the lead this time. Jesse brought up the rear, keeping watch behind us in case this was a trick.

About ten yards back I noticed a set of bars above us, like a drain cover. We stopped and listened. The creaking was overhead.

Even with the night goggles, I couldn't see up through the vent or drain very well. It had to curve or was blocked by something.

"Let's take down the grate," McGarrett suggested.

I reached up and gripped two of the bars. They wouldn't budge.

McGarrett pointed out two large bolts. He reached inside his pack and pulled out a multi-tool that he started working the bolts loose with. Once they'd both dropped to the ground below, I lowered the grate and set it against the tunnel wall.

"Give me a hand; I'm going up," I said.

McGarrett nodded and created a step with his knee, then lifted me into the vent. It was hardly wide enough for my torso, let alone my pack.

"Bring me back down." Mr. Riley did, and I quickly stripped off my excess gear. "All right, here I go."

Once raised back into the tunnel, I used my arms and legs as wedges to move myself up the vent. The walls were slimy with mud, but the vertical tunnel was rigid and narrow enough that I could stop myself from slipping.

I could hear Jesse and McGarrett speaking below, but I couldn't understand what they were saying.

The creaking was getting louder as I got closer. The vent curved and slanted back and forth, blocking the view ahead. I'd left my sword below, and was armed with only a dagger at the moment. If the HowlSage or gray mist were up ahead, I'd be nearly helpless. Escape would be nearly impossible.

I cleared another curve in the tunnel and with my night vision goggles I could see something ahead. It looked like a platform from my angle. Maybe a lift or elevator? This mission was probably a waste of time, and I was probably looking at some remnant from the mines.

The vent widened and I found a narrow ledge to stand on. The lift was swaying side to side, creaking as it did. I'd already come this far, so I wasn't about to leave without seeing the top side of the lift. Of course, the platform was suspended twelve feet above me, and I didn't have a jet pack to blast me up there. I'd have to use my dagger as a pick and pull myself up along the wall.

A noise caught me off guard. It was overhead and sounded like footsteps in sloshy muck.

A beam of light suddenly shone downward onto the lift, some of its rays glancing on the side of the vent.

"You down there," a voice called.

I froze; it could see me.

"Wake up, or you'll not get anything to drink today," the voice said again, its tone malevolent.

I heard the lift creak—someone was on it. Someone was moving. The voice hadn't been speaking to me.

"You see, he's perfectly fine. I promised I wouldn't hurt him," the voice said. Someone else was with it, but didn't respond to the kept promise.

"You—you said I could have something to drink," the prisoner on the lift spoke and, even though the voice was dry and cracked, I knew it.

It was Ike. I knew better than to shout in excitement; I wasn't in any position to fight the voice from above. The light disappeared for a moment.

"But you—" Ike started, but was cut off as a deluge of water poured down. It ricocheted off the lift and icy cold water splattered all over me. I worked hard to hold my position in the slimy wall and keep silent at the same time.

I heard Ike sputtering. Anger burbled in my gut. I wanted vengeance on the tyrant who was treating my friend this way.

"There, now you have your water. Sleep well, your time will come," the voice said, with one last flash of the light. "Good night."

And with that the tunnel was dark again. I used one hand to wipe off the lenses of my goggles and the other to keep hold of the dagger inserted into the wall.

This was still a rescue, and the one in need of rescue was my best friend. I continued up the wall, but remained silent. I didn't want Ike to know I was here, until I was to him. I couldn't risk the voice coming back, or the HowlSage, or the gray mist. I couldn't risk that Ike might be excited and start talking to me.

The chamber that the platform hung in had continued to widen the further I climbed up. It was pitch black, and aside from the sound of my dagger slipping into the muddy wall, and the occasional clod falling from my feet to the ledge below, there were no sounds. When I was nearly even with the platform I decided it was safe enough to speak to Ike. I could now see it wasn't just a platform, but looked like an oversized birdcage.

The spot where the voice had shined its light from and thrown the water was another twenty feet up in the side of the cliff and it was clear as far as I could see.

"Ike, it's me, Taylor," I said softly.

"Taylor!" he shouted.

"Shhh! I know you're excited, but keep your voice down. Whoever put you here might be close. I'm here to rescue you," I said.

His voice was much softer when he spoke again. "Thanks for coming. I really got myself into something this time."

I swallowed hard; before I rescued him I knew I needed to tell him sorry. "Ike...Ike, I'm sorry. I'm sorry for how I treated you. I was mean, and I was neglectful. Can you forgive me?"

Silence ensued for a moment.

"That means a lot, and of course I can," Ike said.

"Good, now let's get you out of here."

"Taylor?"

"Yes?"

"I'm sorry too."

"Don't worry about it, I forgive you."

"Now I'm ready to be rescued."

"All right, I'm going to climb a bit higher and drop onto the top of the cage. Then I'll get you out."

I made quick work of the wall, and pushed off just enough to get myself away and over the cage. The landing was a bit rougher than I'd expected and my right foot slipped right between two of the bars.

"Ouch," I said.

"What'd you do?" Ike asked.

"Nothing, one of my feet just missed the bars." I squatted on the top of the cage and found where a small door had been built in. I used the dagger to pry it open, and then laid across the top of the cage and leaned my upper body through the opening.

"I'm nearly in the center and reaching toward you. If you just stretch your arms a little ways up…"

He did and I grasped his hands; they were icy cold and wet.

"Hold on tight," I ordered, and relying on my abs, I lifted us back out of the cage.

He hugged me, and I hugged back. "Thanks for coming. I knew you would," he said.

I smiled, although he couldn't see it. "Now, we have to get back down. This might not be that easy."

I looked around the chamber, and realized it resembled an old water well. Of course, I knew it was part of the mines and it probably never held any water. The cage hung from a long rope—no, two ropes, but they disappeared into the darkness above. Even with the night vision goggles, I couldn't see where the ropes attached to anything. But then I realized what to do.

"Ike hold on to me. There are two ropes here. I'm going to cut one."

I felt his arms around my waist.

"The cage is going to fall away, and I hope—I think—once the rest of the rope drops down it'll be long enough for us to slide down."

"OK," Ike said. I felt him shiver in the frigid air.

"Hold on." I swiped the dagger across one of the ropes, once, then twice, then a third time. Still the rope didn't break. I sighed, and then—

Snap!

The cage below us dropped away and I hung onto the rope with all my might. I was holding not only my weight, but Ike's as well.

A resounding crash below told me the cage had found the ledge and the narrower drain down.

We had to hurry.

"Your captor may have heard that. We have to be quick. Can you grab the rope and slide down?" I asked.

"Yeah," Ike said as he let go with one hand, and I felt tension in the rope below me. Then his other hand let go. I felt his body pass my knees, then my feet. He was on his way down.

I looked down and could see him shimmying down the rope. But then I saw something I didn't want to see. Something that could be one of two things, but either was not good.

Smoke or mist was rising up the tunnel below us, and it wasn't dust from the collapsed cage settling. It was rising in tendrils.

"Ike, quick. Change course, come up! Come up!" I shouted.

"Why?" His voice called out in panic.

"Because either the gray mist is coming up below us, or the purple smoke you created to stop the gray mist has been unleashed. Either way—"

"It's bad news," Ike finished my sentence.

I watched him hand over hand climb toward me. He was quick. I started up the rope.

At the hole where the voice had been I stopped, Ike was hanging just below me.

"We have to work together and get this rope swinging. We've got to get to that tunnel," I explained. "On the count of three, shift your body to the left."

"Is that your left or my left?" he asked. "It would be counter—"

"Ike, not now, I can see you through the goggles. Your left.

"One—two—three!"

We both shifted our weight to the left, the rope moved slightly.

"Again."

We did. The smoke or mist was getting closer. I even thought I could hear it sizzling.

"Again."

The rope began to swing, we were both moving with it. When it moved left we jerked our bodies left, when it moved right we shifted right.

"Almost there!" I said. I looked down the tunnel, hoping I wouldn't see the source of the voice or its accomplice. Not because I didn't want to fight them, because I did. I was ready to take care of whoever had imprisoned my friend. But at the moment, we weren't in a good spot to defend ourselves.

The rope swung as close to the tunnel as it had yet, and my fingers grasped the ledge, but slipped away. Our pursuer from below was nearly here.

"One more time!"

We swung away and then back. I reached and grabbed. My left hand found a stone, a brick of some sort, and I held on.

"Ike, quick! Climb up."

I watched him get a hold of the ledge and pull his body into the tunnel. Then he grabbed under my armpits and pulled me into the tunnel entrance with him.

We weren't safe yet. The mist or smoke was still rising.

Knowing Ike couldn't see without the goggles, I grabbed his hand and led him down the tunnel. I hoped it was the purple smoke behind us; its pursuit would be purely based on airflow, not on intelligence. I was mindful that at any moment we might come across the bearer of the voice or the HowlSage. But we didn't. The tunnel curved and climbed up. Eventually we came to a split, and I didn't have a clue which way to go. But Ike said he could feel a draft coming from one of the directions, and that the air smelled fresh. So we followed it.

Ten minutes later, we were out in the middle of bare white tree trunks—a grove of aspen that had long lost their golden leaves to the cold oncoming of winter. It was still dark, but the sliver of moon was enough for Ike and me to see without goggles.

"Were you alone?" Ike asked.

"No, Jesse and McGarrett were with me," I said.

"McGarrett?"

"Yah, he wanted to help find you. I think he felt responsible."

"Did he tell my parents?"

I swallowed a lump that had suddenly formed in my throat. "Yeah, they're near."

"Really?" Ike asked. "How close?"

I wasn't sure how to tell him without giving him a chance to panic; after all they were safe. "Well, they're in the tunnel on the road into town."

"How do you know that?" he asked. It was a fair question; it didn't take more than a minute or so to traverse that tunnel.

"They're kind of trapped, but they're safe and they have food."

"They're what?"

I explained about the collapse and that we expected it was the HowlSage, and also that it was no coincidence that a vending machine supply truck had been trapped with them. Plus, a rescue squad was already working to free them.

"Wow, that's amazing. God does some pretty cool stuff," Ike said. "A vending machine truck, ha."

We both laughed for a moment. Ike was always looking on the bright side. It sure took a lot to bring him down.

"Tay, you'll never believe what I saw as they took me to the cage," he said. "I passed through a chamber, and you know what I saw?"

I shook my head. "Nooo."

"A candelabra, a silver one!" he exclaimed.

Now I was really confused. "So?"

"That's right, I hadn't told you. I found out that there's an old storage shed on the backside of the property. I discovered several broken pieces of furniture, discarded silverware and china, things like that. But there was also three silver candelabras, just like the ones in the library, just like the one on Ash Isle."

"OK, keep going," I said.

"The day I was captured, I'd checked the recording from the secret camera I'd placed in there, but it was unnaturally distorted. Something had interfered with it."

"Like the downed communications?"

"No, different, so I decided to go check, and you know what I found?"

I shook my head, which was becoming a common occurrence in this conversation.

"The candelabras were gone, but not the silverware."

I stared at him, clearly confused.

"The candle holders were made of pure silver, the silverware was not. A regular thief wouldn't have been so selective, they'd have grabbed everything and sorted it out later. No, our thief could discern between the two."

"So you're saying that the cloaked figure has come onto the inn property?"

"Maybe. If not it, someone else has," he explained.

Now that Ike had made his point, I understood that there was a clear threat in the appearance of those candelabras. They showed that our normal defenses were not being effective against the enemy. We'd need to ramp that up. And speaking of ramping our defenses up, I remembered about the Raptoryx.

"We saw the Raptoryx again," I said.

"How'd you know what—?" Ike started.

"McGarrett told me that you'd figured it out. Sorry for not waiting for you, for not listening to you."

"It's OK. You're forgiven," Ike said. "You want to hear about it?"

"Yes, you can tell me as we find our way back."

We both agreed that the best thing we could do was to head back to town or The Pink Hippo, whichever was closer, and call McGarrett. Heading back into the mine was not an option. We were armed with nothing. I had a dagger and the goggles, but I'd mistakenly left the radio with my pack when I'd removed the excess gear.

So together we shivered and walked in the direction we thought town was. We were pretty sure we could see the ambient glow of the city lights off a few scattered clouds.

Three hours later we stepped on to a curvy paved road that we recognized as the one leading from the mines to town.

It was another hour before we reached the gates of The Pink Hippo. The sun would be up soon and we only hoped that McGarrett and Jesse had escaped. That they'd survived. The news was grim when we dragged ourselves up the stairs and through the front door.

Mrs. Riley, through a forced calm, let us know that neither Mr. Riley nor Jesse had returned. We followed her to the dining hall, where we ate a couple of her oversized, gooey, warm cinnamon rolls. We were ravenous from all the walking, and I'd never seen Ike's small frame put down so much food. As soon as we were finished, Mrs. Riley told us to get some rest and that she'd wake us when they returned.

I felt like I should go back out looking for them, but I knew this wouldn't be helpful. As tired as I was, I'd be more likely to get in trouble or drop over from exhaustion then perform any sort of rescue. So Ike and I both found comfy spots on the couches in the foyer and crashed.

I woke to someone shaking my shoulders.

"Tay," the voice said. "Taylor, wake up." It was Ike. "They're back and it doesn't look good."

I rubbed my eyes and sat up, then yawned. There were at least a dozen people in the lobby with us. Most were in uniforms. I looked at Ike.

His eyes were glassy as if he was about to cry.

"Who are all these people?"

"McGarrett and Jesse are back. Chief Rutledge brought them in with the paramedics. The chief is comforting Mrs. Riley now."

"What happened?"

"Apparently, a tunnel collapsed on McGarrett and Jesse. Both of them are unconscious. They're alive, but they're not responding."

I knew why they'd been brought here. The Pink Hippo had very good medical equipment, as good as the local hospital, but more so because it was likely the wounds that McGarrett and Jesse had could reveal more about what we did to a regular citizen than was desired. Chief Rutledge knew our line of work—he wasn't a hunter, but he was a believer.

I didn't recognize the paramedics, but some of the other people in the room I did. The mayor and his wife, believers, the Friggs, and a few other members from the local churches—deacons, elders, etc.

The chief walked over to where Ike and I sat. "Why don't you guys come with me for a moment?"

We followed him outside on the porch. The circular driveway surrounding the fountain was filled with several vehicles, some with lights flashing blue and red. Several personal cars filled in the gaps.

"Taylor and Ike, what I'm about to tell you isn't something I'd normally tell to an eleven and fourteen-year-old, but you guys won't be surprised by any of it."

We both nodded to the chief.

"McGarrett and your cousin were lying in a wide chamber when we found them. A circle of stones had been placed all around them, and there were large wax candles burning everywhere," he explained. "Their bodies are covered in bruises and scrapes, but there are no bites; there are no mortal wounds as far as I can see."

"Wait, you said they were in a chamber with candles. I thought the tunnel collapsed?" Ike said.

"Well, some of it did, but it was the story I leaned on when I dragged the bodies out to the paramedics."

"So if they don't have any serious visible injuries, why are they unconscious?" Ike asked.

"That's what we don't know, and that's what I'm worried about. You see, there was more in the chamber than just candles and stones," Chief Rutledge explained grimly. "There were three bowls of liquid and there were amulets everywhere."

"Amulets?" I asked.

"I saw a dagger, a locket, a crown, two bracelets, a couple anklets—all of which were adorned with rubies and diamonds."

"Amulets are often used in rituals to raise spirits or transfer powers," Ike muttered.

"So you think all these things were being used in a ritual, and that McGarrett and Jesse were being used too?"

"I absolutely do," the chief explained. "I'm not sure how far they got. When Mrs. Riley called me she let me know where you guys were supposed to be, and I used the tracking device McGarrett had given me to find them. Due to the nature of the situation, I could only take the mayor, the minister, and Mr. Frigg with me." Chief Rutledge took a hanky from his pocket and wiped it across his brow. "I have to admit, I'm not sure how you do it, Taylor. How you go in there after a demon." He sighed.

"We found two cloaked figures when we got to them. No HowlSage, but two beings. As soon as I called for them to, 'Freeze!' they took off into a side tunnel. As our mission was just to rescue, we didn't pursue. By the time we'd navigated the mine, the paramedics had arrived and we delivered McGarrett and Jesse to them and that brings us to now." The chief looked at Ike.

"What about the stuff? Didn't you get it out?" I asked.

Chief Rutledge shook his head. "We couldn't..." The chief paused. "McGarrett set up a series of contingency procedures for me to follow. As you know, I'm not a hunter, and McGarrett instructed me to avoid contact with the demons as well as their tools. In this case the amulets." The chief sighed. "It was hard. I knew it'd make it easier on you to have collected that stuff. But I've given my word and that is something a man does not break."

I understood, but it seemed sort of crummy of McGarrett not to have shared these contingencies with me.

Chief Rutledge looked at Ike. "There is some good news also. We've estimated Ike's parents will be rescued sometime tomorrow afternoon. The equipment used to bore through the rock arrived, and so far the progress has been very good."

Ike released a pent-up breath.

The chief cleared his throat. "Taylor, I want to be clear. I think it would be best that you remain at The Pink Hippo the rest of the night. Go to school tomorrow, both of you, and I'll pick you up as soon as we are about to reach the survivors."

I nodded. "Should I call my aunt and uncle?"

"I'll take care of that. I'm sure they'll want to come down right away. For now, the best thing you can do is pray, and rest."

"Can we go see McGarrett and Jesse?" Ike asked.

"Tomorrow morning you can; for now get some rest."

"But we just slept for a long time," Ike retorted. "I need to invent, to plan."

"You can tomorrow; just find a nice non-hunt related book or something. Maybe go for a swim in the pool."

"OK," Ike agreed.

Ike and I followed Chief Rutledge back into The Pink Hippo; the crowd was there. People were chatting and sitting in the foyer. Mrs. Riley had been crying, but Mrs. Frigg had her arm around her and there were several other ladies gathered around.

Ike and I headed to the elevator together. When we reached his floor, he stepped out, but stopped the doors from closing.

"I just realized something."

"What?" I asked.

"Do you remember what McGarrett had in his trunk the night he and Jesse first crossed the gray mist?"

I smiled. "The belt."

"What were all the things the chief saw again? A dagger, a locket, a bracelet, an anklet," Ike recalled. "Do you remember?"

I exhaled a thoughtful breath. "There was a crown, and it was two bracelets, not one."

"Right, and two anklets," he corrected. "So a dagger, a locket, two bracelets, two anklets, a crown, and we have the belt."

"Something for every body part," I joked.

"Almost." Ike put his hand on his chin in thought.

The elevator doors started to close automatically. I shoved my hand forward, stopping them. I should mention that the elevator was not original to the hotel, so the technology stopping the lift doors from chopping off your hand was included.

"I need to research. I'll be in the library if you need me; I'm going to pass on that swim," Ike said. He was never one for athletic activity, but certainly not if put against reading.

I almost reminded him of what the chief had said about non-hunting activities, but reading was, I knew, the most relaxing thing Ike could do.

I nodded and let the doors close. I was going to make use of the hot tub. It was time to let my nerves unwind.

Chapter Seventeen

October 18th—Wednesday

I'd tried to visit Jesse and McGarrett in the infirmary, but an elderly lady had told me to come back in half an hour. She asked me if I'd had any breakfast yet, and when I shook my head, told me that some of the ladies from the church had prepared a great spread this morning.

I obeyed and took the elevator down. To my surprise, the foyer was filled with people still. Some of the same from the night before, but some new faces as well. I made my way past them and into the dining hall.

Ike was already at the table, as were two others. The police chief and another man I didn't recognize. I sat and was happy to see that there were several options for breakfast. French toast, waffles, and St. John's breakfast casserole. Yum.

"Morning, Taylor," Chief Rutledge said. "I hope you don't mind me joining you this morning for breakfast. I wanted to come up and check on Mr. and Mrs. Riley. It looks like The Gathering is doing a good job of supporting in the best ways they can."

"The Gathering?" I asked.

"It's what we call the body of believers who have come together to pray," the chief explained.

"Don't you mean have gathered?" Ike said with a smile.

The chief shook his head, "Funny. You'd better be careful, I'm taking the two of you to school today, but I might just take you all the way down to the jail."

I laughed.

Ike was pouring sugar into his coffee, "You mean we get to ride in a squad car?"

"I guess you do," the chief answered.

I scooped some breakfast casserole onto my plate. St. John's could be made with ham, sausage, or even bacon. This one was ham. I looked at the man next to the chief.

He was gone.

"Where'd that other guy go?" I asked.

Chief Rutledge frowned, his bushy white eyebrows furrowed. "Who?" he asked.

"There was someone else sitting next to you when I came down."

"No there wasn't," the chief said. Ike nodded in agreement. "Look," the chief continued. "I know it's been a crazy few days and there are a lot of new people at the inn today. Let's just finish breakfast and we'll go up and see Jesse and Mr. Riley before we leave for school."

"Any change in condition?" Ike asked.

"Afraid not."

We'd seen McGarrett and Jesse, and nothing had changed. They looked just like they were sleeping. So we headed off to school.

It got me thinking about what might have occurred within that chamber last night. About the people and the ritualistic stuff.

"Do you think you could show me how to get back to the chamber?" I asked the chief.

"He doesn't need to," Ike interrupted. "It'll be recorded in the tracking software. We can get there ourselves."

Chief Rutledge nodded as he pulled up next to the curb to drop us in front of the school. "Sounds like Ike's got it figured out. I'll see the two of you after school."

We exited and headed for the front door of the school. Three steps in, I saw Mel. After our weird meeting the other day, I wanted to find her and see what was going on. But as I approached, the boy appeared, stepping out from behind her.

Either way, I wasn't going to let his presence stop me. Ike stood back, but I moved ahead.

The boy turned and glared at me. His eyes were black as coal. He scowled. "What do you want?" he asked.

The frigid voice caught me off guard and I stopped. Mel turned and stared at the boy, a look of surprise on her face. But the moment she saw me she stepped back, awkwardly bumping into the locker bank behind her.

The boy stepped toward me and cracked his knuckles. "I think it's time for you to go."

I looked around his shoulder. "Mel?"

My body launched backward as two hands shoved me in the chest. The boy had attacked. I fell to the ground, sliding across the concrete floor a few feet. I felt my anger rise like a serpent inside my chest.

Ike was at my side and pulling me to my feet, whispering, "Shake it off, you can't risk getting into trouble and getting detention. We have to find that chamber."

I took a deep breath and exhaled. I was still angry, but I knew Ike was right. I watched as the boy put his arm around Melanie and they headed down the hall and turned a corner.

"What was that all about?" Ike asked.

"I don't know. I guess he was just jealous."

For the rest of the day, I watched for a chance to find Mel alone. I only saw her once more, and the boy was with her, hovering like the secret service over the President of the United States.

When the chief of police picked us up, he had bad news. The boring machine had broken. Something about a cooling system, and the bore overheating and snapping. Ike understood all of this, of course. It meant repairs were needed, and if that didn't work a new machine would have to be brought in.

I could tell Ike was disappointed, but he seemed confident that his parents were safe. Protected.

Later on, Ike persuaded me to follow him to the workshop while Chief Rutledge went to check on the status of McGarrett and Jesse. We found out that my aunt and uncle were going to catch a train down and should be here in the next day or so. They wanted to fly in, but the airport's radar and communications had been damaged. The news report said it had been vandals, but we knew one of our enemies was responsible.

Ike loaded the tracking software and quickly eliminated most of the sensor alerts using his animal registry tactic. It was clear that demons, possibly the HowlSage, had been at the tunnel. Likely they were responsible for the malfunction of the machinery. The other three hot spots were the canning factory, the park, and the mines.

We knew the mines were our goal for the night. Regardless of whether the chief wanted us to hunt, Ike and I had determined at lunch we would be finding that chamber.

The boy genius loaded up the tracking from the night before and located the chamber, or so we believed. We couldn't positively see each mine tunnel we needed to traverse to get there. But we would at least get pretty close.

Chief Rutledge came back in and let us know that McGarrett's and Jesse's conditions had not improved, nor had they worsened. He told us that he'd appreciate it if we'd wait to seek the chamber, but I knew why he stopped short of ordering us or making us promise. He knew it'd be in vain. And he was right.

The second he left, Ike was suiting me up. He would watch me from the workshop and keep track of my surroundings, trying to watch for the tell-tale signs of the HowlSage.

With the Raptoryx ruling the sky and primarily living aloft at all times, we hadn't been able to track it. Ike had linked to the local airport radar, but this hadn't been successful in locating the creature—it appeared that the Raptoryx was impervious to radar.

The same with the gray mist—we couldn't technically track it; however, Ike had noticed that light sensors had typically failed in the presence of the smoky matter. Whatever the gray mist was, it consumed or shrouded light.

Basically, I would be going solo, and without any concise information. Basically blind.

Ike had gotten out the belt and laid it on a table. He then drew a chalk line body across the table, the belt at its center. He made marks where the crown, bracelets, anklets, and locket would go. The dagger was placed near the body's right hand. Ike's puzzle was designed to figure out what else there might be.

Ike hadn't bothered to explain what all of these things were to be used for, but I was sure they would adorn the HowlSage in some hope of making it stronger or invincible.

As the last rays of sunlight disappeared over the horizon it was time for me to go. Ike waved goodbye as I flew into the night.

The new moon had gone, and a sliver of the Earth's satellite now glowed clearly in the sky. The sky was a dangerous place with the Raptoryx still on the loose, but it too had to be destroyed.

I watched a logging truck slowly making its way down the narrow road from the mines. Sustainable logging had been one of the ways Ashley Meadows' economy had survived; it had boomed in recent years with everyone "going green."

I could hear the wind whistling over the semi's cargo and its taught chains. The high-pitched noise grew louder, unnaturally so, and then Ike's voice broke in over my radio.

"Taylor, watch out, the Raptoryx is near."

"How do you—?" I didn't finish my sentence. The screeching sound hadn't been coming from the truck below.

Rolling to my back, I looked up. High above, the creature soared over me, clearly visible through my night vision goggles. Its head looked like that of a raven, but its body was long and scaly like a lizard. It had two sets of wings, all flapping independently of each other. The forward two were half as long and less pointy then the back set.

Why hadn't I thought to borrow Jesse's invisibility suit?

To my surprise, the Raptoryx folded its wings and angled into a dive down, heading straight for me. A pair of long arms, each with three talons, stretched out before it as if reaching for its prey—me. Its legs looked powerful, like those of a dinosaur or dragon.

I wasn't afraid, but it currently had the advantage. First, I didn't know what could kill it; second, if you've ever read anything about the World War II dogfights over Europe or the Pacific, you'll know that the diver always had the initial advantage. It's the same with modern-day birds and rodents. In this case, I was the rodent.

I dove backward, but kept my eyes glued on the creature speeding toward me. I felt for my sword, then recounted the other gadgets I had at my disposal. I grasped a smoke grenade and pulled the pin, but kept hold of it. Then, with my other hand, I pulled out my grappling hook launcher.

As the smoke grenade ran out and its trail dissipated, I sighted the winged beast. It'd pulled out of its dive—the smoke had provided enough shroud to disrupt its lock on me. I was nearing the trees, and I hoped it couldn't follow me into the branches. The area of forest I was heading into consisted of tall pines, narrowly planted together. The sustainable forest I'd mentioned. I collapsed my wings and shut off my J-Pak. I was in freefall. I turned my body so my feet were down and my head up.

As my feet pierced the pine canopy, I saw the Raptoryx slow its descent. I watched a few branches fly past and fired my grappling hook. It connected and planted itself into the wood. A sharp jerk to my body stopped my descent and I hung several feet above the forest floor. I released more of the wire, and lowered myself to the brown, pine-needle-strewn ground below.

"Ike," I said into my radio. "Raptoryx avoided. I need directions to the mines on foot. Can you guide me?"

"Of course," he countered.

For the next thirty minutes, Ike provided me turn by turn directions down several paths and over a few small ridges until I was overlooking the mines.

I used my goggles to scour the area and the sky. No sign of the flying creature, and no sign of the HowlSage. "It looks clear," I said. "Anything from your side?"

"Negative. The sensors haven't shown any spikes for the HowlSage."

I slowly made my way down the rocky slope of the ridge overlooking mine entrance number seven. My foot caught a patch of loose rocks, and I slid twenty feet down before getting a handhold on a long, dead root. The final thirty feet went smoothly.

I stared at the mine entrance, knowing that somewhere in there was a chamber with a lot of stuff for a purpose I didn't know. Somewhere in there might be the gray mist, the HowlSage, the cloaked figures, and a myriad of other things.

"Ike, I'm going in."

"Copy that," he said. "Can you start recording?"

"Yes." I'd almost forgotten. I switched on the streaming for the small camera Ike had given me. He'd fitted it to a cord so it could hang loosely around my neck. He'd wanted to put it on a helmet, but I was not about to wear one of those around all night.

"It's pretty clear, go ahead."

As if I needed his permission. I started for the black hole, which glowed green through my goggles. It was close to what Ike was seeing on the screen back in the workshop, but his video also flared up with heat signatures. He'd be able to give me a half second warning of something living at best. Of course, that'd only work for the cloaked figures. If the HowlSage had recently eaten and the contents of its dinner were still warm, it might show up.

Ike continued to guide me through the tunnel, his voice a whisper. After twenty minutes, he said I was close. And in five more I'd found the chamber.

As I approached, a flicker of light lit the tunnel leading to the room. I slunk along the mine walls and pulled my goggles down, knowing the firelight would interfere with them. I peered around the corner into the room, and there were two figures hovering over a table. Three bowls before them. From my angle I couldn't see what exactly they were doing. I took the camera from my neck and held it around the corner, to capture the scene.

They were busy working on something. A spark shot up from before one of them.

"Be careful, my sweet," the other spoke calmly, a male voice. "We mustn't waste our supplies."

The figure working where the spark had come from nodded in agreement.

The boy spoke again. "Yes, just like that. Be sure they are secure. I will prepare the incantation."

The boy moved toward the ring of stones, the same I assumed Jesse and McGarrett had been in. The boy was cloaked—only his hands were exposed in which he carried a large silver vase.

He moved in an odd pattern of circles, pouring out a red liquid, which I assumed was blood. The dirt at his feet became mucky, but he didn't seem to mind. A whisper was coming from his lips, like a song.

I whispered into the radio, "Ike, you getting this?"

"Yes," was his nearly silent reply.

The boy continued to move in his circles, a never-ending stream of red liquid pouring from the vase.

The boy stopped. The vase dropped from his hands and gave off a resounding clang when it struck the floor, red liquid splashing across the ground.

In three swift moves he'd gone to the table, pulled off a dagger, and now stood facing the tunnel in which I hid.

"I know that you are here. Reveal yourself to me," he spoke, his voice deadly.

I swallowed, but I didn't feel scared.

I slid my sword from its sheath and stepped into view. "I am here and I do not fear."

His head rose, and his hood slipped backward, but at the same moment all of the candles in the room went out. I was blind without my goggles and could not see the boy's face.

Then I heard a clang as if two swords had met in midair. The sound was only feet from me. I pulled my goggles up, and the boy was before me within arm's reach, his dagger raised, but stopped. It'd been countered by another weapon. His face was shrouded again, behind an unnatural darkness.

The boy took four steps backward and entered the circle. He looked toward the table, as did I. The other figure swept their arm across the work table, dumping all of the contents into a large burlap sack.

"You will not stop us," the boy whispered. "We are more powerful, and he will rise. The signs have shown it and the stars and planets have aligned."

A brilliant flash of light momentarily blinded me, and my body flew backward. I hit the ground hard; my ears rang. Had there been an explosion?

I shook my head, trying to clear the ringing from my ears. I removed the goggles and rubbed my eyes. Someone stood over me. They offered a hand and pulled me to my feet. The cavern smelled of burnt rubber or something.

The person spoke, "Are you all right?"

I didn't recognize the voice.

"Yes, I am," I said as I ran my fingers over my arms, legs, and through my hair. Everything was still intact.

But then the person was gone and I was again alone.

Chapter Eighteen

October 19th—Thursday

Midnight rolled around and Ike and I were still watching the video. Since I'd returned, we'd viewed it at least fifty times, slowing the footage and using all sorts of enhancement techniques. It was amazing what Ike could do with lighting, reflections, zooms, and heat signatures. But regardless of what we did, we could not see my defender.

He was able to capture the cloaked boy's facial features, shadowed and grainy as they were. The unnatural darkness that had shrouded his mug from me in the chamber was surpassed by Ike's blending of the information captured by the camera. Neither of us recognized him; we flipped through our old yearbooks. Ike even pulled up a list of all Friendbook users in Ashley Meadows—still none matched. We were quickly running out of suspects. And there was no good video of the second cloaked figure, so we moved on to another piece of the puzzle.

I'd not seen any sign of the amulets, as the chief

had called them, and surmised they'd been on the table.

Ike went to one of the many desks in the workshop and flipped an old book open. "Taylor, it's time I show you what it is I read the other night."

I felt guilty; I knew what night that was. "You mean the night I went swimming?"

"Well, yes," Ike cleared his throat. "But that's forgiven."

I smiled at the truth of that statement.

"So I was reading further in *The HowlSage Haunting* and…" Ike used his finger to scan the page he'd opened to. "Here it is. Listen to this, 'I realized my mistake a bit too late. The HowlSage wasn't the real threat; no, it was the man who controlled it. For while demons are evil, it is man who is intelligent, it is man who was born into sin, it is man who has been given free will.'" Ike started flipping through the book some more.

"Wait, is this book fiction?"

"No. It's been taken as a work of fiction because of what it talks about, but it's not. In fact, I think it might have important information for us. Listen to this." Ike found his spot on the page and began to read again. "'I'd focused so long on the HowlSage that I'd not even noticed the greater threat growing. The day of the full moon had come; I was so caught up in the hunt that I'd not realized it was also October the 31st, nor had I realized Friday the 13th had preceded it. Now it was too late, and it had been awoken.'" Ike stopped reading.

"What had been awoken?" I asked.

Ike's face was pale. He swallowed hard before speaking. "A BloodSage."

I knew this was the worst news yet. BloodSages were the template for the modern-day fictional vampire. These demons were far more powerful then HowlSages, and they didn't just come into existence—they had to be summoned into existence by a human through incantations. They were the foulest of demons; BloodSages were one of the reasons for all the secrecy of the society. So many wars had been started because of man's insatiable desire for power. Hitler's S.S. had been set on creating an army of demons, and they'd succeeded so many times. Had the society not been in place to defeat them, the world may be a different place today.

While the person doing the summoning is clearly not on the right path, they are further doomed should they succeed. Man cannot control a demon, it is impossible—demons try to control man. But in the folly of greed, man will be led to believe he can control that which he is creating. This is simply not true.

The BloodSage is rare; many factors have to line up perfectly for them to be brought into existence. I don't believe my dad had ever even faced one.

"But wait, I thought the book was about HowlSages?" I asked.

"It is," Ike started. "But in this instance, the demon that was really being summoned was the BloodSage. The HowlSage was simply being used to summon the BloodSage. It so happened that Friday the 13th of a month with 31 days, was October. It's actually not that big of an anomaly."

"I get that, but shouldn't someone have caught this before? Like McGarrett or your dad?"

Ike shook his head. "This book is really old. I don't even know if either of them have read it. Plus, HowlSages appear any time a full moon falls on the 31st day of a month, which more often than not is in October. What doesn't happen as often is Friday the 13th preceding the 31st full moon, nor do you have a human with the knowledge to summon a BloodSage. And—" Ike stopped midsentence and his face looked sheepish.

"What were you going to say?" I asked.

"Well, I mean—" he stopped again.

"Go ahead," I insisted.

"Well most of the time the HowlSage is stopped in its first day, so while there isn't a lot of research on what happens if a HowlSage lives longer, there isn't usually an opportunity to learn, let alone a reason," Ike concluded.

I nodded. I'd failed to banish the HowlSage on its first day, and that only further complicated everything.

"All right, so what you are saying is that a whole lot of crazy coincidences had to be perfectly aligned for this to happen?"

"Sort of, but in the scheme of things, angels and demons aren't like us—they aren't mortal like us. These alignments have happened many times before, and will happen many more times."

It was hard to believe that something this devious, something this meticulously planned could be happening right under our noses.

"Ike, do you know everything that is needed to create a BloodSage?" I asked.

"There's a summary in the book." Ike quickly flipped the pages to the end of the book. "Here," he said, sliding the book in front of me.

"Signs that a human is involved?" I read.

"Check," Ike said.

I took a pen from the desk and got ready to put a strike through it.

Ike's hand grabbed mine, "You can't do that. This book is really old."

I sighed and put the pen down. "The creation of amulets?" The list below this line was long.

1. Crown

2. Locket

3. Breastplate

4. Heart

5. 2 Bracelets

6. Dagger

7. Scepter

8. 2 Rings

9. Belt

10. 2 Anklets.

"We saw most of these in the chamber. But what is a heart?"

"I don't know for sure, but I hope it's not a real heart," Ike said, his face a light shade of green. "There also wasn't a breastplate, ring, or scepter."

"I saw them working on something; maybe they still had a few more to create," I said, then read further. "The presence of the BloodSage's steed."

"That's the Raptoryx," Ike explained.

"That's why Jesse and McGarrett were so worked up about that flying beast."

Ike nodded.

"OK, there's a few more things. The body of a former Sage." I looked at Ike. "Wait, how is that possible? Wouldn't its body be long deteriorated?"

"A long time ago, the bodies were preserved by the followers, often stolen, or dug up after they'd been disposed."

"Like a mummy?"

"Exactly."

"Well, at least we don't have one of those nearby."

"As far as we know," Ike corrected. "But I very much doubt that the person who is doing all of this would be if they didn't have all the pieces they needed to make it happen."

"So, what else is missing?" I asked.

"The breastplate, whatever the heart is, the scepter, the rings, and we have the belt. We also don't know of the mummy."

"We had better protect the belt."

"They can make another one if they want to, but yes, it might slow them down."

"What do the dates have to do with anything?" I asked.

"You know how we celebrate Easter as the day Christ rose from the dead?"

"Yeah."

"Well, in the demonic world, Halloween is a day for rising, a day for spirits to be released. Friday the 13th is considered a day of evil as well. That's where the superstitions come from," Ike explained.

"I remember McGarrett talking about that in my training," I admitted.

"And, in accordance with the summoning for a BloodSage, one must begin to prepare the potions on the 13th of Friday for delivery on the month's 31st day and full moon."

"That's a lot of things that have to work out."

"Hence why we don't face BloodSages that often. They are very difficult to summon, not to mention how the summoning procedures aren't exactly common knowledge."

"And what is the HowlSage's role?"

"If you read further in the book, the HowlSage is acting as a servant to the human. It's used to collect the things needed for the rituals, to protect the one who will do the summoning. Once it is done with its service, it will bring forth its demon legion and start biting people, spreading hate and weakening their resilience against evil. This makes the smaller demons' jobs easier." Ike put his hand to his chin. "However, in this instance, I would assume the HowlSage will continue to serve the BloodSage; after all, a BloodSage is a top tier demon, or a Supremus."

"It sounds like we need to search the mines." I yawned.

"Or figure out who is behind all of this," Ike suggested. "You did see someone handing the locket to the HowlSage."

"Yes, but we looked for the house. I couldn't find it," I explained. "If I could just kill the HowlSage."

"Yeah, that would certainly affect their ability to create the BloodSage, but it wouldn't stop them."

"What of the gray mist?" I asked.

"That's something I haven't been able to determine for sure; it wasn't mentioned in the book."

"Hmmm," I closed my eyes for a moment and yawned. "I think maybe we'd better get some rest. School tomorrow and hunting."

"You mean today," Ike corrected.

I nodded. "I think I'm going to take the belt with me to my room."

"I wouldn't, it's better protected in here."

"I disagree. Besides, let someone try to steal it from me, then I'll be able to face them. Think of it as a trap."

Ike shook his head, "I don't like it, but you're in charge."

In charge? Was I really? I mean, McGarrett was out, Jesse was out, Mr. Swigart was still trapped. It was true I was the oldest one from our group still active.

"Why don't you camp out in my room? We can protect it together," I offered.

Ike smiled. "I'll grab my sleeping bag!"

When I awoke, the belt was still by my side. I'd slept solid and hadn't even dreamed as far as I could remember. Ike had already woken and left, but his sleeping bag still lay over near the fireplace.

Shower.

Breakfast.

School.

All flew by a little less quickly than I would have liked.

But what mattered was Ike and I had made it home. The news was that the tunnel excavation was going again, but they were still a day or more away from reaching Mr. and Mrs. Swigart. Jesse's parents would arrive sometime this evening. The train had been delayed and then rerouted when a freight train overturned on some tracks, blocking their direct route toward town.

We of course suspected the HowlSage. It was clear that the creature and its master didn't want Ike and I to have any help. Regardless, Ike and I knew what we needed to do.

Stop the BloodSage from rising.

Ike fitted me out with my gear and I was off for the mines. Our goal was to first find that chamber and to take all of the amulets that had been created. This would require a lot of searching, but it had to be done. If I ran into the HowlSage, I would face it and hopefully slay it. If I ran into the gray mist, I would use the canister to block it.

There were only eleven days after tonight, and two of them were Sundays.

Unfortunately, the search didn't go well. The skies were clear, the tunnel was clear, the town slept in silence except for the operation of freeing the trapped people in the tunnel.

Another failure to get and destroy the HowlSage.

Chapter Nineteen

October 20th—Friday

I woke up early and went to sit by Jesse and McGarrett. The Gathering still held vigil at The Pink Hippo with Mrs. Riley. Their condition hadn't improved, but neither did they seem any worse.

Ike apparently had visited several times throughout the night, asking odd questions of whomever was on watch. But I knew by odd questions, they were likely scientific in nature. If the boy genius could figure out how to awaken them or heal them, he would. And knowing what we were up against, I was in full support of that.

Ike and I got to school and went our separate ways for class. Just before I rounded the corner for homeroom, a hand reached out of a janitor closet and yanked me inside. The door slammed shut and the closet was dark, but there was a flowery smell before me.

A light clicked on. It was Melanie. She looked, well, horrible. Her face was pale, and there were shadows under her eyes. It was like she hadn't slept for days.

"Are you OK?" I asked. Had our separation been that traumatic for her?

The warning bell rang in the hall.

She shook her head.

"What's wrong?"

She shook her head again. Then I felt a cold draft behind me. An icy cold hand suddenly slid over my mouth. I felt an arm around my neck tightening, but when I moved to use my hands to fight off the attack, I couldn't, for they'd been bound.

I looked at Melanie's sad eyes. In her hand was the end of the rope.

My eyes began to close as my head filled with static. My legs lost feeling and they started to buckle.

Chapter Twenty

October 25th—Wednesday

I woke to icy water splashing onto my body. Everything was black around me and the air was frigid.

There was a laugh overhead. "Finally awake? It's about time, you've been asleep for four days," the voice said.

Four days? I was lying down on something hard, possibly the floor. Pure blackness surrounded me.

"Did you hear me?" the voice called again.

I didn't speak.

My body jolted backward as another deluge of freezing water poured over my body.

"You should answer me if you wish for the water to stop."

I swallowed and spoke. "I'm here."

"Of course you are. You can't go anywhere," the voice said in a sarcastic tone. "I asked if you were awake."

"Of course I am, I'm talking to you," I said, returning the voice's sarcasm.

Another splattering of cold water.

"Mind who you are speaking with!" the voice bellowed.

"Who might that be?"

"One more powerful than you."

"Is that so? You have a name?"

"You may call me Albert."

My body was shivering uncontrollably now.

A beam of light landed on me, its source a flashlight in the hands of the voice. "You look rather cold down there."

I wouldn't give Albert the satisfaction of admitting it. The light revealed beams all around me, I was in a cage, much like the one I'd rescued Ike from.

"You may change into these."

A bundle of cloth dropped down before me and I made no attempt to reach for it. I kept my arms across my chest as I shivered.

"Fine, have it your way, but you are likely to get hypothermia and there is no one here to help you."

The light disappeared and I heard footsteps patter away from me. I was alone. The voice was right about hypothermia. I retrieved the parcel of clothes and opened it. I couldn't see what it was, but it felt like a robe to me. It would have to do. I stripped off the wet clothes and put on the long cloak. It had a hood and was long enough to graze the tops of my feet.

I hung my own clothes as best I could from the bars. Hopefully the draft might dry them so that I might change back before the voice reappeared. Wearing the robe gave me a creepy feeling, like I was becoming one of them.

Hours had passed with no sign of the voice. I'd listened for a long time, but heard nothing.

I felt my way around my cell. Like Ike's cage, mine was suspended in the air. I could get it to rock back and forth, the rope creaking on a hinge high above. Ike's had been destroyed, so this must be a new one, which meant I was likely in a different part of the mines. I'd kicked the bars, but they didn't break. I climbed to the top and yanked on, pushed at, hung from the small hatch built into the top of the cage. Nothing worked. I was stuck.

Worse, I was alone. And I felt it.

Who would come for me? My dad was gone, McGarrett and Jesse were hurt, Mr. Swigart was a scientist, Uncle Matt couldn't hunt anymore. The job was too dangerous for anyone else. It could be days before a hunter from somewhere else in the world could make it back. A sinking feeling in my heart brought me to sit down. I was an orphan, fatherless, motherless, abandoned. I had no one, except maybe Ike. But he couldn't make me feel loved.

And Melanie…she may have looked sad when she betrayed me, but that didn't make the knife in my back easier to pull out.

The sound of footsteps got my attention. Someone was coming. I could hear the voice, but it was talking to someone.

"Set her down here, I'll watch her. Now raise the cage," The voice said.

I heard an odd wheezing and then my cell jerked up. The rope groaned as it lifted the weight of the wooden cage.

"Stop, right there," the voice ordered.

Something growled. Was it the HowlSage?

"Now open the door and drop her in."

My cage shook violently as something jumped onto the top. I heard the door at the top squeak open, and a muffled scream. Then something landed on the floor beside me with a painful-sounding thump. The door slammed shut and the cage shook again as the HowlSage bounded off of it.

I reached forward. I knew it was a girl, but who was she? I cautiously felt for an arm or leg. The first thing I found was her hair.

The cage started to lower again—we were being sent back down the shaft.

I moved my hand down her eyes, her nose, her mouth—it was bound. She'd been gagged.

"This might hurt," I whispered to her.

I felt her nod, then I yanked the tape from her mouth. She sputtered and spit something out of her mouth. A piece of cloth.

"Tay—Taylor, is that you?" the girl asked, her voice raspy and dry.

"Yes, who are you?"

"It's Melanie," she said.

I backed away. "What happened?"

For a moment she didn't speak. When she did, her voice was solemn. "I was taken, as you were."

"Have you been here for long?"

"No, they kept me somewhere else. But when I refused to help them with their plan, they brought me here."

"Who are they?" I asked.

"My hands and feet are bound. Can you untie them? I'll tell you everything I know as you work on the knots."

"Of course, sorry. I can't see anything down here." I moved my hands to hers and started to undo the knot at her wrists. Once she was free, she made quick work of the rope binding her feet.

"So, who are they?" I asked again.

"The boy is my friend, Albert," she admitted.

"Wait, the cloaked boy is your friend?"

"Yes, the same you saw with me at school."

"It can't be. I was face to face with the cloaked boy only days ago; he looked nothing like the boy at school," I said, dumbfounded.

"He's a master of disguise; what you see at school is not who he really is," she explained. "And now he has betrayed me. And the other…" her voice trailed off. "The other is a hideous beast—a werewolf. I never would have believed they existed if I hadn't seen it with my own eyes," she rambled. "Albert told me we could control it; he said that it'd be fun."

"It's not a werewolf," I said. "It's a HowlSage, also known as a magician of the moon. And how could that possibly be fun?"

"It started out with some small tricks—a Ouija board, incantations and stuff. Nothing that seemed, you know, real. Next thing I knew, we were summoning control over a werewo—HowlSage."

I shook my head. I knew that the path to evil was often slow and unassuming; the evil one and his demons were masters at deception, and all she'd mentioned were just some of the "harmless" ploys they used.

"You don't just come across the incantations and spells to call on a HowlSage. This had to have been going on for some time."

Silence for a moment. "I guess it has."

"Of course you've realized that this Albert kid is bad news, and I'm not just saying that because I like you."

"How do you know so much about this? And you like me?" she asked.

"Melanie, I'm not a normal boy," I said. "I'm a hunter."

"A hunter?"

"Yes, a demon hunter."

I felt the cage shake as if she'd just backed as far away from me as the cage walls would allow. "Demon hunter?"

"Yes."

"So demons exist."

"Of course they do, and yes, I like you. I didn't understand why you left me that one day."

"Oh, that. Well, I realized that I know someone you know."

"Who?" I asked.

"Your cousin is a friend. I met him in Egypt."

"Jesse? He never mentioned that."

"I asked him not to."

"Oh, well…" I didn't know what to say. It sort of hurt to think that Jesse would be hiding something from me. And what was worse, it had to do with the girl I liked. Of course, he didn't know that. I'd never told him who she was, just about her.

Silence.

"Can you kill it?" she asked in a hopeful voice.

"I've been trying."

The kind of quiet that goes with deep thought ensued for a few minutes.

"If we escape from here, do you have somewhere safe we can go?"

"Yeah, The Pink Hippo. Do you have an idea of how to escape?"

Silence again.

"Well, there is this one incantation I know—"

"No. We can't do that," I said, my tone sterner than I'd meant it to be.

"But it's always worked for me in the past. It only calls on a minor demon," she whispered.

I couldn't believe what I was hearing. I knew demons existed. After all, that's what I fought daily. But to hear this girl speak of summoning a demon as if she was deciding what to wear tonight was craziness. And after what I'd just said a few minutes ago. "I thought you were a missionary."

"My parents are the missionaries," she retorted. "Besides, do you have a better plan?"

It was only a second of silence, but that was enough for her. "That's what I thought," she said, "It's the only way."

Those who would come to my aid were either injured or dead. I was alone.

"Besides, if you are a demon hunter, couldn't you just slay it once it frees us?" Her voice was sweet now and I felt her hand on my arm.

It was a fair point. "But I don't have any of my weapons."

"That's not true," a voice whispered, but it wasn't Melanie. "You always have the Sword."

For some reason I felt my side—no sword. I'd already known it, but I still checked. It was then I realized I was only wearing a cloak. My clothes were still hanging next to me on the bars of the cage. I was sure glad that we were in pitch black. I tucked the cloth a little tighter around me.

"It's easy to perform," her hand squeezed my arm tighter. "And I think you'll enjoy it." She slid closer to sit next to me.

"I don't know."

"I'm telling you, this one is just a minor demon," she paused and I heard her giggle. "In fact, it's kind of cute."

Was I really hearing this? "Cute? A demon is never cute."

"They can be."

I shook my head, knowing she couldn't see. "No, they can't. Demons are evil. You should know this."

"Well, suit yourself." She shifted away from me. "I'm not staying in here any longer. I won't end up like Jesse."

"Wait…how do you know about what happened to Jesse?" I asked.

She didn't say anything.

"Of course. The boy in the cloak was Albert," I realized aloud. "You knew about all of this, you knew that I was a demon hunter."

"No, Albert doesn't tell me everything," she promised. "He only asks me to help him on occasion." But I didn't believe her.

Neither of us spoke.

"The Sword you seek never rusts, it can never bend, nor can it break. The Sword never fails," the voice was deep and I knew it wasn't Melanie. It was the same as a few minutes ago.

I shifted from a sitting position to my knees. A word flowed through my mind. Pray. I folded my hands as I knelt.

I heard Melanie make a whimpering noise, but I couldn't see her.

It was time for me to pray, to speak again to the One I'd shut out. To the One I blamed for my losses. To say, "I'm sorry."

"Lord, I am so sorry," I prayed. "I've been lost without You. I've felt that my hope was gone when my mom disappeared and then my dad fell. I feel so alone. And instead of leaning on You in my time of need, I pushed You away."

In my heart I felt His presence, and a Bible verse came to mind: *I will never leave you nor forsake you.*

I knew that though my earthly father was gone, my Heavenly Father was still there. Always.

"Lord, I pray right now for Your forgiveness. Please help me to lean on

You. Please send Your help to us. Our fight is for You. Amen."

I already felt better, like a huge weight had been lifted from me. I'd been carrying that weight for quite a while, all the way back to the loss of my mom; I'd blamed God for taking her from me. I'd been angry with Him. Worst of all, I hadn't prayed since my dad fell. It was the last straw for me. God had made me an orphan. But try fighting a demon without asking for God's help. It's just not possible. And now I realized why the fight had been going so poorly.

A light appeared next to me, growing brighter. But then I heard a whispering in the background.

"Throw off our bindings and come to my aid," the voice chanted. It was Melanie. "I command you to set me free."

The light next to me grew brighter. I knew what was happening. I closed my eyes.

"Lord, send your help. Banish that which is being called to this place."

Melanie's voice grew louder. "I call to you to release my bonds. We serve the same master and you must obey." Melanie let out a piercing shriek.

I opened my eyes. I could see her in the green glow emitting from the demon that now hung above her. It was scaly, with a tail and two arms. No legs. Its head round and plump sitting just on its shoulders, a long curling pink tongue twitched in and out of its mouth rapidly.

"I am Swipe; I have come to steal you from this cage. You shall be free," it whispered gruffly.

"No!" I shouted. "You are not welcome here. I command you to leave," I called.

It turned to look at me. "You have no weapon; you have no power over me." It lurched forward to hover directly in front of me, its talons only inches from my face. "You dare to challenge me?"

I stared into its eyes, small glowing red globes.

It cackled loudly, and turned to look at Melanie as if waiting for a command. "May I?"

I looked at her face, silhouetted in the green glow being given off by Swipe. I couldn't read her expression. It was solemn, calculating. "You—"

"I don't, but there is One who does," came a soft male voice from outside the cage.

A puzzled look crossed the demon's ugly face, followed by shock as he realized what the voice meant.

I tried to see who was out there, as did the demon and Melanie.

"Jesus," the voice said.

At the sound of the name, the demon was sucked toward the cage, against the point of a sword poking between the bars.

Its mouth agape in silent horror, a loud sizzling noise resounded from the small demon. And there in its center, glowing brightly, was the end of a sword. The sword glimmered green from the demon and then shone blue as the demon dissolved right before my eyes.

Melanie stumbled backward against the cage walls.

"Taylor!" the voice across from me shouted. "We have to go now."

The voice was clear to me. I knew who it was. "Ike, how did you find me?"

"I prayed."

That was good enough for me. "What's your plan?"

"I'm going to cut through the bars with a laser," he explained. "Stand back."

I stepped back next to Melanie, who was shifting her weight back and forth, making the cage rock. Then I wondered what command she was about to give the demon before it was destroyed.

"Ike, you killed a demon!"

"I know," he said, his voice shaky as he activated the laser.

"You're a hunter!"

"Greater is He that is in me than he that is in the world, right?" Ike clarified

I nodded. "You're absolutely right."

"Don't be angry," he said as he worked the laser on one of the bars.

"Why?"

"The sword—it's your dad's," he admitted.

"I see." A section of one of the bars dropped away.

"Are you—?" he asked.

"No, how could I be? What better a way to honor him then use it to rescue his son?" The words came out even better than I'd expected.

Another section of bar fell away. "One more and the hole should be big enough for you to escape."

"Melanie, are you OK?" I asked.

She didn't speak, but I felt her hand slip into mine. She squeezed my knuckles like a little girl about to cross a busy highway.

The last section of bar slipped away and fell to the bottom of the chasm.

"Where did you come from?" I asked.

"I repelled into the shaft," Ike said.

"Can we get back out that way?"

"Yes, but I only brought one other harness." Ike stared at Melanie.

"Take her up first and then come back for me," I said.

I helped Melanie get the harness on and made sure it was tight. Then we hooked her to the rope, directly above Ike. They started their ascent, and I decided to take the opportunity to get out of the cloak and back into my clothes. They were still damp, and my boxers were especially chilly.

Twenty minutes passed before Ike returned. He'd left me my sword and a set of night vision goggles, but the time had seemed like an eternity. We were now on our way up the rope. Melanie was waiting somewhere above.

Ike explained that I'd been missing three days. Everything seemed to be falling apart; my aunt and uncle hadn't arrived yet. A winter blizzard had blown in and blocked the train tracks and roads into town. Meteorologists had never seen anything like it before—the storm had formed and basically sat over the range in which Ashley Meadows sat, but had not pummeled the town, inn, or mines.

Further, the boring machine being used to reach the trapped people had broken down again. A smaller machine had been used to create a narrow tunnel which supplies could be passed through, but a person couldn't fit through it yet.

Earlier this morning, Ike had decided to fast. He was kneeling when a book fell off a shelf next to him. He picked it up and a loose sheet of paper fell from it. It was an old map of the mines, and on it was a small penciled cross. The marking was over the position of a former air shaft. His eyes were drawn to it and he knew immediately that I was there, the feeling had overwhelmed him. He set out on his own to rescue me. It'd taken all day to find me, and now it was nearly midnight.

At the top of the shaft I realized how little time we had left. The moon was so bright and growing fuller every night. I'd have to hunt the HowlSage. Tonight. No time to eat and rest.

Ike opened a large pack and pulled out a fresh set of clothes for me, as well as my hunting gear.

"I have a location that has ninety-five percent probability the HowlSage will be there tonight, but you'll have to go now if you want to get there in time."

"What about you? And Mel?"

"I'll take care of her. We'll head back to The Pink Hippo and wait for you."

An alarm started beeping on Ike's watch. "You have to go, it's almost midnight. I've programmed the coordinates into your phone; it'll navigate you. Just be careful—I think the Raptoryx is near."

Melanie seemed to be in a daze; she was standing off by herself, staring up at the moon.

Chapter Twenty-One

October 26th—Thursday

One minute past midnight and I was flying at full speed toward the stone circle. How Ike had such a high probability the HowlSage would be at these coordinates had not been explained, but I knew he had a plan. I had learned that regardless of Ike's failures thus far, he was really smart.

I put the throttle up and let the J-Pak reach its maximum speed. The streets and houses below were a blur. As I neared the park, I decreased speed and landed on a trail. The air was so chilly, but not as bad as inside the shaft in which I'd been held prisoner.

I'd traveled the path a couple times before, but this time was different. My adrenaline was pumping and I felt sure that I could defeat the HowlSage. A branch ahead swayed in the wind, causing me to look twice, but nothing was there.

A shadow sliding over the empty soccer field next to me caused me to look up. There, gliding in circles over the woods, was the Raptoryx. I knew what was below it—the circle.

I stepped through some branches and onto the trail. It felt spongy, like it'd absorbed as much water as it could before it would turn to muck. The branches were shiny green from wetness and moonlight.

I was nearing the pine trees that blocked the circle from view. Would I find the HowlSage there, or would it be Albert?

I slowly parted the branches that blocked my vision of the clearing. In the center of the circle I saw the thick matted fur of the HowlSage standing like the Egyptian god Anubis. The creature's arms were raised high; in them was the belt that had been captured by McGarrett and Jesse.

How? I thought it'd been secure within the workshop, unless…but he wouldn't have. Someone else moved into view—a cloaked figure that could only be Albert. He was moving in a slow shuffling dance around the exterior of the circle.

At the moment, I was horribly outnumbered—the Raptoryx high above, the HowlSage, and the boy. If there was any time I needed help it was now. I'd have to do this myself, so I formed a plan.

First I'd strike the HowlSage with the point of my silver sword through its heart. After that I'd go for Albert. I'd need to get him out of the clearing and into the protective cover of the trees so that the Raptoryx wouldn't have the opportunity to strike. Once Albert was restrained, then I'd mess with the overgrown bird above. It had to be a precise slash and dash attack. Success hinged on the element of surprise and how fast I could run.

Sure, all of my previous attempts had failed, but now I knew why. I'd stopped trusting in the One who was at my side, whose help was always there waiting for me to ask for it. But tonight, suspended in that cage, witnessing a demon being summoned next to me, my eyes were opened again to how real this battle was. The evil one and his minions were still working hard to steal away the souls of humans.

Albert kept doing his freaky dance, getting closer to me; I'd wait until he was at the farthest part of the stone circle from me. Quite possibly I could move in, skewer the creature, and then tackle Albert into the woods.

The cloaked boy was nearly there. It was time. I slipped my sword from its sheath. Something jingled as I did and I looked at the HowlSage and Albert; neither moved.

Wrapped around the hilt was a cross on a chain. My heart sunk for a moment. This cross had been my mom's. I'd used it the first night, but since then left it in my drawer. I knew Ike had retrieved it and placed it on my sword. He'd had hope all along; he'd never checked out of the battle. The cross was significant, because the sight of it could weaken any demon.

This was the moment I'd waited for, and it seemed as if everything was coming to a head. Five more seconds.

Four…

Three…

Two…

One…

A hand on my shoulder caught me off guard, forcing me to spin around. I wobbled backward and nearly into the clearing.

Jesse?

"What are you doing here?" I whispered, it took every ounce of control to keep my voice down, I was so excited. Why wasn't he dressed in his hunting gear?

"Hello, Taylor. I'm glad to see you," Jesse said.

I half smiled. "You came just in the nick—"

Jesse's hands slammed into my chest and my body flew backward through the air, bursting through the trees and into the center of the stone circle.

My sword remained in hand and with the other I rubbed my eyes and looked into the snarling face of the HowlSage. The belt was still in its paws, but now an odd glow came from each of its jewels. A drip of saliva fell from its lips and I rolled to the side real quick to avoid the acidic liquid. I seized the moment and rolled to my feet, then crouched in a defensive position.

Jesse and Albert walked toward me. The HowlSage stood to its full height, nearly ten feet, its long arms bulging with muscle.

"Taylor, come with us. Join us," a voice said. It wasn't Jesse, Albert, or the HowlSage. "Your father is waiting for you."

My dad?

"Yes, your dad. He is a prisoner, but we will let him go should you choose to join us."

Was it possible?

"Indeed."

It was hearing my thoughts.

I clenched my fingers around the cross wrapped around my sword's hilt. I looked at Jesse, unsure of what he was doing. Why was he helping the HowlSage? And Albert was sliding sideways, making it difficult for me to keep him in my peripheral sight.

I started to back away. The HowlSage moved forward, Jesse and Albert continued to close in from their angles. I, their prey, was in the center of a triangle.

A scream resounded overhead, and I looked up to see the Raptoryx circling us. I felt an odd pain in my shoulders, sharp and numbing.

I slowly closed my eyes to the pain. "Please make the pain go away," I prayed. "Help."

A stroke of lightning blasted a nearby tree. I closed my eyes against the light as resounding thunder shook the ground. Albert, Jesse, and the HowlSage were swept off their feet and hit the wet earth. But I remained standing.

I opened my eyes and found three giant men standing around me, swords drawn before them. They moved forward, each advancing on my assailants.

A squeal came from overhead and I watched the Raptoryx bank into a dive, descending toward us. The three protectors moved back toward me and raised their swords over my head, pointed directly at the flying beast. The creature's wings opened wide and it slowed, then began flapping and climbing back into the air. When I looked back to Jesse, he was gone, as were the HowlSage and Albert. Then, with another bright flash of lightning, the three swordsmen were also gone.

I was alone in the center of the circle. A terrifying thought crossed my mind. Jesse was awake and he'd joined them, which left in question the status of anyone at The Pink Hippo. Was anyone there hurt? Ike, Mrs. Riley, McGarrett…Melanie? If Jesse had attacked me, he may have attacked any one of them.

I spread the wings of the J-Pak. I had to get back to the others, no matter what.

I landed on a section of the old inn—the curved metal roof. Entering any other way would be too obvious if The Pink Hippo had been overrun. A small hatch atop the roof provided access to the seventh floor.

As I stepped down I saw the door at the center of the room. It was open and kneeling before it was Ike. He was alone and his shirt was torn; I could see three red streaks running across his back.

"Ike," I whispered. "Ike, are you OK?"

He turned slowly to look at me; one of his eyes was black—he'd been punched in the face. "Is that you, Taylor?"

"Yes."

"Do you believe in Jesus Christ as your Savior?"

That was an odd question. Of course he knew I did. "Yes."

I heard him sniffle; he got to his feet and hobbled toward me. "It's you, really you."

"What do you mean?"

He looked around the empty seventh floor. The skylight glowed with the early morning sun peaking over the horizon. "When I returned with Melanie, she needed to rest, so I showed her to an empty guest room on the fourth floor. I went to the workshop and not more than ten minutes later I heard lots of shouting outside. I came out to see Jesse and her running from the inn. The chief of police stumbled out the door, shouting at them, his arm bloody. He was passed by Mr. Frigg who charged after Jesse and Melanie." Ike paused and took a deep breath. "Jesse turned and slashed at Mr. Frigg with his knife. I ran from the workshop and tried to jump Jesse from the back, but Melanie saw me and she shoved me to the ground. I fell on my face and then felt something sharp drag across my back, like fingernails." He turned around and lifted his shirt, revealing the bloodied scrapes I'd already seen. "Then they fled together in McGarrett's Rolls. But after the car had left the property I saw Jesse fly into the air. The extra J-Pak must have been in the car, I don't know. But either way, I knew where he was headed—for you. I tried to raise you on the radio, but I only got static. So I ran past Mr. Frigg and Chief Rutledge, and as I passed Mrs. Riley I told her to pray. I headed straight for the seventh floor. I used the door to focus all my prayers on your safety. I knew Albert and the HowlSage were already there, but now with Jesse too, you'd need all the support you could get. This is where I've been since."

It was a lot to take in. It didn't give reason to why Jesse had betrayed us, how Melanie could turn him so quickly. "How did the HowlSage get the belt?" I asked.

"I planted it there in the circle. That's why I knew you would find the beast there. They needed that, and I knew it was a sure thing. See, I discovered that the amulets are used to give form to the spirit of the

BloodSage; each piece must be handcrafted and a ritual is performed over it, that's why the stone circle and the Raptoryx are significant. Further, it is likely that Jesse and McGarrett were both put into The Dark Night, which is a curse of nightmares. The only way to bring them out is to kill the demon carrying out the ceremonies, in this case the HowlSage."

I nodded. Ike had created the perfect opportunity for me.

Ike shook his head and looked at his feet. "I failed you. I hadn't counted on Jesse's actions."

I did something I would have never normally done—I grabbed Ike's chin and lifted it, looking right into his eyes. "No, you've done great, Ike. It was the perfect opportunity. I was seconds from making my strike when Jesse appeared. None of us knew, but I'm the one who should have sensed something was wrong. I followed him the other night; I caught him in the workshop with the belt, alone. At the time I didn't think too much of it."

"So what do we do now?"

I shook my head. "Is McGarrett awake?"

"No."

"Well, let's go check on the chief, then maybe we should get some rest. It's been a long night, and tonight I have to hunt."

We spoke with the wounded police chief in the infirmary. As Ike had returned and explained all he'd seen, the chief was sending patrols to the park to block any escape for Albert or the HowlSage. The night before, he'd been on the phone in the lobby when Melanie and Jesse stepped off the elevator.

When Chief Rutledge had attempted to approach the pair, Melanie ordered Jesse to attack. And before the chief could do anything, Jesse was on him, dagger out. The chief used his arm to fend off the attack, and

Jesse ended his assault as soon as Melanie had exited through the front doors of The Pink Hippo. That was when Ike had come outside and seen the rest of the fight.

A patrol was sent to Melanie's address to inform her parents that she was missing and when she was last seen she was exhibiting dangerous and violent behavior. Her whereabouts were currently unknown. The parents knew nothing of a friend named Albert, and there were only two Alberts registered in the school district, one a kindergartner, the other a fifth grader. Where had the cloaked boy come from? Was his name really Albert?

We decided that the first priority was to find Melanie and Jesse. They were in great danger, and we still had a few days to kill the HowlSage as well as stop the BloodSage from being summoned. It would happen on the full moon, as Ike informed me.

I was to first check the canning factory and then the mines. But I was only to check as far as the entrances. The Swigarts were about to be freed from the tunnel, and my uncle and aunt would arrive sometime tomorrow. A snow plow had been dispatched specifically to bring them to Ashley Meadows. The police helicopter had been grounded at the chief's orders due to the Raptoryx's presence.

We hoped that together we might be able to come up with a search, rescue, and attack plan. Without discounting Ike's or my abilities, we knew that the years of experience of my uncle and aunt and Ike's parents would be valuable. The chief, while tactical and a believer, was not a demon hunter.

So after I checked the assigned locations, I returned to The Pink Hippo. We'd have to wait until tomorrow.

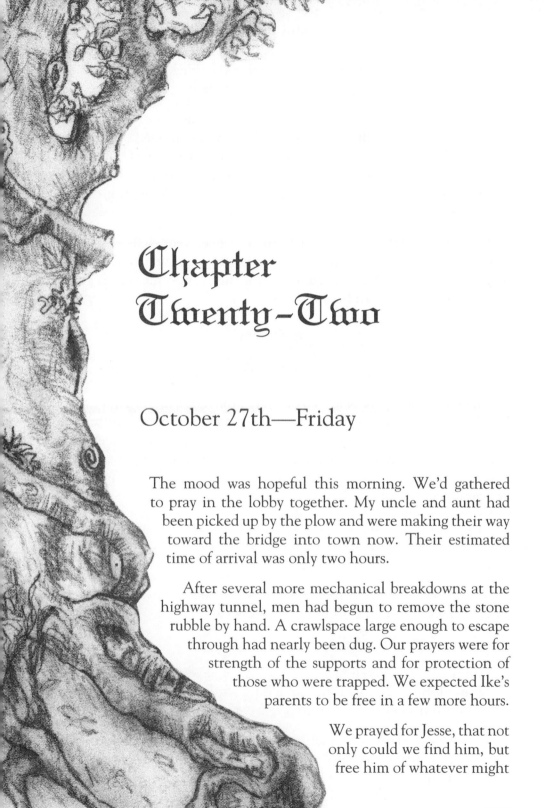

Chapter Twenty-Two

October 27th—Friday

The mood was hopeful this morning. We'd gathered to pray in the lobby together. My uncle and aunt had been picked up by the plow and were making their way toward the bridge into town now. Their estimated time of arrival was only two hours.

After several more mechanical breakdowns at the highway tunnel, men had begun to remove the stone rubble by hand. A crawlspace large enough to escape through had nearly been dug. Our prayers were for strength of the supports and for protection of those who were trapped. We expected Ike's parents to be free in a few more hours.

We prayed for Jesse, that not only could we find him, but free him of whatever might have possessed him. But praying together had helped keep me calm. If I'd been in my earlier state I would have felt totally lost.

But we would soon have a full team for the hunt and from there we could take on the multiple situations that had compiled. We were no longer only hunting the HowlSage, we were rescuing Jesse, awakening McGarrett, stopping a BloodSage from rising, and looking for a human who'd become power hungry. Neither Ike nor I would even pretend we knew how to deal with these things alone.

So while we waited, Ike and I checked over gear, fixed things that were broken, restocked supplies that were needed, and researched old maps of the mines. We wanted to have as much information as possible ready for Ike's dad when he got back.

The rumbling sound of an old diesel engine signaled the plow's arrival. I ran out of the workshop followed by Ike, and there in the rotunda was an old orange snow plow. Climbing out of the passenger side was my uncle Matt and my aunt Mary. They both looked weary, but when my aunt saw me a smile exploded across her face. She went straight for me and embraced me in a full hug.

"Taylor, I'm so sorry. I'm so sorry you've had to face all of this alone," she said. She released her hold and turned to Ike, embracing him. "And you, too. You've both been so brave."

My uncle Matt came over and shook his head. "Taylor, I'm sorry as well. I've been racking my brain over all of this."

"He has," my aunt agreed.

"The chief has been updating me, and I believe that I know how all of this started. But I'll explain that in a bit. First I want to know everything you've seen. It's best we get started right away," Uncle Matt explained.

Ike and I explained everything for my uncle. It took only an hour, but he needed time to think through all of it. He'd taken notes while we talked and was now at a large white board in the workshop. He was writing places, times, people, drawing arrows, connecting things.

We were briefly interrupted when Chief Rutledge arrived. They had begun bringing the survivors from the collapsed tunnel out. He offered to take Ike and I.

We rode with him and were there just a few minutes before people started emerging from the crawlspace. One by one they came out, but nearly fifteen minutes passed between each escape. We learned that Ike's parents had chosen to be the last two out. Likely they'd figured should any demons reappear in the tunnel they should be there. While they weren't hunters, they had a better chance than anyone to defeat the evil spirits. Ike had proven that when he rescued me from Swipe.

When Ike's mom emerged, Ike ran through the police line and embraced her. Something tugged at my heart. A moment like that wouldn't ever come here on earth for me, I'd have to wait until I crossed through the pearly gates. Mrs. Swigart was covered in dirt, but she was healthy and in good spirits. Mr. Swigart soon appeared, followed by two rescuers. They were all free. The reunion was cheerful to watch. Ike was so happy and his dad hadn't been out for more than thirty seconds when he started to tell him everything about the hunt, his words flowing a mile a minute.

The entire ride back to The Pink Hippo Ike jabbered on and his parents listened. Every time I looked in the rearview mirror at the happy family, Ike's parents were staring at him, huge smiles on their face. It was clear how worried they'd been when the news had come that the HowlSage had kidnapped Ike, but now he'd been returned. They'd gotten their son back.

At The Pink Hippo, Mr. and Mrs. Swigart went first to see McGarrett and Mrs. Riley. McGarrett hadn't improved, but instead remained in a coma of sorts. My aunt had joined Mrs. Riley on the medical floor. But what had happened to McGarrett was beyond a physical ailment—this was deeper, and from what we understood only the beast being destroyed could free him, which was my goal. The HowlSage must be banished back to the underworld.

So to work we went. Mr. Swigart and Uncle Matt discussed and worked through the details of the previous weeks. Ike and I joined them as they filled us in on their theory of what led up to this.

"We've had time to evaluate what you told me as well as bring in the events that I believe started this." Uncle Matt walked to the white board. He pointed to the word Egypt. Next to it was a date of September 15th. "It starts when we were still in Egypt. As you may know, a sarcophagus with Sage traces was recently transferred to a museum in New York. That's where I've been. We'd gone to Egypt when a new catacomb was discovered by some archeologists. When we arrived, we ran into all sorts of issues." Uncle Matt pointed to a list of bulleted items.

Passport revocations

Transportation breakdowns

License issues

Excavation restrictions

Weather delays

"Clearly, demons were at work trying to stop us from reaching the tomb." He pointed to a last name—the Trundles. "A missionary family helped us work with the local politicians to secure the sarcophagus for transport." Uncle Matt frowned. "Do any of you know a Melanie Trundle?"

Melanie? The girl who'd befriended me and then betrayed me? I nodded.

"She and Jesse became friends while in Egypt. I'm not sure, but something happened to each of them. Somehow, they're under control of the Sage."

"The HowlSage?" Ike asked. "I thought the HowlSage was being controlled by them."

Uncle Matt shook his head. "No one can ever truly control a Sage. In the end, they control us. But no, I am talking about the BloodSage." Uncle Matt paused for a moment and stroked his jaw, apparently deep in thought. "There was a night when Jesse and Melanie were discovered in the warehouse where the sarcophagus was being held. Melanie said she'd just wanted to see it herself. She'd asked Jesse to come along. I am sure he was taken by her, a bit of a crush. She's a cute girl."

I couldn't argue with that or fault Jesse. I'd been taken by Melanie as well, so much so that I lost sight of the fight. How shallow had I been to be blinded by her beauty? Sure, I was a fourteen-year-old boy. But I wasn't a typical one; I was supposed to be grounded, faithful to the Truth. I'd gotten to a place where the Truth was hidden from me, and it'd been because I'd stopped talking to God. I'd stopped listening for His guidance. That had all changed now; I was headed back in the right direction.

"I believe that Jesse and Melanie have been working together to raise the BloodSage. Jesse was the one to suggest that he come stay with you while we were in New York. And Melanie's parents may have come here under their daughter's control. Last I remember, they were committed to Egypt for at least two more years."

"What of the boy? Albert?" I asked.

"I do not believe he is a boy at all," Uncle Matt explained.

"Then what is he?" Ike asked. "He sure looks and acts like a boy."

"I believe he is a jinn," Uncle Matt explained.

"A jinn?" I asked.

"Jinn are evil spirits who can take human form," Mr. Swigart explained.

"And they are very dangerous. Regardless of what some cultures think, jinn are never good. They may act as such to humans, but only to get whatever it is they are after," Uncle Matt added.

"So, you think that Melanie and Jesse planned all of this?" I asked.

"Not entirely, but I do think they were influenced by a jinn, one that is a subject to the BloodSage. I believe the gray mist that you have encountered is the spirit of the BloodSage," Uncle Matt explained.

"I agree. Demons are evil, but they are not stupid. C.S. Lewis' *The Screwtape Letters* displays accurately just how smart they can be. They are calculating, and they plot against us every day," Mr. Swigart said. "The jinn would have known about the Etherpit here in Ashley Meadows. This would be the closest Etherpit to the BloodSage's mummified remains, once transported to New York."

"So all this time I've been fighting the wrong demon?" I asked.

"No, you haven't been fighting the wrong demon. The HowlSage must still be defeated, and it has an integral part in all of this. The jinn is a master of trickery, but it does not have the magical powers needed to raise the BloodSage. That falls to the HowlSage," said Uncle Matt.

"So how do we defeat the jinn?" Ike asked.

"There are two simultaneous steps that must be used to defeat the jinn," said Mr. Swigart. "First, remove its cloak. This can—"

"Wait. I've seen this happen. At school with the maintenance guy. Albert had a pitchfork, and a ball of light hit him square in the chest. He disappeared, but his cloak remained. I went to look at it, but my hand burned when I tried touching it, and then the cloak deteriorated right before my eyes."

"Albert?" my uncle asked.

"That's what the jinn said to call him," I explained.

Mr. Swigart and Uncle Matt looked at each other fearfully. "Teddy, you don't think?"

Theodore was Mr. Swigart's first name; Teddy was his common name.

"Texas?" Mr. Swigart responded.

Uncle Matt nodded.

Ike's dad firmed his jaw. "If that's true, than we have to rescue Melanie and Jesse immediately."

"I agree." My uncle looked at me. "First things first—have Ike help you get dressed into your gear. Teddy, see if you can adjust the trace settings and search for a level 13 at the mines or the canning factory."

Mr. Swigart nodded. "I'll also check the woods where the amulets have been presented."

Uncle Matt nodded and then looked at Ike and I. "Why are you two still standing here? Get ready."

I stumbled backward and bumped into a desk. His words had caught me off guard. I wasn't used to the authoritative voice of my uncle. He'd been a hunter, and after that he'd investigated and commanded several operations. It was clear he was in charge, and I was his soldier. I was under his command.

I regained my composure. I changed and then Ike helped me gather all of my gear and fit it on.

When we joined my uncle and Ike's dad back in the main room of the workshop, the large screen on the wall displayed several glowing crimson blips. But one stood out, one glowed brighter, one was larger than the rest. But it wasn't at any of the locations previously mentioned. It was just a few miles away.

Mr. Swigart tapped something on a screen in front of him. The map before him grew and centered in on the crimson blip. The location was a small stone island located on Coal Chase Lake. A lake that happened to be on The Pink Hippo Inn's vast property.

"Is that where I think it is?" Ike asked.

"If you're thinking of Coal Chase Lake, then yes," Mr. Swigart said.

"It's time to go, Taylor. Mr. Swigart and I will make our way to the lake. We will be prepared to support you in any way we can. Ike, go let The Gathering know they need to pray. And then go to the attic and open the door."

Ike smiled at me and then ran from the workshop. He was off on his mission.

I stepped out onto the rotunda and prepared to take off. A few snowflakes drifted down around me. The clock tower bells began to chime. The time was now midnight.

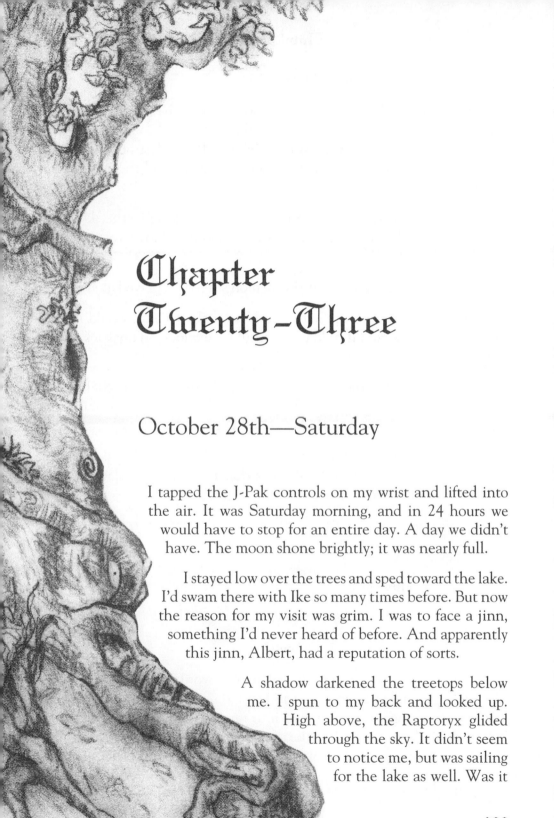

Chapter Twenty-Three

October 28th—Saturday

I tapped the J-Pak controls on my wrist and lifted into the air. It was Saturday morning, and in 24 hours we would have to stop for an entire day. A day we didn't have. The moon shone brightly; it was nearly full.

I stayed low over the trees and sped toward the lake. I'd swam there with Ike so many times before. But now the reason for my visit was grim. I was to face a jinn, something I'd never heard of before. And apparently this jinn, Albert, had a reputation of sorts.

A shadow darkened the treetops below me. I spun to my back and looked up. High above, the Raptoryx glided through the sky. It didn't seem to notice me, but was sailing for the lake as well. Was it going to collect my cousin or Melanie?

A moment later I had my answer. It dove toward the island, letting out a deafening screech that echoed across the lake. I had to kill it before it did something awful to my cousin or Melanie. Regardless of what they'd done or how they'd sinned, they were still humans and they could still be saved.

Besides that, it was a menace to me, always lurking in the sky. This was my chance. I rolled back to my stomach and slid my sword from its sheath. It glowed blue in the moonlight.

"Lord, please help me defeat this demon's steed," I prayed aloud.

I pushed a button on my wrist controls for the J-Pak. I would take it to its top speed. Would it hold up, or would it explode on my back? I was about to find out.

The wind blew through my hair, and without goggles I would have been blinded. At 178 miles an hour, the ground zipped past in a blur. I felt my ears go numb from the cold air whistling past.

I was closing on the Raptoryx, but it was closing on the isle. I could see a fire burning on the pile of rocks that made up the island. Three silhouettes were clear in the fire's ring of light.

One hundred yards…

Seventy-five yards…

Fifty yards…

Twenty-five yards…

Wham!

I slammed into the Raptoryx. I felt my sword slide into the beast. My arm was yanked upward as the beast screamed in pain and jerked in surprise. A huge wing slammed into my head, my grip on the sword loosened. I held on and pulled the sword from the creature's side. A blast of crimson flame and gray smoke spewed from the wound I had inflicted.

It screeched again and rolled away from me. I watched as it writhed in the air. Its flight was unbalanced; I'd severed muscles to one of its wings. "Thank You, Lord. Help me to expel this beast back to the depths from where it came," I prayed.

I moved to strike again. Raising my sword high, I flew over the creature and then thrust my sword down. The silver blade plunged into the Raptoryx's neck.

I jerked my arm back, ripping the blade down its neck. A row of crimson flames spurted into the air at the incision. The creature shuddered and jolted left, then right in an attempt to knock me loose. Neither its arms nor its beak could reach me. It rolled over and its disabled wing nearly knocked me from the sky. But I was quicker, my mind was clearer than it'd ever been. The belly of the Raptoryx was exposed to me. A beam of moonlight seemed to highlight an area on the underside of the beast. And somehow I was sure I needed to strike that exact spot.

I dived again and drove the tip of my sword through the skin. Suddenly I was thrown backward by a blast of body parts. The beast had exploded before me. A mucky red goo covered me.

But the beast was gone. I looked toward the island below. There were only two shadows remaining. I set down on the far end of the rock isle, my sword drawn before me. I was ready for any attack.

A fire burned in the center of the island and two figures stood near, facing the fire. I was pretty confident it was Jesse and Melanie. Neither wore cloaks and I could see Jesse's curly hair and Melanie's long hair. Approaching slowly, I called to them, "Jesse? Mel?"

Neither moved at my voice.

I lifted my radio to my lips and whispered, "Uncle Matt, I think I found them."

"Jesse, Melanie, and Albert?" he asked.

"No, I think just Melanie and Jesse," I explained. And then I remembered that I had seen three figures. I turned sharply and scoured the island.

"Don't do anything yet. Keep your eye on the water around you. The jinn is very tricky and he may have gotten Melanie or Jesse to summon other Sages to his aid. The HowlSage may even be close. The scanners didn't show any signs of the HowlSage near you, but that doesn't mean it isn't there," Uncle Matt said.

"I killed it," I said, "the Raptoryx, that is."

"We saw. Congratulations, that is a big accomplishment. But we can discuss it further when you are safe again." My uncle's voice was stern and unexcited. "For now, just wait. Teddy and I will be there shortly. We have to row out to the island."

I was a bit upset that my uncle hadn't seemed excited at the death of the Raptoryx. That thing had caused Jesse and I all sorts of problems. Plus, wasn't it vital to the BloodSage? After all, it was its steed. I shrugged and inched closer to the pair near the fire.

"Jesse? Melanie?" I asked again. No response. I looked around the island and at the shore. I scanned the water for any disturbances. But the lake was calm, a glassy surface shining brightly from the nearly full moon overhead.

I turned back toward the fire and my body involuntarily jerked backward at what I saw. Jesse was standing right before me. A dark smile crossed his face. He jumped forward, his hands clamping around my neck. His weight took me to the ground. My sword clattered on the rocky terrain as I lost hold of its hilt. Jesse planted his knees on my arms, pinning me down. His grip on my neck tightened and it became harder to breathe.

"You shall not defeat us. We are united as one." He cocked his head to the side. "We have seen the way and we will win the war. Do you not wish to join us?"

I grimaced and forced a breath. "Never."

"Then you shall die," he said.

"No I won't," I said, and thrust my knee into his gut.

Jesse released me and fell back, grabbing his ribs and wheezing.

I searched for my sword, but instead found a pair of girl's pink converse shoes. I looked up into the face of Melanie. She held the sword in her hands.

"Looking for this?" she asked in a mocking tone. She lifted the sword over her head as if to strike me. "You must understand, everything is set. There is no stopping the rise of the BloodSage now. He will return, and when he does he will bring great power to I and he who is at my side." Melanie lowered the sword and smiled at me. "Why shouldn't he be you?" she asked, her voice nearly as sweet as when we'd talked at lunch, or on the scooter, or at Starbucks.

A grunt from behind us caught our attention. Jesse was on his feet again, he was staring at Melanie in anger. "You said that it was over between the two of you." He stepped forward.

Melanie turned and held the sword toward him. "Not a step further."

"Or what, you'll run me through?" Jesse asked. "You can't complete the task without me."

Melanie glared at Jesse. Her eyes narrowed with anger. "The HowlSage will return tonight with the cargo and Albert can help me finish."

"I am the one who taught you how to summon the HowlSage; it answers only to me," Jesse argued.

I'd been listening from my position on the ground. I slowly shifted backward to get out from between them.

"Ahh, but as you just said, 'you taught me.' I summoned it. It answers to me now," Melanie retorted. "Now step back."

"No!" Jesse yelled and stepped closer.

I noticed a dagger in his hand. It was raised.

"Fine then," Melanie screamed and darted forward, sword raised. She brought it down, but Jesse parried with his dagger. He stepped back. She charged again, but Jesse was quick and rolled to the right. Mel swung left, and Jesse leapt into the air. He landed on his feet and then rolled forward.

I stood up, unsure of what to do. I couldn't let them kill each other, but I was unarmed. Wait, that wasn't true, I had my grappling hook. I could use it to restrain one of them. Melanie had the sword, so she was the obvious choice.

I took aim, but before I could shoot, Jesse and Melanie dropped to the ground, their bodies limp. What had happened?

The creak of a wooden stern bumping against the island caught my attention. "Good work, Taylor," Mr. Swigart said as he stepped out of a small row boat, a blow dart pipe in his hands.

"Great shots, Teddy," my uncle Matt said as he stepped onto the island. "Taylor, help us get them into the boat. We have to bind their hands and feet." He handed me a long coil of rope. "You take care of Jesse's hands."

The three of us made quick work and carried the two unconscious kids to the boat. My uncle clearly had no problem with the binding of his own son, but I knew it was for Jesse's protection.

"What next?" I asked.

"Fly back to the workshop; tell Ike we are on our way. Also, tell him to do a cross scan for SwampSages within a seven mile radius of the inn. Then I want you to go to the seventh floor. There is someone waiting for you there." My uncle turned away, clearly dismissing me.

Mr. Swigart launched the boat into the water and jumped in. "We'll see you in a little while." I watched as they set to rowing for the shore.

A cold breeze blew over the island, picking up water and spraying my exposed face. Everything went black around me as the fire went out. The rocky surface of the island still glowed from the moonlight, but soon that too faded. There were no clouds; something else was at work. The answer came in an eerie voice that I recognized instantly.

"Taylor, it is good to see you again. And imagine the two of us here and alone. No one to…to distract us."

"I know it's you, Albert. There is no need to shroud yourself with this darkness."

Albert cackled. "Oh, but darkness is what I like. It makes me feel alive," he said. I saw his cloaked figure a few yards off. He moved forward, his hands clasped before him.

"You will never be alive. I know what you are," I said. I fingered the cross in my pocket with my left hand, my right grasping the hilt of my sword. I knew that my sword would not be enough to kill the jinn. Mr. Swigart had begun to explain how I could do it, but he'd never finished. The truth was, I didn't know how to defeat the demon before me.

"Do you want to see your father?"

The question made my heart leap, as it had every time before. But I knew these words were being said by a master of deception. He would say anything to control me.

"You cannot show me my father," I said.

"I can." Albert waved his arm toward the water and then to the center of the island. A stream of glowing water erupted from the lake and poured into a pool in the middle of the island. It glowed from something other than the moonlight.

The water swirled and an image began to appear. I saw someone sitting on the ground with an eerie gray mist circling around. The man looked toward me and I instantly recognized his face.

"Taylor?" my dad asked.

Could he see me? "Dad?"

The man nodded with a smile, but suddenly he frowned. "No, Taylor, close your eyes. Do not—" The image suddenly disappeared as the water began to boil and then blasted into a spout of steam.

"You see he is alive," Albert whispered. "We have him and he is ours. But you can be reunited with him. What is there left in the world for you? There is no one who—"

"You're wrong," I interrupted. A dreamlike stream of faces passed through my mind's eye—my uncle and aunt, Ike, his parents, Mr. and Mrs. Riley, even Jesse. "There are many reasons."

"So be it, but you will not win against me," he said.

I heard the tell-tale ring of a dagger being slid from its sheath. I knew that if I fought him alone I could not win. I didn't know the first thing about defeating a jinn; I needed help.

"Lord, please send someone; please give me the strength," I prayed aloud.

I heard Albert hiss. I knew prayer was a weapon in itself against a demon.

"Your word is a Sword against evil," I prayed.

Albert hissed louder, but I watched as he prepared to strike. He wasn't going to let me continue. He leapt into the air, dagger raised, held with both hands. A screech of anger burst from his lips.

Then everything seemed to slow to a snail's pace. As Albert flew through the air, his dagger glowing orange, I felt a warmth course through my body, one I hadn't felt for a long time. Two balls of white light flew by me on either side, coming together on Albert's chest. The hood of his cloak fell backward, and for the first time I saw his face. It looked human, but even in this light I could see it was as white as a ghost. His eyes were pure black, no pupils, no white. His expression was one of pure agony. The dagger he'd held came loose and flew from his hands. Albert's body cartwheeled backward and crashed onto the island's rocky surface.

Two giant men stepped up next to me. They wore white cloaks and their hands remained together, palms facing out. The one on my right spoke.

"Taylor, you must be quick. Use your sword to remove the hood from the cloak," the man said.

I ran for the crumpled form of Albert. But his body was already gone, only the cloak remained on the ground. I took my sword and jabbed it into the neck of the cloak, then slid it across. I lifted the hood up with my sword, but it was still attached on one side.

"You must sever it entirely," the other man said.

I reached to take hold of the cloak, but stopped as the first man shouted.

"No, do not touch the cloak. You must only allow the sword to do the work," he ordered. "We have banished the jinn with the light of Truth, but its cloak must not feel the touch of a human. If it does, the jinn will be called back."

I yanked my hand backward and lowered my sword. It dropped to the ground.

"Be quick, the time is short," the second called.

A wave of water leaped onto the island, surging over my feet. I stumbled backward, then looked for the cloak. Where had it gone?

"Quick, it's there," the first said, and pointed toward the lake.

The cloak floated about five yards off the island. I started for the water, knowing I had to get it before it sunk.

"Wait," called the second, then added, "Andrew, prepare."

I looked at the cloaked men. They each removed swords from invisible sheaths at their sides.

"Taylor, prepare, they are coming," the one called Andrew said. "Phillip, you must retrieve the cloak. Taylor and I will fight them off."

"Fight off who?" I asked.

Andrew lifted his hands and blasted a ball of white flames into the air. It hovered ten feet above and illuminated the entire island.

It was then I saw them. They looked exactly like the one who'd banished my father. At least a dozen SwampSages were emerging from the lake, each green and scaly. SwampSages are not like HowlSages, they are not as smart or as powerful. But in numbers they find their strength.

Three crossed onto the island at the same time. Two went for Andrew, one for me. I knew that the sword would work to sever limbs and expose the creature's insides, but the weapon needed to finish them off was salt, pure rock salt. I'd learned that in my training. I always carried a supply, but not enough for twelve SwampSages.

I unclasped one of my four pouches and dumped a small bit into my hand. I had to make quick work and be accurate, before more joined the fray. The SwampSage's eyes were bulbous and black, its eyelids like that of a lizard. This was a weak spot for the SwampSage. A little salt and the eyes would melt away, which would kill the creature.

I saw Andrew charge his two opponents, his movements were crisp and clean. He severed the arms off the first and then took the legs off the second. Two more had come on land and he turned to face them.

I dashed forward, knowing I could not wait any longer. The SwampSage's tongue flicked from its lips and then disappeared. It clasped its hands together and a burst of murky water shot forward. I dove right and rolled. The ball of dark liquid hit the island and sizzled. This was not water you wanted to swim in. I stood and charged at the creature.

My sword cut through the air in an arc and came down on the creature's left arm, separating it. It swiped at me with its right hand; its long yellowed claws ripped across my chest, but did not pierce the armor I wore. With my other hand, I pitched the salt I held at the spot of the severed limb. The small clear crystals made contact and a nasty green flame erupted and sizzled from the exposed wound. The creature screeched and fell forward, writhing in agony.

One down.

I looked at Andrew; several SwampSages had been injured around him, some legless, some armless, a few limbless. He was parrying against two others who held long staffs. The weapons appeared to be a combination of vine and driftwood.

Phillip hovered over the water, but I saw no J-Pak on his back. He was slashing at three SwampSages who were attempting to capture the cloak. The creatures opposing Philip were submerged deep enough in the water that he could not get at their limbs, and you never wanted to decapitate a SwampSage. This only caused them to multiply. In this way, they were like the Hydra. Thankfully I hadn't had to face one of those yet.

The final three Sages were coming for me. They climbed from the water and stood together. I lifted my sword and charged them. In sync, they clasped their hands and a trio of murky water orbs flew at me. I ducked and then leaped back as the water crashed at my feet. The rocks sizzled and cracked as the acid melted them. I started forward, but the creatures blasted a volley of water at me again, forcing me to roll to the left.

I popped up and launched myself at the one on the left flank of the three. I swiped my sword down and threw a handful of salt at the same time.

It worked.

The SwampSage's right leg dropped to the ground and the salt made contact with the open wound. It sizzled and green flames burst from the wound. The SwampSage's green scales shimmered from the firelight. It dropped to the ground and disintegrated.

The remaining two turned to face me. But I was too quick and slashed at the center SwampSage's arms, removing them quickly with two sweeps of my blade. I launched salt at its face and caught it with its eyes wide open. It sizzled and fell to the ground in a pile of green ash.

I was on a roll. I swept across the remaining creature, but in my excitement I lost my accuracy. I'd gotten cocky. My sword swept through the SwampSage's neck, sending its head to the ground. It was too late; the damage was done.

I was amazed how quickly the new SwampSages formed. Not even a second remained to strike the severed parts of the original Sage. I was surrounded by two new SwampSages. Its head had rolled behind me, while its body fell before me. You can imagine how dangerous these creatures could be. A hunter could quickly find himself surrounded if his attacks were not accurate.

"Taylor, jump!" Andrew yelled.

I obeyed and propelled myself into the air. Two orbs of acidic water collided right where I'd been. I landed hard on the ground a few feet away.

Andrew called for my sword and I tossed it to him. He grabbed it out of midair. With two blades, he spun and in an instant split each of the Sages in half. "Salt!" he called.

I undid a pouch and threw salt on the upper torsos of the injured

Sages. They sizzled and deteriorated.

"Now take care of the rest!" Andrew ordered. "I will help Phillip."

He tossed my sword back to me and I made quick work of the many injured SwampSages. Most were now defenseless, but left to themselves too long and they'd get back into the lake where they could regenerate. I'd just finished when the two men floated down, landing next to me. Where had these hunters come from? I'd thought that our forces were spread too thin and no help could be sent.

"I am sorry, Taylor; I have failed you," Phillip said.

Andrew shook his head. "It is not failure, brother. All has been decided. It is part of the plan."

"Yes, brother," Phillip said.

"The cloak escaped. A SwampSage retrieved it and disappeared beneath the waves," Andrew said. "We must go and so must you. Return to the workshop; your uncle and Mr. Swigart are nearly there."

The two men bowed and then flew into the air like rockets without the fiery trail.

I stood for a moment in awe. Who had they been? Hunters? Angels?

My radio buzzed to life, and brought me back to the task at hand.

"Taylor, come in," said Mr. Swigart's voice.

I lifted the radio to my mouth. "It's me."

"Where are you? Is everything OK?" he asked.

"I'm fine. I just finished fighting SwampSages," I explained.

"SwampSages? But we didn't see any on the island when we left. We saw you blast off," he said.

"No, I never left. The moment you rowed away, the fire went out and Albert appeared," I said. "He tried to convince me to join him again. That my father was still alive."

"Taylor you know that—" Mr. Swigart started.

"My father isn't alive," I said.

"No, I was going to say that…we have reason to believe he is," Mr. Swigart said.

My heart skipped several beats and my mind began to spin.

"I told you he was," a voice said in my mind. A searing pain shot through my head. I braced my skull with my hands as hard as I could. "You could have—" it began.

My limbs started to go numb, the pain continued in my mind.

My vision started to blur, I felt my body dropping to the ground. It was all happening in slow motion.

There was only one thing I could do. I cried out, "In the name of Jesus, leave me!"

The last thing I felt was the cold gravel against my cheek.

I woke to the clock tower bells chiming nine o'clock. I opened my eyes and saw Ike sitting in a chair at the end of my bed. Sun was shining through my windows. Was it morning? I looked at my alarm clock for confirmation.

My eyes felt thick with sleep; I rubbed them clear and looked around. Ike was not alone, his mother sat next to him, as did my Aunt Mary.

"You're awake!" Ike cheered.

Mrs. Swigart patted his leg. "Give him a moment," she said sweetly.

"What happened? How did I get here?" I asked.

My aunt looked at me very seriously. "We aren't exactly sure, but Theodore heard you banish something in Jesus' name. They went back to the island when you—"

"I went too!" Ike interrupted.

"—didn't respond," my aunt finished.

"And yes, nothing could keep Ike from going along," Mrs. Swigart explained.

I didn't remember exactly what had happened, only that I'd learned my father was still alive. A smile crossed my lips; I watched as my aunt's and the Swigarts' expressions changed to that of curiosity.

The world looked different to me. At the moment I didn't even care what I'd banished, only that my dad, one of my parents, was still alive.

"Thanks for being there, Ike," I said.

He nodded and tried to look tough. "No problem."

My stomach felt empty. "So what's for breakfast?" I could feel an uncontrollable grin on my face.

My aunt and Mrs. Swigart laughed.

"Typical teenage boy, always hungry," Aunt Mary said.

And then I felt something in the pit of my stomach. "Aunt Mary…" I started. "How is…how is Jesse?"

She frowned, but recovered with a forced smile. "He has been better. He's upstairs under supervision for the time being."

I knew that meant he was restrained. Demon possession was a very serious thing. And while most times prayer could help to lift the hold the demons had, I knew this was different. Jesse had called to the demon, he'd been in league with a jinn. He would have to ask for cleansing, his heart would need to change. The battle was his.

"He'll be OK," Mrs. Swigart said as she slipped her arm around my aunt. "I heard you say you were hungry and I think The Gathering has cooked up something extra special this morning in celebration for this morning's victory."

"Victory?" I asked.

"The rescue of Jesse and Melanie, the defeat of twelve SwampSages, and the arrival of the Angels," my aunt explained. "We'll give you a minute to change. Meet us downstairs when you are ready."

The two women and Ike headed for the door.

"Aunt Mary?" I said. "How is McGarrett?"

She sighed. "Nothing's changed yet. But there is still hope."

I nodded and the three left.

I quickly changed and headed downstairs. When I stepped out of the elevator, I was greeted with cheers. I smiled and was offered several handshakes. The Gathering was growing; there were several more townspeople than before.

Three long tables were set up buffet style. There was so much food. I filled my plate at least three times. I was hungrier than I'd been in a long time. Ike sat across from me, eating. He hadn't said much, but I wondered if he knew about my dad and if he was waiting for me to mention it.

"Ike, did you hear?" I asked.

His wide smile gave it away.

"Of course you did," I said.

"Your dad is alive." His eyes were bright with hope and excitement.

I nodded. It was so comforting to see that I had a friend who was as excited for me as I was.

The door to the dining hall opened and in walked Mr. Swigart, my uncle, Chief Rutledge, and another man. I recognized him instantly. It was the monk who'd told me I had the gift. The one who'd said I'd feel no fear. He was the overseer of Legion der Dämonjäger. I knew his presence signaled that our battle was the most dangerous, the most significant one the society was currently facing.

The four men sat at a separate table. They were deep in conversation, but I saw the monk eye me several times.

I finished my meal and Ike and I excused ourselves from his mom and my aunt. I wanted to tell him about the entire battle and I knew he was eager to hear about all of it.

We made our way to the largest library, but found it occupied by several praying men. We went to the second library. It was empty. We sat across from each other and I began to explain the entire battle. Before I knew it, I was on my feet reenacting my attacks for him. Ike sat still, mouth open, watching my every move.

After I'd told him the story for the third time, he asked how I felt about the news of my father. Of course, this conversation made me feel more alive. What could I do but be happy when something I'd lost was found?

Which for some reason reminded me of one of the pastor's sermons, the very same ones I thought were boring. The pastor had once said, "Our Lord is like a shepherd; when one of us is lost, He searches for us, and when He finds us, He rejoices."

"I'm going to find him," I said. I waited for Ike to tell me I was nuts, that I couldn't do that.

Instead he nodded. "I know."

"You don't think I'm crazy?" I asked.

He shook his head. "No, but I do think it will be dangerous and I can help. I've—"

I held up my hands, "Wait, Ike, it's too dangerous for me to ask you to come. My father's being held somewhere in the depths of the Earth."

Ike nodded. "I know."

The door to the library swung open. In walked the monk, unaccompanied.

"Greetings," the monk said.

"Hello, sir," Ike replied.

"Hello," I said.

The monk crossed the room and bowed his head slightly. "Ike, may I speak to Taylor alone?" he asked.

"Of course," Ike said, and in a second he'd left the library. I heard the door close.

The monk wandered to the dark fireplace. He stood and admired a small statue on the wide oak mantle.

I wandered over and stood just a few steps away.

"Are you ready to follow?" he asked.

"Where?"

The monk twisted the statue and I heard the sound of rusty gears trying to move. A moment more and the sound of stone grinding across stone resounded in the hearth. What had appeared to be a brick wall started to move backward.

The monk ducked into the fireplace and stepped through the new doorway. He wiped cobwebs away from an area of the old brick and then pressed a small black button. I heard the buzz of electricity zipping through old wiring. Several dusty light bulbs illuminated in sconces that lined the passage ahead.

The monk started down a long spiral staircase of cold gray stone. I followed.

The air was cold and musty. We were soon standing next to a waterway of sorts. An old wooden vessel bobbed up and down in the water, but there were no openings for the boat to escape from the chamber through.

"At midnight on Monday meet me at this boat. You will not hunt again until then," the monk said.

"But sir—" I started.

The old monk held up his hand. "Trust," was all he said. And then he started back up the stairs. I looked at the boat. It rocked back and forth in the water, creaking each time it bumped the stone wall of the canal.

We'd come down the staircase to see the boat and for him to say one thing to me; it seemed a waste of time and effort. But over the last months I'd learned to trust as the monk commanded and also begun to painfully develop patience. I wasn't a pro at either, but I was learning.

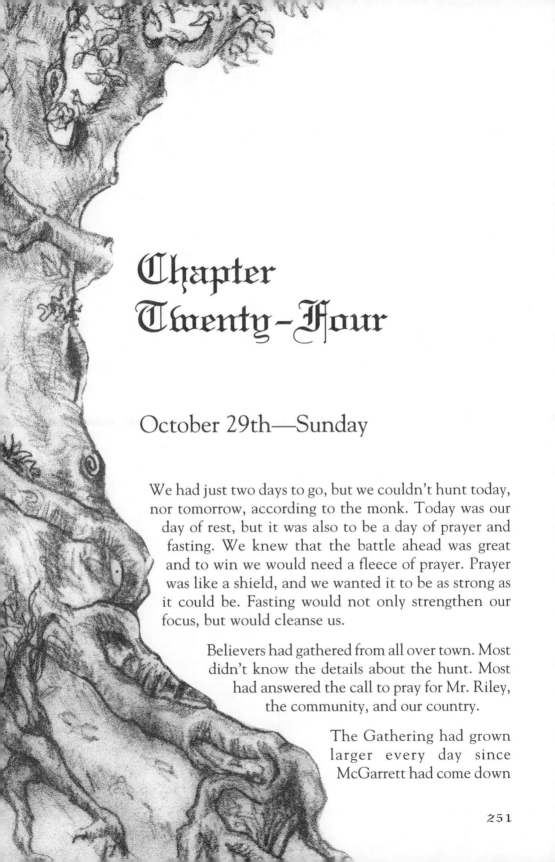

Chapter Twenty-Four

October 29th—Sunday

We had just two days to go, but we couldn't hunt today, nor tomorrow, according to the monk. Today was our day of rest, but it was also to be a day of prayer and fasting. We knew that the battle ahead was great and to win we would need a fleece of prayer. Prayer was like a shield, and we wanted it to be as strong as it could be. Fasting would not only strengthen our focus, but would cleanse us.

Believers had gathered from all over town. Most didn't know the details about the hunt. Most had answered the call to pray for Mr. Riley, the community, and our country.

The Gathering had grown larger every day since McGarrett had come down with his illness, as we preferred to call it. Now The Pink Hippo was filled with prayer warriors. The inn had never been so full in all my time here. I doubted very much it'd ever been this full since the mines had shut down back in the 1800s.

Chapter Twenty-Five

October 30th—Monday

I woke and looked at the alarm clock. The red numbers glowed 1:00 a.m. The bright moonlight from the nearly full moon shone in through the window. It almost looked like daytime. I rolled over and looked toward the fireplace. It was dark and unlit. I should have been hunting right now, but instead I was in bed and supposed to be sleeping. And today I had to go to school. I couldn't believe it, but it was the monk's orders.

I knew that I had to obey, and indeed I trusted that he was wiser than myself.

I never did get back to sleep, but climbed out of my bed when my alarm went off and made my way to the seventh floor to pray. When the elevator doors opened, I was surprised to see Ike. He was already dressed for school; I could only imagine what time he got up or if he'd ever actually gone to sleep. I was sure he was feeling the same anxiety I was.

"Good morning, Taylor," Ike said cheerfully.

"Morning," I said. I looked at the old elevator buttons, the number seven was lit up. Ike must have had the same idea I had. "Heading up?"

He nodded. "I wanted to pray before school."

"Do you mind if I join you?" I asked.

"Not at all."

We rode to the seventh floor. It was empty, but I could feel the presence of prayer. I knew in my heart that members of The Gathering were praying this very moment everywhere throughout our town and members of the society were praying all throughout the world.

After breakfast we were off to school. There were a dozen people willing to drive us, but in the end it was my uncle Matt who took us.

"Taylor, I wanted to let you know that the sarcophagus I'd been analyzing in New York has disappeared." My uncle turned the car out of the driveway and onto the pavement leading toward Ashley Meadows. "This only makes your mission that much more critical. Of course we've suspected for some time that it would eventually be brought here."

Then I remembered the argument between Melanie and Jesse. "That's right, Melanie had mentioned the HowlSage was bringing some sort of cargo here."

Our eyes connected in the rearview mirror. "Why didn't you mention that before?" he asked.

"I don't know, I must have forgotten," I said in a defensive tone.

He shook his head. "You must remember to tell me everything. I must have every fact to use in making the decisions we face," he said. His voice was stern. "Is there anything else?"

I shook my head. "Not that I can remember."

"Well, try, and when I pick you up from school I want you to tell me anything you haven't so far," he said, but it was more of an order.

We rode the rest of the way in silence and he dropped Ike and I out front of the school. Uncle Matt forced a smile as he pulled away and Ike waved. I didn't. Who did he think he was?

And as if Ike could read my thoughts, he said, "I know he comes across hard. But I can't imagine someone better in charge of this hunt." Ike looked at me seriously. "Your uncle has more experience than any other hunter alive."

"Really?"

Ike nodded. It was then I realized that I knew very little about my uncle, and even less about the society. I would need to learn more.

It was weird to be back in the school. Last time I'd been there, I'd been kidnapped. What really got me was none of the kids or teachers seemed to notice I'd been gone or that anything peculiar was happening.

Ike said it was because kids were always getting sick with stuff in the transition from fall to winter. Our absences had easily blended in.

I walked past Melanie's locker and remembered Albert shoving me across the hall and into the locker bank. How had I not known he was a demon, a jinn? Was I really that ignorant, or blinded? It had been Melanie's objective to throw me off; that was clear now, and she'd done an excellent job.

I felt an ache in my chest, my heart for that matter. I recounted her touch on my hand, her smile, our conversations. Had they all just been some ploy to further her efforts in summoning the BloodSage? The lump in my throat told me they had. I felt betrayed, but worse I felt used.

I went to my homeroom and waited as the clock slowly ticked by.

Next was math and then English.

Mrs. Mullen sat behind her desk as I entered. The bell rang as I took my seat.

Mrs. Mullen walked to the white board and started to write across it in large black letters, "What is truth?"

It was an interesting question to pose to a freshman English class.

"Class, today I will be assigning a paper that will take you the rest of the year to write, but I believe the question will take you longer to answer," Mrs. Mullen said. "What is truth?"

Several hands shot up. I looked around, a couple of the hands belonged to the regular geniuses. But one caught my attention; it belonged to a kid I'd often overlooked. I'd seen him talk to Ike after Sunday School a couple of times, but I couldn't remember what his name was.

He spoke without being called on. "Truth can be different depending on one's paradigm," the boy answered.

"Indeed it can," our teacher nodded, "but the question is not for us to answer now. I want this assignment to be an opportunity for you to reflect, for you to look inside of yourselves. What is it you believe truth is?" She sat down on the edge of her desk. "I expect many of you will come to similar findings, but be sure that you can defend your conclusion."

Mrs. Mullen walked back to her desk and picked up a stack of papers. "I have graded your essays on media persuasion. I must say I was quite impressed and I'd like a few of you to share your papers with us." She began handing back the essays.

Mine had gotten a B-, and thus wasn't among those to be read out loud. Instead, I sat back and listened as several of my peers read from their A+ graded papers.

Once the bell rang it was off to my favorite class, Greek mythology with Mrs. Diordean. I'm being sarcastic, if you couldn't tell.

After an agonizing hour on some Titan guy eating his brothers or father or something, it was time for lunch. As I entered the cafeteria, I didn't feel the freedom I thought I would. Instead, I found myself sitting with Ike, unable to eat. I looked at the table where I'd eaten with Melanie. Where she'd touched my hand, where we'd become friends. Had it really all been a lie? She'd been working me over, trying to win me to her side of the battle. To distract me while she and my cousin helped Albert summon a BloodSage back into existence. And within a few hours their efforts would pay off and the BloodSage would be a reality if I didn't stop it.

When Uncle Matt pulled up, I realized I hadn't put much thought into his request. But there was something I could tell him that I hadn't gotten to yet. I climbed into the passenger seat while Ike got in the back.

"I remembered something I needed to tell you," I started.

Uncle Matt nodded.

"One of the first few nights I was on the hunt, I had a dream," I began. "I awoke in my room to a blazing fire and before it sat the HowlSage. He invited me to sit with him, but I didn't. But for some reason I couldn't speak or move."

"I read that that is very common in dreams," Ike added from the back seat.

I'd nearly forgotten he was there and listening.

"The HowlSage called me forward and my feet followed; I had no control over my own body." The dream played like a movie in my mind. "Every step took me closer, until I was staring into the beast's face. The HowlSage remained sitting, it didn't advance on me, nor did it feel like a threat. My body involuntarily sat in the chair across from it. Then it spoke, 'Taylor, you should know something. You are a skilled adversary.'"

I could hear its low growling voice in my head. But I knew it was just an echo from my memory.

"Its mouth wasn't moving, yet I understood its every word."

I decided to leave out the HowlSage's jabs at my cousin.

"'You and I could be a strong team; we could rule this city,' the HowlSage continued. 'We could rule this world, if we wanted. We would be unstoppable.'" I took a breath. The dream was becoming far too real. I closed my eyes.

"Keep going," Ike encouraged.

"Yes, Taylor," my uncle said. "This is important, you must explain what happened next."

"Well, after that I felt something cold on the back of my neck. An icy gray mist slid over my shoulders and pooled near my heart."

A shiver coursed over my body as I relived the gray mist sliding across my body.

"The HowlSage spoke again asking for me to, 'let them in.' It said they could change me. But then a bright light flashed across the room; a rumble followed."

I looked out the windshield toward the winding road that would lead to The Pink Hippo's driveway. "Somehow, my voice returned to me, 'You would change me to evil,' I accused. The HowlSage laughed and asked 'What is evil?'"

That reminded me of Mrs. Mullen's assignment, "What is truth?"

"How did you respond to the HowlSage?" Ike asked.

A shiver coursed my body again. "The gray mist swirled over me again. And my mind became blurry, but I tried to think of an answer for the HowlSage. What was evil? Who decided what evil was?" I crossed my arms over my chest. I felt so cold. I continued; the dream was so clear. "Lighting flashed again, shaking my windows. Then the HowlSage asked for me to join them. But first he wanted the belt. For some reason, I obeyed and started for the belt. But the lighting flashed again and I saw my father's face. His sword was in his hand. He spoke, but I couldn't hear what he said. I tried to ask him to repeat it, but the HowlSage interrupted. 'Yes, your father, we can bring you to him. We have him,' it said."

I frowned; it was true they had him. I knew my next mission—should I live through this one—was going to be near impossible.

"Is that it?" Uncle Matt asked anxiously.

"Yes, after that the room swirled in light and I woke to find myself sitting next to my door. But it was closed. That was it." I paused. "Can we turn the heat on?"

My uncle tapped the dash and adjusted the temperature. "It is rather cold," he mumbled. "And look, is that snow?"

I looked out the passenger side window. Sleet had started to fall. It'd been cold for the last few weeks and it'd snowed off and on, but nothing significant.

"Wow, it's really coming down," Ike said. "The trees are already white."

Sure enough, the branches of the pine trees were becoming heavy with snow.

"It wasn't even sleeting at the school," Uncle Matt said.

"Yes, but the road to the inn does increase in elevation by nearly a thousand feet," Ike explained.

Uncle Matt turned on the windshield wipers and they swiped back and forth across the window. A moment later, he had to increase the intervals of the wiper blades. The snow had begun to fall more quickly.

Soon, the roads were slick and the car began to fishtail left and right, so Uncle Matt had to decrease his speed to twenty miles an hour.

"I've never seen it come down so heavy," Ike said. "There was no weather predicted for tonight when I checked this morning."

Uncle Matt sighed.

"It is October," I added. "It's not unusual for it to snow."

"No, it's not, but Ike's right, there was nothing like this in the forecast for this evening." My uncle frowned, his brows narrowed just above his eyes as he concentrated on the road, both hands gripping the steering wheel.

"But when is the weather man ever right?" I joked.

My uncle ignored me, "Ike, I want you to pull the seat beside you down and get the gear that's in the trunk," he said. "Set it beside you on the seat."

I heard Ike pulling on something and I turned around to see the backseat cushion next to him lean forward. He strained against his safety belt to retrieve the gear.

"Why does he need to—?" I started.

"Taylor, in just a minute I'm going to come to a stop, I want you to climb in back and change into the gear," Uncle Matt said.

"But what—?" I was cut off.

"This isn't just weather. It's a spell."

I looked back again and saw Ike. He'd unstrapped himself and half his body was in the trunk.

Wham!

My body flew forward. A strip across my chest burned as my safety belt dug in. The front of the car was lower than me, the back rising upward. I looked at the windshield as the glass splintered like a spider web. I felt myself being inverted as the car flew into a front-over-end somersault. It came down hard on the pavement with a deafening thunder of metal against asphalt.

I was suspended upside down, restrained in my seat by the safety belt. I looked to my left and saw Uncle Matt. He was stuck as well. I heard him groan.

Ike! I remembered him crawling into the trunk; he'd been free of his harness.

"Ike?" I cried, and worked to release myself from my belt. I maneuvered to see between the seats. I could only see the backside of Ike. He wasn't moving.

"Ike? Are you OK?" I called.

"Taylor, quick, in the dash. There's a pack of flares. Get them now!" Uncle Matt ordered.

"But Ike—"

"In a moment, but if you don't get those flares, we won't be alive long enough to save Ike."

I turned back for the glove box and undid the latch. There were several maps and other pieces of paper in the way. Then I saw the small box. I grabbed it and opened it. There were a dozen small orange cylinders, none larger than a Crayola marker.

"Give me a few and—" Uncle Matt started, but the car suddenly spun around on its roof. It didn't stop, it spun faster and faster.

I heard a groan from the backseat. Ike was alive.

"Hang on, Ike," Uncle Matt yelled.

I reached for my seat back and held on. Uncle Matt was holding onto the steering wheel. He reached his hand for me, "Give me one."

I strained and grabbed two from the box, then placed one in my uncle's outstretched hand.

He pushed something on one end, and an orange flame shot out the opposite side. The windshield looked like a spider web, but it was still in one piece; after all, that is what windshields are designed to do. Uncle Matt used his good foot to kick it clear.

The car was still spinning around.

"Taylor, give me another," my uncle said as he chucked the lit flare from the car.

I did and in thirty seconds we deployed all but two. With every rotation, the glow from the flares created what looked like an unabridged wall of fire. The car's spin had begun to slow.

"Taylor, when the car comes to a stop I want you to get Ike free. Then get into the woods and make your way back to The Pink Hippo. We're close," he said, holding the eleventh flare in his hand. "I'm going to distract it. You keep the last flare; you may need it."

"Wait, what are you going to distract?" I asked.

"The BlizzardSage that's outside," he said in mock casual tone.

"The what?"

"Think of the abominable snowman, but five times larger and way more dangerous," he explained. "Its only weakness is fire—that's its greatest fear."

"But should I be the—I mean, I'm younger," I said.

"It's not about speed or strength with a BlizzardSage, it's about the bluff," he explained. "Now go."

The car had come to a stop. My uncle opened his door and crawled from the car. A flare was lit on the ground before him, the one in his hand was still dark. I clambered between the seats and to the back. Ike had rolled over and was looking at me, clearly dazed.

"Whoa, that was quite the ride," he murmured slowly.

I couldn't stop the laugh that escaped my lips. "We have to go." The rear passenger side door opened with a creak and I backed out of the car. Ike was in better shape than I'd thought and climbed free without help. As I stood up, I nearly fell backward in awe at what stood on the other side of the car and across the road.

The beast stood twenty feet high and ten feet wide. It was covered in a thick, stringy, shaggy coat of white and gray fur. Its face looked like an ape's, even black in color. It had large bulky arms, with hands and fingers—those, too, looked like an ape's. I saw it snarl, displaying a top and bottom set of yellowed fangs.

And there, standing before the BlizzardSage at a height of five foot eight, was my uncle Matt, a single lit flare in his hand. He waved it back and forth, and I heard him shouting. Not threats, but a prayer. "For the Lord thy God is a consuming fire, even a jealous God," He was quoting Scripture.

The giant beast seemed to be transfixed by the flames. It didn't move, but its lip quivered. I wanted to go to my uncle's side, but I remembered his orders. And from what I'd learned so far, it was smart to obey my uncle's commands.

"Come on, Ike, let's go," I said, but Ike was already at the tree line. He'd pulled his hood over his head and he held out a small tablet computer before him.

"This way," he called, and started into the trees.

We arrived at the split-rail fence surrounding The Pink Hippo three hours later. My uncle had said we were close, but it certainly hadn't felt like it. The deep snow had slowed us, and we had to climb over several ridges and through several valleys.

I boosted Ike over the fence, then pulled myself up and swung my legs across. The snow had continued to fall and it was now up to our knees in some areas. A cold wind had picked up as well. The moon was blocked by the heavy snow clouds, but I knew that it was nearly full. By tomorrow night it would be, and the HowlSage would be venomous.

Another twenty minutes and we came to the front steps of The Pink Hippo. Ike had tried to radio his dad, but the reception was poor. Inside we found The Gathering gathered together in prayer. As soon as my aunt Mary and Mrs. Swigart saw us, they ran to us.

"What happened?" Mrs. Swigart asked. "Where have you been?"

"We were attacked on the road by a Blizzard—" Ike started.

"Yes, it's quite a blizzard out there," my aunt interrupted in cover, then added in a whisper, "Let's take this to the workshop. Mr. Swigart is waiting for you."

I realized what she was doing. Members from The Gathering were watching. They couldn't know what was really happening. We had to protect the secret. I'd seen what could happen if a human believed they could control a demon. I now knew firsthand why secrecy was so important.

The four of us made our way to the workshop where Mr. Swigart had several computers open, parts everywhere. The moment he saw Ike and I, he stopped and came for us. He gave Ike a giant hug.

"I've been worried. I tried to load your homing devices, but the reception for everything is out," he explained.

"I know exactly how to fix that," Ike said. "I had to do it while you were gone." Then he disappeared down the hall.

"Where is Matt?" Mr. Swigart asked.

"Ike started to mention a BlizzardSage," my aunt Mary said.

Mr. Swigart shook his head and sighed. "All right, I'm going to take the Diesel and go after him. At least it was only a BlizzardSage," he added.

"Only a BlizzardSage?" I asked, exasperated. "Have you seen one of them things? They're like—"

"Thirty feet tall," Mr. Swigart finished. "I know. But they're dumber than an ox."

"Thirty feet? The one we saw was probably twenty. You mean to tell me they come bigger than that?" I asked.

He laughed. "Yes, the largest reported was over forty-five feet tall."

Ike reappeared. "All right, try it now."

Mr. Swigart booted up the computer. The screen glowed to life and clearly on the map heading our direction was a small blue dot tagged, 'Matt Rivers.'

"Looks like he's on his way. Let's go get him," Mr. Swigart said.

Ike and I followed him to the back of the workshop and into the motor-pool garage. We headed right for the "Diesel" as it was called.

A large Caterpillar tractor with a bucket bigger than McGarrett's Rolls Royce, the Diesel could get through just about anything aside from solid rock, and even that I wasn't sure it couldn't dig through. We climbed up the ladder and into the closed cab.

Mr. Swigart fired up the engine, and Mrs. Swigart pushed the door opener. She waved to us and blew kisses as we rolled out of the garage and into the falling snow. We lowered the bucket and plowed the lane as we went. Ike held the small tablet computer up and I watched the blue dot representing my uncle get closer. He hadn't stopped and was still moving toward us.

Ten minutes later, we found him. He was hobbling through the deep drifts of white precipitation. He shivered with no coat. His left hand was pressing tightly against his right shoulder, under it a large stain of crimson blood.

The three of us climbed down from the tractor to help him.

"Matt, your arm," Mr. Swigart exclaimed.

"It's fine for the moment. It looks worse than it is," my uncle explained.

We helped him up and into the toasty cab of the Cat tractor.

"What happened?" I asked. "Did you kill it?"

"Not kill, but banished," he said through chattering teeth.

"Give your uncle a moment," Mr. Swigart said as he turned the huge tractor back toward the inn.

My Aunt Mary greeted Uncle Matt with a big kiss and a warm blanket. Once inside, she began to dress his wound. His skin was dotted with thirteen small holes, each allowing blood to drain from his body. My aunt had to put a special putty-type salve over each one. I watched my uncle grimace several times through the procedure. After she was finished, my uncle changed and sat near a warm heater, covered by a blanket. Mrs. Swigart brought us all warm cocoa.

It felt weird, being here with these people. It didn't feel like we were in the middle of a hunt or that demons were lurking everywhere just off the property. Or that my dad was trapped hundreds if not thousands of feet underground. It felt like I was with family, and I supposed I was.

Uncle Matt explained that the wounds had come when the BlizzardSage threw a large icicle at him, but as it came within inches of his chest, a flaming arrow shattered it, sending smaller non-fatal splinters through the air.

Two Angels came to his aid and fought the BlizzardSage. They'd quickly dispatched it and after that they guided Uncle Matt up the road through the arctic wind. But they'd cleared the path by using a shower of flames to melt the snow. They'd only left when Uncle Matt reached the entrance to The Pink Hippo driveway.

Once the account was over, Mr. Swigart said that we needed to take the tractor and clear the car wreck. He doubted anyone would be traveling the road, but nonetheless the wreckage would be suspicious.

I had exactly four hours until I had to be at the boat.

I sat on the side of my bed dressed in my hunting gear. After I'd changed and prepared, my uncle recommended that I spend some time in prayer. I did, and my mind felt clear, my heart felt full, I was ready to end this hunt, to finish the HowlSage, to stop Albert, and to break the holds on Melanie, Jesse, and McGarrett.

I decided to take the stairs and made my way to the second library. The fireplace passage had already been opened, and the old lights were lit. I crept down the stone staircase to the waterway below. I knew the old monk would be there waiting for me; what I didn't know was where we were about to go.

Even this far beneath the inn, which I wasn't exactly sure how far that was, I could hear the loud ring of the clock tower bells. Twelve times they rang.

It was midnight, and I'd reached the beginning of the end.

Chapter Twenty-Six

October 31st—Halloween —Tuesday (Full Moon)

The back of the monk was to me as I stepped into the water chamber. His hood was over his head and I could hear him singing. I knew the song—an old hymn we'd sung in church called "How Great Thou Art."

I stood beside him while he sang.

He didn't greet me until he'd finished each verse and refrain. Listening to him soothed my nerves. I felt goose bumps on my arms, but it came from the energy of excitement, not fear or cold.

"Come, Taylor, it is time for us to end this evil," he

said, and waved his hand at the boat.

I stepped into the wooden vessel and it rocked ever so slightly. A weak smile crossed the monk's face, and then he turned toward the door and waved his hands.

The lights in the stairway went out. We were in darkness.

I could not see, but I heard and felt the monk step into the boat. A light appeared before me. The monk had lit an old, wrought-iron lantern. The small yellow flame provided enough light to see each other and cast an eerie flicker on the walls, increased by the reflective properties of the water. The monk sat facing me.

Where were we going? We were in a twelve by twelve by twelve cube, with no doors except the one we'd come through from the stairwell. The boat took up six feet of the length, leaving only three feet on either side.

"Grab the oars," the monk said. I watched as he lifted the looped end of a mooring rope from a hook on the landing.

I hadn't noticed them before, but the oars were attached to either side of the boat. I took the handles in each hand and straightened my back. I'd rowed many times on Coal Chase Lake before. This would be no different; I only hoped that we wouldn't have to go against the current. Of course, I wasn't sure we were going to go anywhere, besides bumping against a stone block wall.

The monk pointed to the wall behind him. "Row," the monk ordered kindly as he used his hand to push away from the dock.

"But sir, there's—" I started.

"Row," he said a bit more firmly. "You must have faith."

I shook my head and rolled my shoulders. The oars dug into the water and the boat moved forward.

An agonizing creak groaned from the wall before me, the sort an old person makes when they get up from their chair after sitting for a long time. The water foamed and bubbled as the wall began to lower into the water. An opening appeared and, as I rowed forward, we passed freely over the submerged wall.

"Faith and trust are very important, Taylor," the monk said.

The light from the lantern illuminated his face in such a way that it cast shadows on his old wrinkled features. He was far older than I'd realized.

"We will be rowing some time before we reach our destination. At times, the current will cause you to work hard, but it is making you stronger, and at others it will assist you as it is now. Your arms will become tired, but you mustn't give in to the temptation to quit. I will encourage you and counsel you along the way," the monk explained. "The current is like that of our Lord and the trials we face on Earth. Sometimes there are challenges that strengthen us and other times we feel as if everything is perfect. Both are times to seek and learn, for God is teaching us and guiding us, should we choose to listen."

I nodded my head. The words were good advice and I knew over the last twenty-nine days I'd failed to listen to God and what He was leading me to do. I'd been tempted, and instead of seeking counsel and wisdom, I gave in to my own selfish desires.

"If you listen and can find peace in your heart, our fight will be directed. Tonight will not end in favor of the evil one," the old monk continued. "But do not be discouraged, if you feel inadequate. Remember the story of David and Goliath. David was but a shepherd boy, and in the eyes of man he was put against someone far superior in battle. And the Scripture says in First Samuel seventeen verse thirty-three: 'And Saul said to David, Thou art not able to go against this Philistine to fight with him: for thou art but a youth, and he a man of war from his youth.' God had chosen David for that battle and later to lead His people. God has a plan for all of us."

The words were from the ultimate Sword. Over the last twenty-nine days, I'd failed to listen to God and what He was leading me to do. I thought about the cost of my neglect. Ike's capture, McGarrett, Jesse—could this have been avoided had I stuck to my task?

"Prepare to row hard. We must take the next left and it will be against the current," the monk warned. He held the lantern over the left side of the boat, his right, so that I could see the way.

Ten feet later and we reached the turn. I rowed each arm in opposite directions to turn the boat into the oncoming tide of water. The boat bucked as the first surges of water hit it.

"You must row!" the monk said.

I dug in. Each roll of my shoulders, each turn of my wrist, moved the boat only inches. Nothing like the three feet per stroke I'd been doing before.

This was tiring. The light was dim and I couldn't see how long I'd have to keep up the rowing.

My arms were growing sore. I couldn't do this. It was too hard. I was too weak. Sweat beads formed on my forehead and slid down the bridge of my nose.

"You are doing good," the monk encouraged. "Persistence."

It felt like an hour, but I knew it'd been only ten or so minutes, when the monk spoke again.

"Good work; turn right at the next junction. It's about nine feet away."

The rays from the lantern revealed the next split in the tunnel. Water rushed from one opening and the current I was in streamed down the other. I dug one oar in and back-paddled with the other. The boat turned quickly and the bow dipped. The boat started to slide and I couldn't row fast enough to assist.

Just a moment later the monk called out his next instructions.

"Turn right," he said, the lantern light revealed an oncoming split.

Again, as I made the hard maneuver I found myself hit with a strong current of water. It felt almost as though I was driving the boat uphill, but I couldn't tell for sure. The light from the lantern seemed to be showing more, but still it was hard to see how far it would be before the next turn.

My muscles had hardly had a reprieve and I was fighting again. They burned. Yes, I felt a chill on my chest. The moisture from the sweat was cold against my skin.

"Keep going," the monk encouraged. "Do not give in to the pain of your arms, the weakness of your earthly body. You must seek a higher strength. The battle we fight is not only physical, but mental, and more than anything, spiritual." He held the lantern out for me to see. "We are nearly there."

But ahead of me I could only see a flat wall. The tunnel turned into a "T" and it was time to choose. I noticed I'd either be continuing against the flow, or with. I hoped I'd be going with.

The monk pointed and I sighed with relief. "Turn left."

The water picked up and carried the boat again. I lifted the oars out of the water and we cruised down the tunnel. "God provides exactly what we need and He will never give us more than we can handle. It is written, 'There hath no temptation taken you but such as is common to man: but God is faithful, who will not suffer you to be tempted above that ye are able; but will with the temptation also make a way to escape, that ye may be able to bear it,'" the monk quoted.

But my rest was short-lived as the monk pointed to the left. "The turn must be made quickly; the turn is tight. We mustn't get sucked down the other tunnel by the current."

My aching arms reminded me of the strain from the last upstream paddle. If I was lax in the turning, the current would take us, but was that such a bad thing? The current would carry us and extend my rest. My arms were so tired. The monk would never know that I'd let us be taken; it would be easy for him to believe that I had just underestimated.

No! What was I thinking? I would know. What had the monk just quoted from the Bible?

There hath no temptation taken you but such as is common to man: but God is faithful, who will not suffer you to be tempted above that ye are able; but will with the temptation also make a way to escape, that ye may be able to bear it.

This was a temptation—to give in to weakness, but further to be dishonest in order to give my earthly body rest. I could not give in—I had to fight.

The monk clutched the lantern and cleared his throat. "'But Jesus beheld them, and said unto them, With men this is impossible; but with God all things are possible.' It is through Christ that you stand against temptation, Taylor! He will strengthen you."

I made the turn and again felt the current pressing against the boat. My muscles burned and the force of the water seemed stronger than it'd ever been.

I cried out, "Lord, give me the strength!" My words sounded hollow in the narrow waterway.

The monk looked at me with a firm smile. "Good, Taylor, keep rowing. This is not impossible. You have chosen wisely; you did not take the easy way out."

Did he know that I'd thought of letting us slide down the other waterway? He couldn't.

I grunted. Where were we even going? I wanted to be done, to give up. But I knew I couldn't, I had to resist this time. This time? The thought came into my mind and I realized that I'd given in to temptation before.

"Lord, I need Your forgiveness; I shirked my duties the day I went with Melanie. I know now that she was misleading me, that she was using her beauty to distract me from what needed to be done." I realized then that I was praying aloud…screaming it, in fact.

"Do you know the story of Samson?" the monk asked.

I nodded, sending droplets of sweat flying.

"Samson was tempted by a beautiful woman; her name was Delilah. He ended up giving away the secret to his strength and she used it against him. He was captured and broken by the Philistines. But when Samson called on the strength of God, he was still able to complete what God had planned for him, even though he'd messed everything up along the way."

The monk lifted the lantern. "Right turn."

I followed the command and felt the relief of the current taking over. The boat slid through the water and I allowed my arms to rest. It seemed to last longer than before. I noticed that I could see more of the monk's features as he sat across from me. I could also see further down the tunnel ahead of us. The light in the lantern had grown brighter.

The water was shallow around us and green in color, and I could see the bottom of the tunnel. We were coasting along slowly now.

The monk began to sing; his choice: "In the Garden." His voice echoed around us, sounding as though many were singing with him. The light reflecting off the water and its flicker provided a surreal setting for the song.

An odd feeling of strength came over me, a shiver of excitement and anticipation.

As he finished the song, the lantern light revealed another split in the tunnel. I knew we'd be heading against the current. I prayed for strength.

The lantern light grew brighter and, as I made the turn, I could see that this tunnel was longer than any I'd gone through before.

I rowed, propelling the boat forward, but the resistance was strong. At the pace we were going, it'd take an hour to get to the end, and I didn't think I had the strength to last that long. The sweat was running down my cheeks and my armpits were soaked. Was this ever going to end?

Then the monk caught me off guard; he began to sing. But the songs were from my childhood, from Sunday school. He started with "The Lord's Army" and ended with "This Little Light of Mine." And as he finished, on the final line the lantern seemed to brighten and he pointed toward the oncoming wall. "Turn right."

The turn came quick and the lantern's light hit the entire tunnel ahead. It was long, but the current was with me and it was picking up speed. We were cruising along and the monk began to sing again, this time, "Come Thou Fount."

Although this was the longest tunnel we'd be in, it hardly took the entire song to navigate. As we neared the end of the tunnel, I wondered when the boat trip would end. It seemed we should be getting somewhere, and while I wasn't as worried about whether I could continue, I was feeling confident—not overly, but prepared for the fight ahead. My adrenaline was pumping and I was ready to dispatch the HowlSage, confront the jinn, and even go head-to-head with the gray mist.

"Turn right," the monk said.

The bow of the boat was breached by a strong surge of water. We were headed into the current again; the lantern light seemed to dim and then extinguish. I was fighting the current with every stroke of my arms. My muscles burned, but worse than before. The monk said nothing, and I could no longer see his face. I suddenly felt the boat begin to slip backward. I had to row harder.

"Lord, give me the strength!" I cried. I dug deeper, the oars rotated— into the water, out of the water, in again.

Then for some reason I just let go. The boat began to slide backward. "Please, Lord!" I called. "I need Your strength."

A surge of air blasted me in the back, pressing me forward. The entire boat moved forward. I grabbed the oars and dug in. The boat began to move, I...no, *we* were beating the current.

Still the monk had not spoken, but the lantern was again lit, and the flame growing brighter every moment. Soon I could see the end of the tunnel.

It was near.

Twenty feet...

Fifteen feet...

Ten feet...

Five feet...

"Left," the monk said, and a smile flickered across his face. As we turned, we came into a small chamber. A gurgling in the water behind me caused me to look back. A stone wall was emerging from beneath the water. Growing higher and higher, soon it reached the ceiling and the wall stopped.

I looked around. It couldn't be.

We were in the exact chamber we'd started in. The old monk took the rope from the bottom of the boat and looped it back around the mooring hook.

The old monk stepped from the boat and offered his hand for me to join him. "You are ready."

"But where are we?" I asked. "Are we back at the beginning?"

The monk shook his head, "No, no, my dear boy. You are far from where you were when we began."

I wanted to clarify, but then I understood. This was never about going somewhere to meet the HowlSage. This was a test not only of my physical strength, but that of my strength in Christ. All of it was to prepare me for what I would face. I knew it without the old man telling me.

He touched a small switch and the staircase lit up. I followed him up in silence, and when we were back in the library, he spoke. "Rest, my boy. For at dusk you defeat the HowlSage."

I nodded and left the library for my room.

I woke to Ike's shaking. His hands were on my shoulder.

"Taylor, get up," he said. "It's time to go. It's only an hour before dusk."

I rolled to my side and looked at my alarm clock—4:20 p.m. My arms ached and my eyes were so heavy. What had I done last night, or this morning? I knew I'd rowed in the dark, but why had I done that?

Most athletes I knew didn't work that hard the night—I mean—the morning of their competition. But I'd been put through the most intense workout I'd ever endured. I tried to sit up, but my abs felt like they'd been ripped out of my body.

Ike reached out his arms and pulled me up, which I groaned through. Then I tried moving my legs to the edge of the bed. I'd never realized how much rowing utilizes your entire body.

I finally got into a sitting position on the side of the bed. Ike reached for my night stand and handed me a cup of something. It was thick and from what I could tell in the light of the setting sun, green.

"Drink this," he said. "It's from the old monk."

I started to move it toward my mouth, but Ike stopped me.

"I'd hold your nose. It's a bit strong," he explained.

"What is it?"

"Not real sure. I wanted to test it, but the monk wouldn't let me. He said it was just what you needed for tonight."

I sighed. "Bottoms up!" Plugging my nose with my free hand, I drained the green, grainy liquid into my mouth. It scratched its way down my entire throat and I was pretty sure I could literally feel it land in my stomach.

I sputtered and then swallowed hard. "Wow."

For a moment, I thought I might barf it all back up. My stomach seemed to turn over and the room seemed to swirl just ever so slightly.

Then I had clarity. My vision cleared, my stomach mellowed, and I suddenly realized the aching in my legs, arms, and abs...was gone.

"*Whoa!*" I shouted. I jumped to my feet and stretched out my arms. They moved quickly in several jabs, like a shadow boxer. I kicked my legs up, finding a flexibility I didn't know was there.

Ike stood and watched me, his mouth open. He was as surprised as myself. "Wow, what was in that stuff?"

"No idea, but I feel good."

"Excellent, because they want you downstairs at 4:30. That's just six minutes from now." Ike sat on the edge of my bed. "There's one more thing I need to give you."

"Please don't let it be some sort of equally nasty bread or sandwich," I joked.

Ike reached into a pack he'd brought with him. I hadn't noticed it before.

"It's this," he said as he lifted a small, metal, insect-shaped thing toward me.

"It looks like a spider," I said.

"That's exactly what it is," he explained happily.

"Uh, what does it do?"

"It's an arachnadroid," he said.

"A what?"

"I'm still working on the name." Ike shrugged. "It's a camera bot. You can use it to check something out without getting into a risky position. For instance, this can fit into narrow holes or climb up walls for you."

"How do I—?" I started.

"It's all controlled from your web phone. Watch."

Ike grabbed my phone from my night stand and started tapping. He set the small silver arachnid onto the ground. I watched as he slid his finger across the phone's screen. The little spider bot began to move.

"And look, you can see through its eyes here." Ike held the phone up so I could see.

On the screen was a live video from the cameras embedded in the arachnadroid's eyes.

"Wow," I said.

Ike scooped it up and placed it back in the pack. "We'd better go now."

I dressed quickly and the two of us made our way down the elevator.

The lobby was cramped. Apparently, The Gathering had grown even greater. Somehow, more people had made it up the mountain road, despite the heavy snow fall. I soon found out that Chief Rutledge had had some fun using the Diesel and clearing the entire stretch of road.

As I walked through, Mr. Frigg stopped me. This was the first time I'd really ever talked to him.

"Taylor and Ike, we want to pray for you," he said.

The Gathering bowed their heads, and over the next ten minutes they prayed fervently for our safety and our strength. I knew most did not understand that I would be facing a demon that'd taken physical form in combat tonight. Most just believed that our town and the youth of our nation were on a troubled path, and that we needed their prayers.

It was true. As I'd mentioned before about the church service and my peers' activities during, we were in trouble. Most of us had closed our ears to the Truth, and if we didn't reconnect soon, the battle would only get more difficult.

Mr. Frigg closed the prayer and sent us on our way.

Once in the workshop, we found my aunt and uncle and Ike's parents huddled together. Their heads were bowed and their eyes closed. They looked up as the door latch clicked shut.

"Boys, just in time," my uncle said. "Now, the orders are simple. Taylor—"

"Where is the monk?" I asked.

My uncle looked only slightly annoyed that I'd interrupted.

"He's gone," Mr. Swigart said. "But he told us that your training this morning went well and that you passed."

I nodded. "He told me the same. But I don't understand. Is he not going to help me?"

"There is no need," Mrs. Swigart said. "You are ready."

I rubbed my chin. I wanted to be confused, to be worried. But I wasn't. The monk had said I was ready. The question was, did I believe I was?

"As I was saying," my uncle began. "Taylor will enter through the canning factory."

Mr. Swigart tapped the computer screen before him and the large wall screen displayed a map of Ashley Meadows, but centered on the factory.

"He will travel through the drain," Uncle Matt explained.

Another tap on the screen and the old drainage tunnel was highlighted.

"Once he reaches the mines, he will proceed to the chamber," my uncle said, then he turned to me. "Taylor, you must wait until you see the sarcophagus being opened, but do not delay. The HowlSage and the jinn will begin their rituals and the gray mist will be called. Once it comes, it will be too late and we would risk the BloodSage being awakened."

"What do I do when the sarcophagus is opened?" I asked.

"The HowlSage will be the one to open it. The moment it lifts the lid, it will be frozen in place for a few minutes," Mr. Swigart explained. "It's a defensive effect of the coffin on the one who breaches it."

"A few minutes, like three?" I asked.

"It's hard to say for sure," Mr. Swigart added.

"The jinn will be carrying the amulets to the sarcophagus. He will be weighed down by them, as he must wear them and lay into the sarcophagus. This is the moment you need. You must strike the HowlSage through the heart with your sword, and then you must ensure the lid of the sarcophagus closes with the jinn and amulets inside."

"You mean Albert?" I asked.

"Yes, but we do not give the jinn name recognition. It only strengthens their appearance as a human," Aunt Mary explained. "This is not a boy; it's a demon."

"What if the gray mist comes?" Ike asked.

I looked at him with a frown. I didn't want to be reminded of any additional complications that might arise.

"Well, if the gray mist comes, Taylor will be using the canisters you invented," Mr. Swigart said.

Ike looked surprised, "But I haven't worked on those for several days. They aren't finished."

"Son, don't worry," Mr. Swigart began. "McGarrett worked on them and I've further tweaked them," Mr. Swigart finished. "Do you know how to use the glove?"

I nodded, "Ike showed me a while back."

Ike was clearly proud at the praise from his father. But who wouldn't be? I hoped I'd have a dad again soon.

"Now, once you've locked the jinn in, we will come to assist you. There is no way for the jinn to escape from the sarcophagus on his own," my uncle said.

I nodded. It all seemed on the up and up. And if I had a moment where the HowlSage could not move, and where the jinn wasn't in a position to fight or escape, it seemed I couldn't lose.

But if it was all this easy, than why the intensive training last night?

"Are you ready, Taylor?" my uncle asked.

"Yes, as ready as I can be."

"Then let's get you suited up," Mr. Swigart said. "You won't be flying tonight."

"Why not?" I asked.

Uncle Matt sighed and looked at the large screen on the wall. The map still showed the drainage tunnel leading to the mine. "Because another Raptoryx has been called, but this one is older and larger."

I swallowed the lump in my throat. "Fair enough; the car it is."

"We weren't going to tell you yet, because there was no reason to worry about it. Your fight will take place in the tunnels where the Raptoryx has no effect on you," my uncle said.

"Another fight for another day," Ike said with a smile.

Mr. Swigart looked at his son un-amused, my uncle shook his head, and I laughed.

I geared up and went to the car. Mr. Swigart was driving, Ike next to him in the passenger seat—our on-demand tech support, if you will. My uncle and I were in the back.

"Taylor, I want to come with you," my uncle explained.

"But you can't, Matt, and you know it," Mr. Swigart said firmly. "Your shoulder injury would only make you a liability."

My uncle grunted. "But Taylor hasn't—" he started.

"The monk said he was ready," Mr. Swigart retorted.

"I know but—" my uncle tried again.

"And we must listen," Mr. Swigart finished.

I looked at my uncle sitting next to me, his arm in a sling. "I'll be fine. I am ready."

He nodded but didn't say anything.

The sides of the roads were piled high with snow from the chief's work. So much had fallen last night at the arrival of the BlizzardSage that the autumn sun could not melt it away during the daylight hours.

When we pulled into the parking lot of the canning factory, I didn't feel nervous as I had the times I'd come before. I was ready for whatever was inside, and the good thing was that I had a pretty good idea of what that was.

The factory was quiet and empty. Almost too quiet and too empty. But

I would leave well enough alone. I found the old drain and climbed in. Using my night vision goggles, I quickly traversed the old drain. I passed under the shaft that Ike had been held in. The sides of the drain were blackened, and I knew this was where the gray mist had ambushed Jesse and McGarrett. It was the last time Mr. Riley had been conscious.

I continued toward my destination. A right turn here, a left here. We had a pretty good idea of where the chamber was. It'd been marked; we only hoped that the jinn had chosen to use it again.

A soft orange light flickered on the side of the mine tunnel walls. I knew that we'd chosen correctly.

A male voice resounded quietly, chanting something. Over and over again it spoke. I knew the ceremony had begun.

I crept closer and then deployed the small spider-looking robot Ike had given me. I moved it up the wall and sent it toward the chamber that was just out of sight. I watched through the screen as it neared. The video was a bit jerky, but good enough that I could see.

The chamber came into the visual range of the arachnadroid. The room was lit with hundreds of burning candles. In the center was the large sarcophagus, black smooth stones surrounded it in a wide circle. Someone in a black cloak was working at a table at the far side of the chamber. Its back was to me, but I knew it was Albert—I mean, the jinn.

The HowlSage entered from one of the other mine tunnels. It ducked until it came into the chamber. It was nearly fifteen feet tall and fierce as ever. Foam covered its muzzle and its tongue licked back and forth across both of its blackened lips. It was infectious now—the full moon had brought its venom to potency.

The beast moved across the room in a few long strides. It stood near the sarcophagus, waiting.

I knew what it waited for.

It was almost time.

My sword slid from its sheath in near silence and I watched for the jinn to move to the coffin that awaited it. I remembered what Uncle

Matt and Mr. Swigart had said.

I would have just a few moments and I had to strike the HowlSage quickly while ensuring the jinn became entombed in the sarcophagus. I zoomed the spider's camera on the jinn. It was working slowly, methodically, still chanting.

A grunt came from the HowlSage; it seemed to be getting impatient. To my surprise, the jinn raised its hand—a streak of lighting zipped from it and I heard the HowlSage squeal in pain.

Truly, the jinn was in control. A human might not have the power to bend a demon to its will, but clearly another demon did.

The next moment, the jinn slipped off its cloak. It wore nothing beneath the garment.

Albert slid the amulets onto his body. First the locket. Then the bracelets. The rings and the belt, followed by the dagger. Next the anklets and the crown. I watched him lift a heart-looking amulet into the air, then bring it down swift and hard to his chest. I reminded myself that this was not a human despite its physical appearance. It was a jinn, a demon. But it was still hard when your eyes saw differently, and Albert's self-inflicting action made me grimace uncomfortably. The demon shook violently for a moment and then stopped. It fitted the breastplate over its chest and then, finally, it took the scepter in its hand.

Turning toward me, it started for the sarcophagus. It was odd to see Albert wearing all of the amulets as if he were a king, but I knew that even he was a servant, not only to the BloodSage, but to the evil one himself. Before the jinn entered the circle it raised the scepter high in its hand and cried out in a tongue I didn't understand.

The moment Albert stepped across the stone line, all of his human features disappeared. I suddenly saw him for what he was—a demon. While the jinn had appeared as a boy at other times, it was clearly not now. Its skin was a sickening gray. A long, narrow, reptilian tail twitched back and forth, a small set of two spikes on the end. It looked like a grotesque, mummified serpent on two legs. A forked tongue slid in and out of its mouth and its nose was flat and round. Long, yellowed claws adorned each finger and toe. This was evil, not a boy.

Albert walked toward the sarcophagus and looked up at the HowlSage, but instead of telling it to open the lid, it jammed the scepter into the fifteen-foot-tall creature's side. The HowlSage roared in anger, but immediately obeyed.

Its large clawed hands gripped the edge of the lid.

This was the moment. It was time. I prepared to dash in and strike. Shock and awe, baby!

The lid started to lift open.

Thirty degrees…

Sixty degrees…

Ninety degrees…

A blinding flash of red lit the chamber. An agonizing scream erupted from the sarcophagus. It didn't stop.

I saw that the HowlSage was pure gray, like stone. This was it. The jinn had moved to the sarcophagus and began to lower himself inside.

I began to run. My sword was out at my side, facing forward. The jinn's body disappeared beneath the side of the sarcophagus just as I broke into the chamber. I closed on the HowlSage.

Propelling myself into the air, I extended my sword at the now-frozen beast. I reached my free hand for the sarcophagus lid. I looked down and saw the jinn lying on top of mummified remains inside, blue chords of electricity were sizzling across the two bodies.

The tip of my sword touched the HowlSage's furry chest. My other hand grasped the lid and pushed it down. The heavy lid lowered quickly and I saw the jinn's reaction on its face as it recognized me. I had foiled its plan and there was nothing it could do.

The lid slammed shut, but then I realized my sword was still free. It wasn't lodged in the flesh of the HowlSage. I looked toward where the creature's head was supposed to be, but it was gone. I landed on my feet and looked for the beast.

My eyes found it. It stood only a few yards away, snarling, foam and potent saliva dribbling from its jaws.

"*Arrrooohhh!*" it screamed, then launched itself at me.

I dived and rolled to get clear. I attempted to swipe with my sword, but only by driving the sword directly into its heart could I defeat it.

I turned just in time to see it make its next pass. This time it was on all fours and it barreled at me like a ravenous wolf—which, for appearance's sake, was exactly what it was.

I slipped out of its way and it slammed head-first into the far wall of the chamber. Several loose stones fell from the ceiling and bounced off the sarcophagus and nearby table, knocking at least a dozen candles to the ground. Most went out, but one found Albert's cloak. The garment burst into flames, but didn't deteriorate.

I heard the HowlSage snarl again. I held my sword before me as it leapt into the air. I thrust my sword at it, but the beast twisted in mid-air and landed near the sarcophagus. It looked at me and gave its version of a smile. Then it grabbed the coffin, tucked it under one arm, and on all fours scrambled into one of the mine tunnels.

Shock thundered through my brain. This wasn't how things were supposed to go. I had no choice but to follow.

As I ran, I wondered if the gray mist would appear. After all, the jinn had gotten into the sarcophagus with all the amulets, and the HowlSage was still alive.

The air around me became cold; I remembered that this often happened when the gray mist appeared, but also that the mines were simply cold, and I had just left a room with a hundred candles burning and producing heat. But to be safe, I took one of Ike's canisters and threw it behind me. I did not put on the glove used to control the purple smoke, but instead let it fill the tunnel behind me. I only hoped I would not have to go back that way. I knew what the purple stuff did to clothing and I didn't want to end up naked if Ike's dad hadn't actually fixed that issue.

I could hear the HowlSage ahead, but I knew it was pulling away from me. It was bigger and faster than when I'd seen it last. Another of Ike's inventions crossed my mind. The blood bombs—I only hoped that the HowlSage would smell it from this distance and still be interested.

But what did I have to lose? I pulled one from the pack on my belt. I hurdled it as far down the tunnel ahead of me as I could. Just a few seconds later I crossed over it—I ran right through the red puddle.

I couldn't hear the HowlSage any longer. No sound of its footfalls, no wheezing, no growling. I'd failed. I continued to run, but I wasn't sure why.

Roar!

I tried to stop, but my body slammed into the down and charging shoulder of the HowlSage. It'd come back. The blood bombs had worked.

I bounced off the beast and my right shoulder hit the nearby cave wall. A yell ripped from my mouth. The HowlSage tumbled forward into a somersault; the sarcophagus was nowhere in sight.

I clambered to my feet and took off down the tunnel. Had the demon been so dumb as to leave the coffin behind? Maybe its bestial desires had taken over.

I charged forward through the mine.

The angry call of the HowlSage behind me told me it'd discovered the ruse.

I'd not gone that far, so I only had a minute at most before it'd catch me. But that minute was all I needed. I came to the end of the tunnel and saw something that incited both anger and hope. I was at the edge of the Etherpit.

A frigid wind rose out from the gaping mouth of the hole. The void wasn't just black, it was empty, the absence of anything.

This is where I'd planned on coming later. This was where I would descend and free my dad.

Another cry from the HowlSage, louder this time, told me the beast was closing on my position.

I saw the sarcophagus sitting next to the Etherpit. Why was it there?

The furry, wolf-like demon burst into view. It instantly leapt at me and I raised my sword to meet it. It flew over me, but its chest was exposed. I jumped up and rammed my sword into the beast's chest.

It was dead before it hit the ground. Its limp body landed just on the other side of me, rolling to the edge of the pit. Its arm twitched, bumping the sarcophagus. The coffin teetered and began to slide toward the pit.

"No!" I screamed aloud and dashed to stop it. The tips of my fingers brushed against it just as gravity took hold.

It was too late and I stood helpless as the sarcophagus, jinn inside, disappeared into the darkness of the Etherpit.

My knees felt weak and I dropped to the ground. I bent over on all fours. I'd lost the jinn and the BloodSage's body. What would happen now?

The air became freezing cold and a blast of air hit me like a ton of bricks. I rolled to my side. I watched as a cloud of gray mist rushed down the tunnel and then flew into the Etherpit like it was being sucked through a vacuum.

I let out a deep breath. I had no idea what would happen now. I turned around and saw the oversized wolf body of the HowlSage. It was dead, but it was not yet banished. I knew what I had to do as I pulled my mom's cross from my pocket. This would finally send the magician of the moon, as it was also called, back to the underworld.

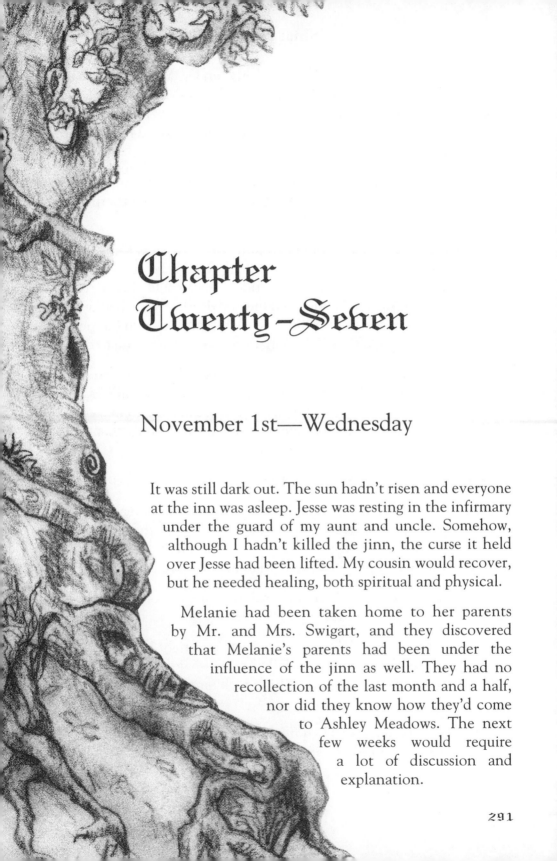

Chapter Twenty-Seven

November 1st—Wednesday

It was still dark out. The sun hadn't risen and everyone at the inn was asleep. Jesse was resting in the infirmary under the guard of my aunt and uncle. Somehow, although I hadn't killed the jinn, the curse it held over Jesse had been lifted. My cousin would recover, but he needed healing, both spiritual and physical.

Melanie had been taken home to her parents by Mr. and Mrs. Swigart, and they discovered that Melanie's parents had been under the influence of the jinn as well. They had no recollection of the last month and a half, nor did they know how they'd come to Ashley Meadows. The next few weeks would require a lot of discussion and explanation.

McGarrett was awake and recovering under Mrs. Riley's careful nursing. I snuck in and saw him. He was asleep, as was Mrs. Riley. But I took his hand and told him what I was about to do. I knew if he was awake he might try to stop me; I'd realized that he loved me as a father would love his son.

Everyone was back with their loved ones—everyone but me. But I was about to change that. Now that I knew exactly where the Etherpit was; I could start my journey immediately.

In my room I tossed an extra black shirt into my pack. I was going to head into the pit. No hunter had ever attempted this before. I'd believed that the Etherpit was a portal of sorts, not one we could choose to enter and exit at will. Only God controlled life and death. Albert had revealed a chamber at the bottom of this pit, one that was still within our physical world, one that I could get to. And that was what I was going to do.

My heart felt hopeful now. I knew that God would provide the support needed to fight the host of hell and his minion army. Not all was lost. It was true that demons were everywhere, lurking, waiting to make us slip up, to take advantage of our weaknesses. I'd always known that, but I'd been neglectful. I hadn't been living in Truth.

Not anymore.

I'd gathered all of my gear in secret and I was nearly ready. I wasn't abandoning my post; instead I was taking the battle to the enemy. They would not be expecting me, and I hoped that I could find my dad and free him. Together we would be stronger than myself alone.

No matter what I'd find and face below, the emotional drive to find my dad would be all I needed.

I snuck through the lobby, glancing left and right. The inn looked normal; you'd never guess that a daily war was being fought from here, that this old building housed a high-tech group of demon-hunting Christians.

The large entry doors of The Pink Hippo creaked as I exited. The next time I crossed that threshold, it would be with my dad, I was sure of it.

I walked across the rotunda and stood near the fountain. I knew where one of Ike's secret cameras was. He deserved more than just a note.

I looked directly into the largest hippo's right eye. "Ike, I know you're going to be upset that I left without saying goodbye in person. But honestly," I paused and took a breath. "I know you'd want to come with and I'm afraid I wouldn't have the willpower to turn you down. But this journey is going to be dangerous, and I could never ask anyone to join me. You have been the best friend anyone could have."

"Ditto," said a voice behind me.

I turned to see Ike standing there. He was dressed in black and had a jet pack strapped to his back.

"Ike? What are you doing?" I asked.

"I'm coming with you," was his simple reply.

Ike's

Visual Guide to Demons

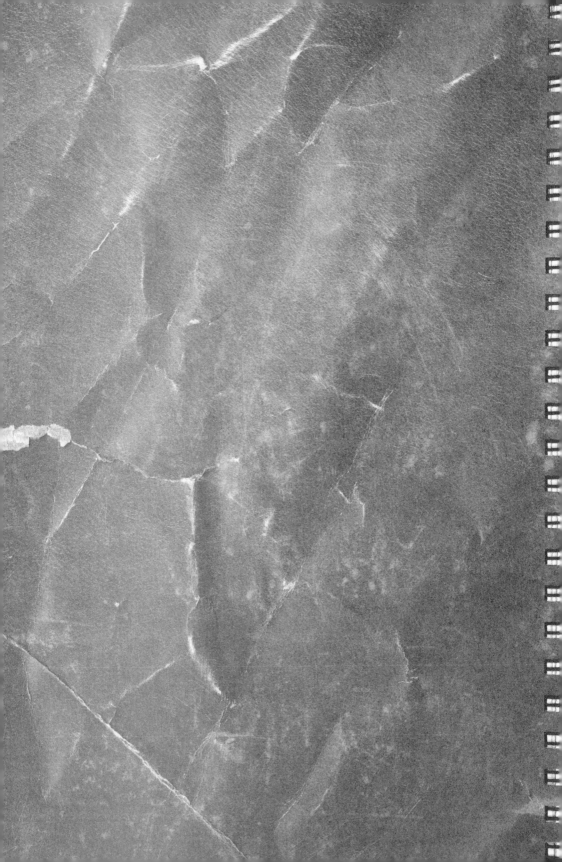

Levels of Demons —
1. Masterum
2. Supremus
3. Magnum
4. Quantus
5. Regulus
6. Minor
7. Microus

BASED ON

Strength, Magic, strategy and deceit.

There are seven levels of demons. Level refers to a combination of strength, magic, strategy, and deceit. Masterum is the highest level, but no Masterum level demon has entered into the World for nearly two thousand years. The Supremus is also rare, they do not need EtherPits in order to pass into the World. These type of demon are usually strategist but are known for infighting amongst themselves. Magnum level demons are more common and rely heavily on brute strength, but can also play a powerful game of deception. These types of demons must pass through an EtherPit to enter our world, and their presence rarely goes undetected. Quantus are far more common and while they must too pass through EtherPits are much harder to detect. Once through Quantus demons can multiply within our World, their strength usually lies in numbers and they are not known for brute or mental strength. Regulus demons are very common, and can make themselves look like humans or other beasts. Known to cause general havoc such as accidents and dangers for humans, they also use deception to trick humans into doing the Regulus demon's bidding. Minor demons are often summoned by humans delving into the magic arts. While humans can summon Regulus demons, they more often summon Minor demons and because those demons quickly can take control of a human's heart and mind, the magician progresses no further. Microus demons are the smallest and least powerful, often felt simply as bad thoughts and small accidents. Microus demons are very common and are a continued pest against human's moral choices.

ETHERPIT
Gateway to the Underworld

An EtherPit is a gateway from the underworld and often appears deep in a cavern or mine. EtherPits provided entry for demons into our world. When unguarded demons of any level can slip into our world and begin to spread evil. Not all EtherPits have been discovered and new ones can open at any time. Man can not enter through the EtherPit, for only God controls life and death.

BLOODSAGE

The BloodSage is a Supremus level demon. It is perceived as royalty within the demon world. They are strategists of the underworld, seeking to create vast armies of minor demons, they fight amongst themselves to create huge territories from which they can feed and siphon strength from human sin. Often believed to be the most dangerous demon faced this side of an EtherPit. They were the foulest of demons; BloodSages were one of the reason for all the secrecy of the society. So many wars had been started because of man's insatiable desire for power. Hitler's SS had been set on creating an army of demons, and they'd succeeded so many times, had the society not been in place to defeat them, the world may be a different place today. Blood-Sages are the template for the modern day fictional Vampire. These demons are far more powerful than most others, and they don't just come into existence—they are summoned into existence by a human through incantations. The BloodSage is rare, many factors have to line up perfectly for them to be brought into existence.

Template for the modern day fictional vampire.

turn Page for More →

More info. on the BloodSage

In accordance with the summoning for a BloodSage, a human must begin to prepare the potions on the 13th of Friday for delivery on the month's 31st day and Full Moon. Usually this means a HowlSage will also be involved as they appear anytime the 31st day of a month falls on the Full Moon. Many things are needed in the summoning. A human must create a series of amulets, that include a crown, a locket, a breastplate, a heart, two bracelets, a dagger, a scepter, two rings, a belt, and two anklets. The amulets must all be adorned with rubies, diamonds, and opals and set in pure silver. These are placed on the body of a former sage which has often been mummified. Rituals are performed over each amulet to give strength to the mummified remains, while the spirit of the BloodSage is summoned. They are then presented to the BloodSages' steed often from the center of a circle of stones. The steed is known as a Raptoryx. The BloodSage is known to travel on or commands the Raptoryx to attack. Because HowlSages appear during the same time a BloodSage can be summoned, they are often used by the human undertaking the summoning as a servant to provide the magic needed to summon the spirit of the BloodSage.

Amulets needed to summon the BloodSage.

1. A Crown
2. A Locket
3. Breastplate
4. Heart
5. 2 Bracelets
6. Dagger
7. Scepter
8. 2 Rings
9. Belt
10. 2 Anklets

BloodSage

Raptoryx companion to BloodSage.

HOWLSAGE

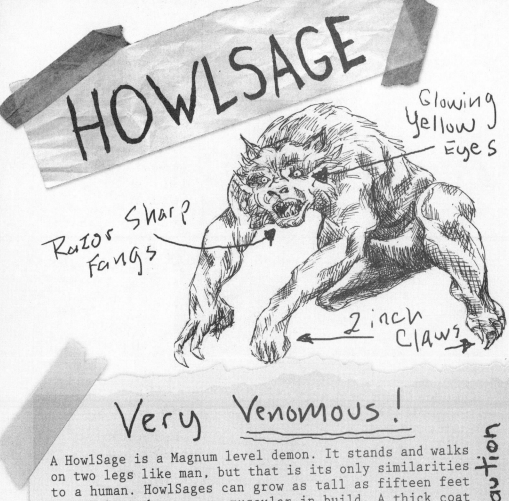

Glowing Yellow Eyes

Razor Sharp Fangs

2 inch Claws

Very Venomous!

A HowlSage is a Magnum level demon. It stands and walks on two legs like man, but that is its only similarities to a human. HowlSages can grow as tall as fifteen feet in height and are very muscular in build. A thick coat of brown, gray, or black fur covers its entire body, but thins on its chest, replaced with leathery skin and a visible set of abs. Its muzzle is somewhat pointed, housing two sets of razor sharp fangs. Its ears also come to sharp points, looking more like cat ears than dog. It also has a small bobbed looking tail. The HowlSage's eyes glow of their own accord, like two yellow bulbs. Nearly two inch claws on its feet and hands are its primary weapons; its fangs were reserved for conversion through the injection of venom. The HowlSage hungers for the flesh of men, but not as dinner. Instead his bite inserts a potent venom, that fills man's heart and mind with hate. This weakens their defense toward the smaller demons seeking to cause man to sin. Its tactical purpose is to act as a landing party and General to a battalion of demons. The creature comes through the EtherPit and fills the role of the strongman, guarding the EtherPit and allowing demons of lower levels to come through safely. more →

Use Extreme Caution

How to kill a HowlSage

HowlSages are incarnated anytime a full moon falls on the 31st day of a month. The key to killing the HowlSage is to get it in the first night or at the very least the first week. It reaches its full strength and its venom becomes potent when the moon becomes full again 27 days after its birth, on the 31st of that month. Only by driving a sword made of silver directly through the HowlSage's 'heart' could it be dispatched. HowlSages were different from the horror film werewolves, they couldn't be killed by a so-called silver bullet. Werewolves were fake, their creation based on peasant sightings dating back to medieval times. The Society had gone to great lengths to ensure their reality remained as a myth wrapped behind the mask of the werewolf. If just anyone knew that these demonic sages existed, they may try and control them, use them for their own sinful plans. The greatest example of this happening was during world war two with Hitler's SS. They were deep into demonic control, and they had thousands of Sages in their service. The modern day depiction of a 'werewolf' has incorrectly made the beast into a being that can portray not only human characteristics but also be a hero, this is simply not possible. The HowlSages' magic is also necessary for the summoning of the BloodSage.

HowlSage

A silver sword directly through the heart.

Exhale's breath of frozen air →

BLIZZARDSAGE

A BlizzardSage is a Magnum level demon, often sent into a battlefield to provide might for an invading demonic force. The BlizzardSage is gargantuan in size, the tallest measuring forty-five feet in height, and twenty feed wide. Most are closer to thirty feet tall. A BlizzardSage's coat of stringy shaggy fur is white and gray, the perfect camoflauge for the Blizzardish weather the BlizzardSage's presence creates. Its face, stomach, pupiless eyes, and ape-like hands are black. The BlizzardSage has razorsharp fangs, and its face is similar to that of a gorilla. BlizzardSages have a range of weapons at their disposal, aside from the artic temperatures and pelting snow their Blizzard spells bring, they can exhlae a breath of frozen air, instantly freezing anything in its path. They can also create man size icicles or boulder size snowballs to hurl at their enemies. The only thing a Blizzard-Sage immediately fears is fire. Even a flame the size of a human's thumb is enough to give the demon pause.

To defeat a Blizzard Sage any size flame will do.

Watch out for:
Man size icicles and
Boulder size snowballs!

SWAMPSAGE

DO NOT Chop off Head

This will produce another SwampSage!

SwampSage are Quantus level demons. SwampSages are common and can be summoned from nearly any lake, creek, or swamp in the world. While not very intelligent or strong, they are formidable in numbers. They're similar in body type and size of the average human and walk upright as well. Their scaly skin is green and earthy in look and they can be mistaken for a swimming alligator if seen underwater. They have long reptilian tongs and sharp yellowed claws. The creatures primary weapon is a burst of murky acidic water they launch from their hands. They often also carried staffs made from driftwood and vines. When battling a SwampSage the hunter must be very careful not to sever the head, this will only produce another SwampSage within moments. The only way to dispatch a SwampSage is to land pure rock salt in either an exposed wound or the demons eyes or mouth. In battle hunters are generally armed with salt packs and a sword. Once a limb is severed or a cut made on the SwampSage the salt is tossed in the wound, causing an eruption of green flames and the disintegration of the demon.

Watch Out! For Quick-sand

Electricity

↑ The most effective weapon against the ↘

SANDSAGE

SandSages are Quantus level demons. SandSages take on many forms, sometimes appearing in the image of a man, however still made of sand. Sometimes they come as a sand-storm on the horizon and sweep against their attacker in a suffocating covering of sand and dust. Sometimes the demon moves through the desert sand dunes like a shark in water. It is often also difficult to determine how many SandSages a hunter is up against, when in storm form, there may be hundreds. The SandSage's best weapon is decep-tion sometimes in the form of a mirage, and sometimes physically like quicksand. SandSage's also use their stormy form to suffocate or bury an adversary. Defeating the SandSage depends entirely on the form which it is cur-rently in. Water can be used against most forms, but alone this often just disperses the demon temporarily. The most effective weapon developed thus far to fight the SandSage has been a concentrated burst of electricty, which crys-talizes the sand into glass, which can then be shattered.

JINN

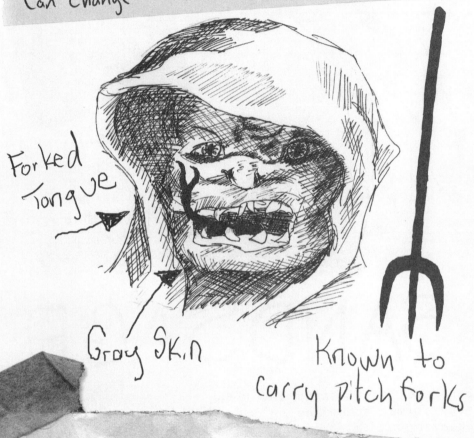

Forked Tongue

Gray Skin

Known to carry pitch forks

Jinn are Regulus level demons. Jinn are able to take the form of a human or other beast. They are very dangerous. Despite what some cultures think, jinn are never good. They may act kind and helpful to humans, but only to get whatever it is they are after. The jinn is a master of trickery, but it does not have the magical powers needed to carry out some of its plans. For those plans it needs higher level demons and often convinces its human target to summon those higher demons. Jinn are known to carry pitchforks, but this is a sort of jibe at the human characterization of Satan with his pitchfork. More →

How to Defeat a Jinn

A jinn can only be defeated when two simultaneous attacks are carried out. First its cloak must be removed and second you must use the light of Truth. Once the cloak is removed its hood must be severed. Many cultures or humans tricked into jinn servitude are convinced to call their jinn by a specific name, this type of name recognition only strengthens its appearance as a human. A jinn's true demonic form is nothing like that of a human, its skin is gray in color and it has a long narrow reptilian tail with a set of two small spikes at the end. A forked tongue and round flat nose adorn its face, while long yellowed claws protrude from each finger and toe. Its closest resemblance is that of a mummified serpent on two legs.

The LIGHT of TRUTH

1. Remove the cloak from the Jinn.

2. Use it!

3. Sever the hood from the cloak.

Steed of the
Blood Sage

Primary Weapons:

1. Talons
2. Beak

RAPTORYX

Caution: Some have been known to breathe fire!

Are best known as the steed of the BloodSage, the
Raptoryx is not a demon but a minion of the Underworld. Their presence often signifies the coming awakening of a BloodSage. Its head resembles a raven's and
its body is long and scaly like a lizard. It has two
sets of wings, the forward set are half as long and
less pointy then the back set. The Raptoryx has long
arms, each armed with three talons. Its legs are
powerful, like those of a dinosaur or dragon. The
Raptoryx talons and beaks are its primary weapons,
some have been known to breathe fire.

more→

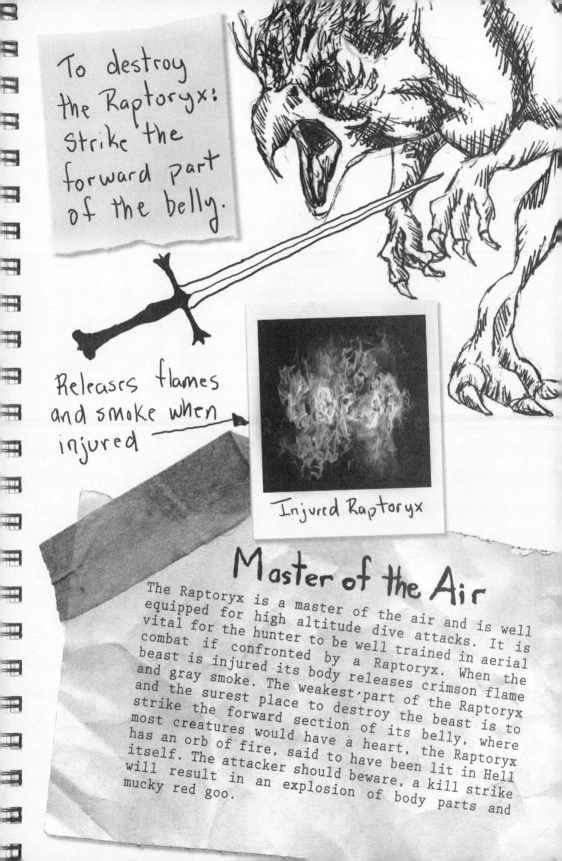

To destroy the Raptoryx: strike the forward part of the belly.

Releases flames and smoke when injured

Injured Raptoryx

Master of the Air

The Raptoryx is a master of the air and is well equipped for high altitude dive attacks. It is vital for the hunter to be well trained in aerial combat if confronted by a Raptoryx. When the beast is injured its body releases crimson flame and gray smoke. The weakest part of the Raptoryx and the surest place to destroy the beast is to strike the forward section of its belly, where most creatures would have a heart, the Raptoryx has an orb of fire, said to have been lit in Hell itself. The attacker should beware, a kill strike will result in an explosion of body parts and mucky red goo.

GRAY MIST

Accompanied by voices and dark feelings

A Weapon of Deceit and Mind Games.

Defensive shroud for HowlSage

The gray mist is believed to be the spirit of the BloodSage. It puts an impenetrable defensive shroud over the HowlSage. Each time an attack was made on whatever the gray mist surrounded it glowed green. Voices and dark feelings often accompanied the gray mist. It seemed that the gray mist was able to seek out its prey with cunning and swiftness. Its weapon was one of deceit and mind games.

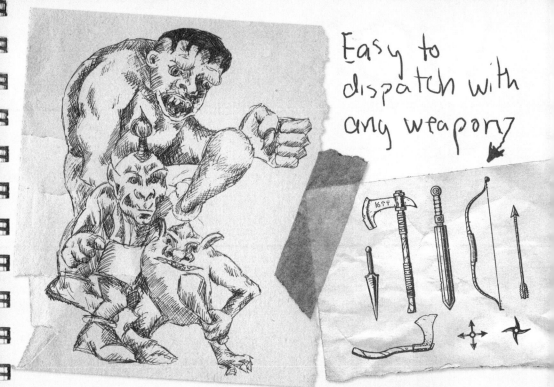

Easy to dispatch with any weapon

GOBLINS

Primary weapons are teeth and claws.

Goblins are not demons, but minions of the Underworld. They come in many sizes and shapes and often attack in hordes. They are invisible to the human eye, unless the human has been gifted to see or the goblin makes itself known. Goblins are only able to enter through EtherPits and only after higher level demons have established a stronghold over their territory. Goblins are rarely encountered above the surface of the Earth, if they are it is considered an infestation. Goblins can be as small as six inches in height and as tall as four feet. They come in a variety of colors and shapes. Their primary weapon are their four rows of needle like teeth and curved claws. Some have been known to spit venom, but this only causes irritation to the impacted body area and is not lethal. Goblins are easy to dispatch, they can be killed by nearly any means used to hunt animals in the physical world. Three cities that are known to be infested with Goblins are San Francisco, Las Vegas, and Miami.

WORMIN

Can accompany Sand Sages and SwampSages.

Large mouth with 3 sets of fangs.

Grows up to 50 feet long.

Can swallow an entire bus.

Rarely found in cold climates.

A Wormin is not a demon, but a minion of the Underworld. They have the ability to travel through the earth like an eel in water. Wormin have been known to accompany SwampSages and SandSages, but rarely are found in cold climates. The Wormin have no arms or legs, and instead rely on their large mouths and three set of fangs. Wormin can range up to fifty feet long and can swallow entire Buses. Wormin can be killed by injecting them with a dose of toxin called Sastryx equal to one one hundreth of their body weight or by getting them to swallow an explosive laced with Sastryx.

Can be killed with injection of Sastryx

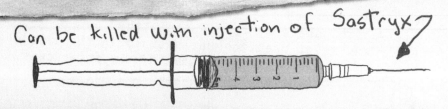

Guardians of the
BloodSage

Can grow
up to 40
feet in
height.

HYDRA

Most <u>Foulest</u> and <u>Dangerous</u> of Minions!

Amount of Heads = 3 to Infinity

Known to be the foulest and most dangerous of the Under-
World minions. They are the guardians of the BloodSage.
Like German Shepherds to the Nazis, Hydra guard and
protect the BloodSage's quarters. Hydras can grow to
forty feet in height, and nearest resemble a dragon.
However their multiple heads and inability to fly make
them different. Hydras can have from three to an infinite
amount of heads.

More ➜

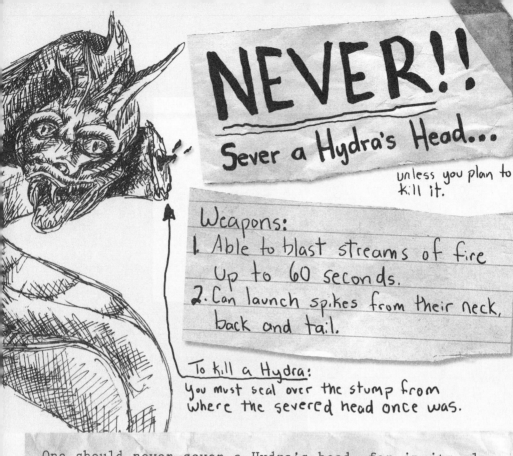

NEVER!!
Sever a Hydra's Head...

unless you plan to kill it.

Weapons:
1. Able to blast streams of fire up to 60 seconds.
2. Can launch spikes from their neck, back and tail.

To kill a Hydra:
You must seal over the stump from where the severed head once was.

One should never sever a Hydra's head, for in its place two new heads will appear. Hydras have the ability to breathe fire. They can only be killed by removing a head and sealing over the stump from where the severed head once was. Hydras can blast a stream of fire over one hundred yards once they've reached full maturity. Hydras although primarily using their fire for attack, can also launch the spikes that line their neck, back, and tail. Most Hydras can only maintain their spray of flame for at most a minute per each head, before they need to recharge. The largest Hydra ever encountered had twenty seven heads and was forty feet in height. It was never killed, but only imprisoned when hunters detonated the cavern around it sealing it within rock.

Fire Breathers

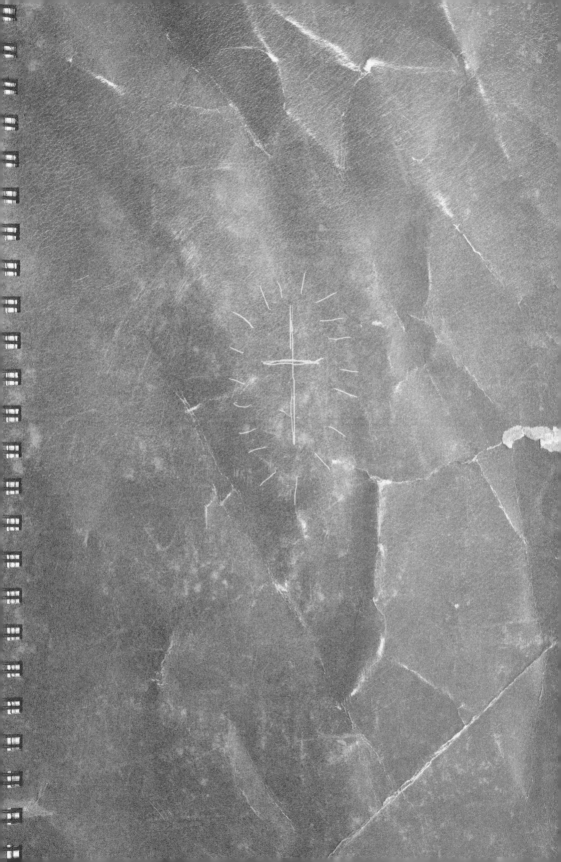

About
Brock D. Eastman

Brock D. Eastman likes to write, but his focus is on his wonderful wife and two daughters. They reside at the base of America's mountain and are learning to call Colorado home, but sometimes need a visit to the comfortable cornfields and hospitality of the Midwest. Especially during spring and harvest.

Brock is product marketing manager at Focus on the Family, where he has the privilege to work on the world-renowned Adventures in Odyssey brand, a show his dad got him hooked on when he was a little boy. He also makes frequent appearances on the official Adventures in Odyssey podcast and has written an article for Thriving Family magazine.

Brock's publishing journey started with the writing of the Quest for Truth series in 2005, and with his wife's encouragement he sought and found a publisher in 2010. Shortly after he signed to write the Sages of Darkness trilogy as well as a book for Adventures in Odyssey's, the Imagination Station series. He is always thinking of his next story and totes a thumb drive full of ideas.

To keep track of what Brock is working on, visit:
www.BrockEastman.com.

Other books Brock has written or are coming out soon:

The Quest for Truth: (P&R Publishing)

Taken (2011)

Risk (2012)

Unleash (2012)

Tangle (2013)

Hope (2013)

The Imagination Station (Adventures in Odyssey):
(Tyndale/Focus on the Family)

Showdown with the Shepherd (2011)

Sages of Darkness: (Destiny Image)

HowlSage (2011)

BlizzardSage (2012)

BloodSage (2013)